TRIXIE T

TRIXIE TRADER

Helen Dunne

ORION

First published in Great Britain in 2001 by Orion, an imprint of the
Orion Publishing Group Ltd.

Third impression 2001

A CIP catalogue record for this book is available from the British Library.

Typeset at The Spartan Press Ltd,
Lymington, Hants
Printed in Great Britain by
Clays Ltd, St Ives plc

All the characters in this book are fictitious, and any resemblance
to actual persons, living or dead is purely coincidental.

The Orion Publishing Group Ltd
Orion House
5 Upper St Martin's Lane
London, WC2H 9EA

To my father Daniel.
You were there at my beginning,
I know you'll be with me to my end.

Acknowledgements

What can I say? So many people, so little space and so many opportunities to offend somebody by leaving them out.

To my mother Lily, for letting me borrow so much of her; John, for setting up the computer and Liz, for the daily e-mail support during those dark days of writing. To Charlotte, for reading daily transcripts and providing a great sounding board, and all the friends who I could not have coped without, who provided advice, alcohol and a shoulder to moan on.

Slainté to Adam, Sheila and Catherine; Anna, Andrew, Becky, Caroline, Chris, Daniel, Garrett, Geraldine, Iona, Jason and Mark, Jackie, James, Joelle, Kerry, Lauren, Lisa, Melanie, Mike, Paul, Patricia, Patricia and Gordon, Philip, Ra, Roly, Sue, Shira, Suzy and Tony. Thanks. I owe you all a drink. Just one, though.

At the risk of sounding like Gwyneth Paltrow, I would also like to thank my boss Neil Collins, for giving me space for the column and a leave of absence to write the book; Amanda Seyderhelm, my agent; Jane Wood, my editor at Orion, who gently nudged me into doing this the right way; and Selina Walker, who started the process.

And, finally, in the time-honoured fashion, I would like to say that all errors and inaccuracies in this book are, of course . . . nothing to do with me.

Trixie Trader can be emailed at trixie@telegraph.co.uk

Tuesday, October 3

God was obviously not an investment banker. He did a lot of good things. Putting Jimmy Choo together with a shoe last and Tom Ford into Gucci were, quite frankly, strokes of genius. As for producing human bodies in two varieties, and then creating Adam and Eve to extol the virtues of sex. I think that could be described as the greatest public relations campaign ever. Maurice Saatchi, eat your heart out.

I have no problems with any of this. Honestly. Take my Philip Treacy hat off to Him. But if God had been an investment banker then He would have sorted out the time zones, and I would not be forced to come into work at 7 a.m. to make contact with my colleagues in the Far East.

SEVEN! A! M! The middle of the night. That's something the careers advisers don't tell you about on the university milk round. Oh yes, they emphasised the money aspect of working in the City. But nothing, *nothing* about early mornings. It was always apparent that getting up early was the downside of working as a postman or milkman, along with no money and lousy uniforms, but the City? I thought it was all champagne, designer suits and huge bonuses.

I'll never get used to early-morning meetings. They play havoc with my social life and if it weren't for my Prairie eye cream would probably destroy my looks. Actually, if my boss Jim hadn't specifically asked me to make an appearance this morning, I don't really think that I would have bothered. Come to think of it, he was pretty terse yesterday. Perhaps he was upset about my long lunch at One Lombard Street. Perhaps he's under stress. Yes, that must be it. He's calculating our bonuses and doesn't quite know how much to give me. My heart is racing in anticipation as I push back the Perspex divider and shout instructions at the black-cab driver.

'Could you speed up a bit?' I love cabs. The only place where you can talk behind people's backs without offending them. 'I have a meeting to get to within the next ten minutes.'

'Sorry, love. Look, it's grid-locked.' The driver points to the traffic clogging up the road. 'It's the police checkpoints and idiots in white vans parked on double yellow lines. You'd be faster walking.'

'Do these shoes look like they were designed for walking?' I ask. If God had meant us to walk places then he wouldn't have created cabs or spike heels.

'No, they don't. But it'll take at least thirty minutes to get to Bank in this traffic. You'd be better off walking. Get those calves into shape.'

I quickly glance down at my calves. My *bête noire*. Do they look fat? Surely they can't have gone to flab so quickly? I only missed one appointment with my personal trainer last week, when I had that party to go to. I flex my feet back and forwards, checking how they look. No! It's just the driver being rude. One careless remark and that chubby red-haired child, who thought that ginger nut biscuits were designed to taunt her, comes rushing back to the surface. These calves are so perfectly honed that Action Man would be proud of them. Panic attack OVER.

I push the exact money through the gap behind the insolent driver. Ha! The twist around will do his back in.

'What? No tip?' He looks irritated.

'Sorry. Forgot. Don't wash in muddy water.' I grab my bag and slam the door behind me, checking my watch. I'm not going to make it to the meeting on time. Blast. I know. I'll keep calm by totting up what I'll spend my bonus on. Saw a nice jacket in Nicole Farhi, the black suit in Emporio Armani, the latest Palm Pilot, one week at the health spa in . . .

What on earth! I wake from my reverie with a bang as some idiot barges straight into me. His latté is all over the skirt of my red wool suit. I look up to see Liam Neeson standing in front of me, with an empty Styrofoam cup in his hand.

'Oh my good God in heaven,' he exclaims. 'I didn't see you. I was looking for somewhere and . . . what can I say? I'm so sorry.'

That Irish lilt! I was about to tell him that I loved him in the film *Michael Collins*, although I don't think the producers should have killed him off at the end, when I feel the warm contents of his coffee cup seeping through my skirt.

'What the hell have you done?' I shout. 'Why didn't you look where you were going?' Froth drips on to my ponyskin shoes. 'Look at me!'

He does, and I have to quickly remind myself that this cretin may look like Liam Neeson but he's ruined my skirt. He is staring at the damp patch, at the little wisps of froth that are settling into the wool. His mouth wide open in horror, revealing a perfect set of white teeth. He gulps, before repeating:

'Oh my good God. I'm so sorry. Can I get you something for it?'

'What? Like two sugars? Or how about a dash of vanilla syrup?'

'Er, no.' He looks awkwardly at me as a dark ringlet falls into his eyes. Blue eyes. Two of them. Nice. 'I meant a damp cloth.'

'No thank you. I think my skirt is quite damp enough. Besides, have you looked around here?' I wave my hand to indicate the buildings that line both sides of Moorgate, one of the main thoroughfares of the City. 'Look. Bank. Bank. Building society. Can't seem to see a shop sign that says "Damp Cloths R Us".'

'Well, I don't know what to say. Oh, here, use this.' He presents me with a cotton handkerchief, white with what look like green splodges, which he has pulled out of his pocket.

'What!' If only he wasn't quite so good-looking. His grey suit hangs well on his lean frame. 'I'm not touching that. It doesn't even look clean.'

'It is. It is. Look.' I avert my eyes as the clumsy man tries to prove his point, by showing that the green marking is part of the pattern. He looks at me in despair. 'Well, at least let me pay for it to be dry-cleaned. I feel awful about it. Prada skirts are simply not designed to be drenched in coffee.'

He recognises the label! I look up, intrigued.

'I don't think any skirt is designed to be drenched in coffee. Not just Prada ones.'

'Look, I know this is really rude but I was in a terrible hurry. I mean, I *am* in a terrible hurry. That's why I bumped into you – although if I'd more time I'd have bumped into you *and* not spilled my coffee.' He looks at me and I can feel my face begin to colour. 'Can I give you my number? So that you can call me about the bill for dry-cleaning,' he adds quickly. 'I have to get somewhere and I'm running late.'

He hands me a card. Liam Neeson is actually called Ciaran Ryan, and the number? If I'm not mistaken it has a Chelsea prefix. Very cool. His own personal calling cards. I quickly check the back. Yep, it's Smythson.

'How do I know this really is your number, Mr Ryan?' I ask. 'Specialist dry-cleaning is expensive. This might just be a ruse to get out of paying, and if this coffee does not come out, I assure you that I shall demand a replacement suit.'

Ciaran Ryan hands me a mobile telephone. Hmm. Latest model. 'Dial it,' he instructs. I press the buttons. It's a compact phone. Rather like it. Might be tempted to upgrade from my current model. Mine is already six months old, which, in the telecom industry, means that it's due for the Queen's telegram any moment. It's ringing. An answerphone kicks in. 'Hello, this is Ciaran Ryan. I'm sorry that I can't come to the phone at the moment . . .'

So he's an I, not a we. I disconnect the phone, and then tell him that I'll call later this afternoon.

'Actually, I won't be in. I'm starting a new job today but I'll be in tonight. Call then.' In tonight? Has he no social life? 'And by the way, I will pay for a replacement suit if needs be, but I think you should knock something off for wear and tear. I mean, you must have worn it quite a lot over the past eighteen months . . . since it first hit the catwalk.' He laughs.

Kerpow! A knockout blow from Ciaran Ryan. I struggle to regain my dignity, which is difficult when you're standing in your very own puddle, and dig into my handbag. 'Here's my

business card, Mr Ryan. Perhaps you could call me this afternoon. I'm afraid that I'm out this evening.' My voice oozes
contempt and I put my eyes into glacial mode. Colleagues
usually tremble at the sight.

Not so Mr Ryan. He smiles as he turns the card over. 'So,
you're an investment banker. No wonder you can afford Prada.'
I shoot him another withering look. 'I'll call you later,' he
continues. 'Honest. And now it's,' he glances at his watch,
'seven twenty and I am really late for my meeting. Ciao.' He
marches off down Moorgate towards the Bank of England.

Seven twenty. Oh no. It should be another five minutes'
walk to the office, but in these spike heels it will take at least
ten. I'm late. What am I going to tell Jim? Perhaps I could
invent another family crisis. Hang on – how many strokes has
my grandmother already had this year? I suppose I could tell
him that I popped in to see a client on the way. That would
sound impressive. But he'd probably casually check up on
me. Or even ask which one. Oh, what am I thinking? I have
the perfect excuse. A Hollywood look-alike spilled his latté
down my skirt. Simple. Even I couldn't have made that one
up.

I arrive at the bank at seven forty-five. As I make my way up
the five stone steps to the glass-fronted lobby, I have a sense of
doom. It's not going to be my day. The security guards, all
puffed up in their military-style uniforms and peaked caps,
snigger at the wet patch on my skirt. God. I wish I hadn't worn
red. Black is the colour for emergencies. I'm only thankful that
I left a little Armani number on the coat stand by my desk after
collecting it from the dry-cleaner's.

As I get out of the lift, I am grateful to see hundreds of people
engrossed in the computers on their desks, ignoring me as I
walk across the vast trading floor, my bag clutched in front of
the wet patch. The electronic notice board that runs around
the top of the walls indicates that it has been a bad night in the
Far East for financial markets. I can see the usual show-offs
jumping up and down, barking commands through their
phones, as they try to get a feel for the way that the London

market will open. Despite the crowds, it is relatively quiet in here, thanks to state-of-the-art soundproofing.

It takes a few minutes to reach my desk, which is at the furthest end of the floor. I sit facing the management's glass offices that edge the trading floor. Not that anybody in those offices can really see me. The trading screens that cover my desk provide a helpful barrier. Besides, another desk, with its own battery of computers, backs directly on to mine.

I sit in a bank of ten desks – five one side, five the other. My workstation (investment-bank-speak for desk) is at the very end of the row, then there is an aisle, with a clutter of coat stands, dustbins, photocopiers and shredders, before another bank of desks begins. Yet despite the fact that we all work on top of each other, it can be remarkably private. I have held long in-depth conversations on the phone, feet on desk, but my colleagues have either been too busy with their own work or too boring to listen in. I never hear what the people on the desks facing me are saying. And I rarely see them, unless I make an effort to stand up and look over the screens, which I never choose to do.

Members of my section are filing out of one of the glass offices. I've missed the morning meeting, when a representative from each division outlines what the day is expected to bring. I suppose I had better ask someone if anything special is likely today. Find out what the bank's economists' take is on the Far Eastern jitters.

I grab my suit from the coat stand by my desk, and turn to walk to the ladies', when Jim taps my elbow.

'My office in ten,' he hisses. 'I'm off to the management meeting but I won't be late. And nor will you.' *Quelle horreur!* He seems to be in a terrible mood. Before I can explain about the coffee and the skirt, he adds: 'I don't want you to pretend that a client has suddenly been admitted to hospital, or that your wisdom tooth is playing up. I have already counted six wisdom teeth extractions over the past two years.' Damn! He knows all my excuses.

Jim begins to walk away, then pauses. His back still towards me, he says: 'And Trixie, your time of the month is still two weeks away. Mary keeps tabs on it in her schedule, so we can order extra biscuits.' Remind me to ladder the tights of Jim's personal assistant later.

What is wrong with Jim? A meeting. In his office. I hope he's put the family photographs away. The one of his wife in a seventies kaftan always makes me laugh.

It's fair to say I owe Jim a lot. I was the first graduate that he ever hired, all those years ago. I had just finished my BA in anthropology at Birmingham, and didn't quite know what to do with myself. I have to admit that I only applied to the City after learning about the salaries, and the pool of attractive young men. A pool I frequently dip my toes into, although less often of late after a bad bout of stubbing. Jim was so friendly and kind – a complete contrast to this morning.

I change my suit in the ladies'. Damn Ciaran Ryan – Liam Neeson looks or not. Even my La Perla knickers are marked. I'm sure the coffee will stain. I touch up my make-up, and tousle my pale red curls back into shape. I know it's arrogant to say so but people have commented that I look like Nicole Kidman. I'll just have to straighten my hair to match her new style. Must make an appointment at Charles Worthington's minimalist salon in Percy Street, but for now, I had better face Jim.

'Come in, Trixie,' Jim says, when I knock on his office door. I sense barging in is not quite the order of the day today. 'Take a seat.'

He appears engrossed with the bank of trading screens on his desk. I can hear the regular beep of e-mails arriving on his PC. I wonder if he's received that film of the zookeeper mucking out the elephant's cage who finds his head stuck up its bottom when Jumbo takes a sudden step back. I could send it on to him.

'Er, Jim, have you got that e-mail—'

'Be quiet, Trixie,' he interrupts. 'I'm just checking on last night's positions. I'll talk to you in a moment.' Glancing around, I see he's got rid of the photograph of his wife Denise. She's not exactly what you could call blessed, being blighted with a rather nasty facial hair problem. A few years back I heard rumours that Jim was trying to get a transfer to the Middle East. It was a big job, and would have been a promotion for him, but I know the real reason he wanted it was the yashmaks! Luckily, his children don't seem to have inherited any maternal genes. They look quite sweet smiling out of the silver frames.

Mary smiles from her desk just outside Jim's door through the glass wall. I'll teach her. Keeping track of my menstrual cycle. I'm sure human resources would be interested in that form of harassment.

I glance behind Jim through the window that makes up one wall of his office. I can see the London Eye in the distance, moving so slowly that it takes a moment to notice. It's one of the advantages of working on the fifteenth floor. The view. If I was only closer to the window I could see St Paul's, the Monument, the Tower of London, all those historical buildings that make working in the City so special. How could anybody ever think Frankfurt, with its stark modern architecture, could displace London as the financial centre of Europe?

'Right, now let's get on with it.' Jim focuses his steely eyes on me. I can usually read his expressions, but today I'm baffled.

'I don't know how to say this, Trixie, but you're skating on very thin ice. Several people have complained about your attitude of recent months. You've missed so many morning meetings, and when you are here it's as though you couldn't really be bothered.'

Wow! Where did that come from? I feel I must interrupt. Explain about the alarm clock that has trouble telling the time. Mention those pesky leaves that keep falling on my line. Tell Jim about the Liam Neeson look-alike who spilled coffee down my skirt. He listens intently to my litany of problems, but then puts up his hand to stop me.

'Good one, Trixie. I wouldn't put it past you to have spilled the coffee yourself. Anyway, I was going to say something even if you had shown up for this morning's meeting. Things aren't going well here. The bank's had a tough year and drastic action needs to be taken.' He fixes me with a stern gaze. 'Our shareholders demand it. They don't like losing money on their investment whilst we pay mega bonuses to all and sundry. We need to take action. Costs will be slashed, and the cheapest way to do this is to cut jobs.'

No! Is this why he has called me into his office? Surely, surely he can't mean me? I look at him in shock. I touch my throat and thank God for Clarins' neck firming cream. Thank God, too, that I can make jokes to stop myself howling. What would I do without my salary? My *bonus*? It's a truly appalling thought.

'Have you anything to say?' Jim is looking at me.

'I thought we had a special relationship. I was your first,' I blurt out. 'You said you'd look after me.'

'Things change, Trixie, and people change. You've changed. I've changed. We're different people from the two who met seven years ago. Look at you now. You're a confident, designer-clad woman. When we first met, you thought Armani was a character in *Little Women*. Now you practically have shares in the shop.'

But I haven't really changed inside, have I? It just makes it easier on him if he believes that I have. I'm not letting him get away with this. I've had to grow up. Fight to be where I am. Does he know what it's like being a woman in this man's world?

'You said you'd teach me everything you knew. You told me that it would be difficult at first. When I struggled, you said that I would soon get there. I found my rhythm and you were right. Everything fell into place.' Tears are stinging in the back of my eyes but I refuse to give in to them. How can Jim tell me so calmly that my career is almost over? How dare he point out my failings in such a callous way? No man treats me like this. Not since Sam. I look away from him and blink hard. I don't think I used my waterproof mascara this morning.

'You learned everything that I could teach you. And at first it was brilliant. You must remember those days when you just shone with excitement. When I only had to say the word and you reacted.' A hint of warmth returning to Jim's voice.

I remember those days when it didn't matter what time of

9

day or night it was. When everything was new, fresh and exciting. When I made it for every morning meeting. When did it all change? When did everything become tired and boring? Routine! That's what made it dull.

Jim looks across the desk at me, pushes his one hair back across his forehead. 'Surely you can understand? It was your spirit that first attracted me to you when I was asked to pick out the graduate I wished to train. Once harnessed, it understood the financial markets, and some of the deals that you put together were truly awesome. Now that spirit is unfettered' – has Jim been taking self-empowerment lessons again? – 'and the difference is startling.'

He grasps my hand across the table. Mary's eyes nearly fall out of their sockets. She's not known as Popeye for nothing. 'Trixie, you've become brittle. There's no need always to have a sharp retort for your colleagues. I think you'll find that they'll like you more if you act like the real you.'

I snatch my hands away. Jim doesn't know the real me. Nobody does in this bank. I haven't let them. But if Jim thinks that he can weasel his way out of this with a few kind words, then he's got another think coming.

'So let's get this right, Jim,' I say. 'You need to get rid of a few people and I am your first choice.'

'I wouldn't put it quite like that.' He looks taken aback by my blunt approach. Perhaps he expected me to collapse into tears like the 'real me' he wants to see.

'So, how would you put it? In a game of musical chairs, say, would I be the one without the chair?'

'Technically, that would be correct.' He nods slowly.

'So technically, then, if I bent my knees and began to move my pert little bottom downwards, how far would it have to go before it made contact with a firm surface? Before I even get to a seated position? At a fully perpendicular seated position? Or when it hits the parquet flooring?' I direct my finger at his floor to illustrate my point.

'Trixie. That's not a useful analogy. You're missing the point.'

'But I thought the point was that I was without a chair. I am the head that is to be cut. The Anne Boleyn of the department.' I place my forefinger in front of my neck and swiftly move it from one side to the other to indicate a slashing motion.

'Look, this conversation is going in the wrong direction. On current trends, you'd be the first choice for the chop, yes, but the situation is not totally unsalvageable.'

'How could it be salvaged, Jim? You've already destroyed my character, my hopes and my ambitions.' Lay it on thick, Trixie. Make him feel guilty. Let a single tear fall now. Don't worry about the mascara. Sucker him in.

'Don't try that line on me. You only have yourself to blame for the mess you're in.' Ah! Not quite the reaction I was hoping for. 'You enjoy the trappings of success, but don't actually want to work for them. If you want to save your job then bring back the old Trixie. The one who worked for a living and loved it.'

'And what would the old Trixie have to do?' It's been so long since work excited me. Can I ever get the adrenalin rush back? Do I want to? Oh, don't be silly, Trixie. Of course you want to. What else could you do? Anthropology is not exactly a useful degree, unless, of course, you want to be an anthropologist. Which you don't. You want to work in the City. You want to earn a high salary and revel in the respect that it brings you.

'She'd have to get a deal. A serious, good deal. One that will bring in lots of fees and earn her lots of Brownie points with her colleagues in the department. You're losing their support. People can't be expected to be sympathetic for ever.' He looks disappointed as he shakes his head at me.

'So, Jim, what sort of deal are we talking about here? Small but perfectly formed? A huge one that makes every other bank blanch with envy? Something small but unusual? Alternatively, what about bringing a company to market for the very first time? A début deal, so to speak?'

'Trixie, if you could bring any of those deals to the bank, I would be pleased. Let's not analyse things in advance. Go with the flow. Realise your inner strength.' Yes, definitely. He's hit those self-empowerment lessons again. 'But your strength was

11

always in bonds. You've helped some of the world's biggest companies raise billions of dollars through the bond markets. Go back to basics. Don't try anything fancy.'

One of the four phones on Jim's cluttered desk begins to ring. He picks it up in an irritated fashion. 'Mary, I told you to hold all calls. What? Oh, very well.' He turns to me. 'Sorry. Got to take this. There's a problem reconciling the trades in Malaysia. Count this as a friendly, semi-official warning. Get your arse into gear, girl, or get it out of here.'

I smile, and rise from the black leather chair. 'Thanks, Jim. By the way, is there a time scale on winning that deal?'

He looks embarrassed. 'Sorry, didn't I say? The semi-official list is being drawn up at the moment. Final decisions on head cuts will be made at the beginning of November, with an announcement towards the middle.' Six weeks! That's not enough time to lose a stone, let alone win a deal.

I reach my desk in a daze, totting up my credit card bills, mortgage, car loan and overdraft on the way. The truth is inescapable. I need this job. If Jim fires me, NatWest will have to issue a profits warning. I have more debts than Tanzania.

My three screens indicate that the world's financial markets are collapsing. How am I going to win a deal in this environment? I press Julie's number on the dealer board in front of me. The wonders of City science. A touch screen to speed-dial numbers because, after all, time is money.

In times of crisis, Julie is the only number to call – well, hers and Jo Malone's delivery hotline. I've known Julie since university, when she was going through her Top Shop phase. I almost didn't talk to her at first – the sparks from the nylon were too disconcerting – but she got over it and now we're best buddies.

Come to think of it, I haven't spoken to Julie since we got back from our mini-break in Cannes on Sunday night. She barely gets the words 'Emerging Markets Desk' out before I launch into my tale of woe.

'Really, Trixie. What do you expect? You hardly put your back into the job. I would have thought that this was inevitable.' Julie's voice sounds cold, and not quite as Concerned of City as I would have liked.

This calls for some emotional output. 'Julie. How can you talk to me like this? You're supposed to be my best friend. Is it too much to expect a "best friend" to be supportive in a time of crisis?'

'Oh, that's right. Call me your best friend now. You weren't quite so friendly at the weekend. Remember the bikini top?'

'Of course I do. I admired it. Gucci, wasn't it? I really didn't mean to spill my vodka and Diet Coke over it, and speaking of spilled drinks—'

'That's not the point,' Julie interrupts. 'Don't you remember holding up my bikini top and saying out loud, in your best strangulated Loyd Grossman voice: "Who lives in a house like this?" It was bloody embarrassing. I didn't know where to look.'

'Yeah, but at least the men did.' I can't help laughing at the memory. Until that moment I really thought goggle eyes was a fictional term.

'That's not funny. You know I'm sensitive about my bust size. It's bad enough that you call me JJ when there's a group of men about.'

'But that's your name.' I think it is time to defend my corner. Julie seems to have eaten more than two Shredded Wheat this morning. 'Your name is Julie Jones. JJ.'

'It doesn't help when you tell people that it refers to my cup size.'

'God, Julie, you're such a grump sometimes. Lighten up. It's only a bit of teasing. One look at your bust and people know that I'm only joking. You're more a double D.' I push the receiver away from my ear as a rush of expletives comes down the line. 'Anyway, you made fun of my calves. Told me that you'd seen better ones under a cow, and you know how much I worry about them. But I don't know why you're complaining. I mean, *I'm* the one who's just been told their job is on the line. It's my problems we should be focusing on now. Sometimes you can be quite selfish.'

It seems that Julie likes being called selfish even less than JJ. She slams her phone down with another expletive that I'm sure her mother never taught her. I didn't mean to upset her, but a bit of support would have been nice.

And then I noticed the coffee. A Styrofoam cup on my desk, with a wisp of froth coming through the hole in the lid. 'What's this? I didn't order this,' I say to nobody in particular.

'A peace offering.' I spin around at the sound of the Irish voice, and look into a pair of twinkling blue eyes for the second time that day. 'Ciaran Ryan, new UK head of bond sales. I've brought you a latté – just as you like it. Two sugars and a dash of vanilla syrup.'

Wednesday, October 4
(D Day minus 41 – and I've only just realised!)

How could I be expected to get into work on time today? I'm under stress, and stressed people sleep longer. Ricki Lake said so. Okay, so perhaps the night out with Julie to discuss Jim and his ultimatum did not help. But what did he expect? That's what women do. We discuss things, and preferably on company expenses.

I let Julie stew for a few hours yesterday, and then rang her back at lunchtime in penitent mood. She seemed to have got over her huff – probably pre-menstrual – and had actually given some thought to my plight.

'Why don't you do an IPO?' she suggested.

'Pio! I thought we'd agreed not to talk about those Italian waiters. The Chianti and the heat just got to me.'

'Not Pio. I said I. P. O. Three initials that stand for an initial public offering. They're all the rage at the moment. Bring in loads of fees. You'd be a hero. Come on, Trixie, how long have you worked in the City?' I can hear the frustration in her voice as she continues tapping away at her Bloomberg screen.

'I'm only teasing. I know what it is; just don't know how to do it. Stock-market flotations aren't really my thing. They never have been, and if I've only got six weeks then it's a bit silly wasting time learning a new skill. I'll just have to ring round the bank's clients and encourage one of them to raise money by doing a bond issue. Shouldn't be too difficult.' Should it?

'But Trixie, you're a coverage girl. You're meant to be constantly on the phone, ringing the bank's clients every day to discuss potential ways of raising funds for their companies. You should know immediately who needs money. All you have to do is ring them today and alert them to a few possibilities.

Ask somebody on the sales desk what investors are demanding at the moment. Match demand with supply. Easy.'

'Er . . .' What is she on about? Has this girl lost her marbles?

'You do discuss with clients, don't you? I mean, that is your job.' Sometimes Julie sounds like my old headmistress. And sometimes, after a late night, she looks like her. But I don't tell her. Obviously. She's bad enough when I mention her ample bosom.

'Well I used to, but then that whole Sam thing blew up and I sort of never got back into it. I sent them all diaries this year, though. Can never have too many of them, can you? Particularly our leather-bound ones. They've got a really handy wine vintage chart. And I'm friends with one or two of them. You remember Sandra? The blonde who's always accompanied by a group of men. She can down a bottle of champagne in one – apparently it's all to do with her double-jointed epiglottis. And Moira – the one who can get designer clothes at cost. Still discuss their needs every day.'

'Why don't you get one of them to do a deal with you?' Questions, questions, questions. Where's the tea and sympathy?

'Don't be silly. Their companies haven't needed to borrow money for years.'

'I think we need to talk properly. It's time to lay Sam to rest and get on with your life. And restore your career.' I'd love to lay Sam to rest. With a marble headstone.

And that's how Julie and I ended up in the Met Bar last night, where we enjoyed three bottles of champagne on my corporate Amex. It's a good number, three. Two is never quite enough. Besides, I'll put Sandra down on the expense claim and tell Jim that one of the bottles went on her party trick. It's strange, but he's always keen to meet her.

So it's not my fault that I slept in this morning. I would have slept later but my cleaning lady Lily arrived at nine, and woke me as she entered my bedroom pushing the Dyson vacuum cleaner before her. She's been with me for years. Actually, Lily grew up just a few hundred yards from my flat in Islington, but she moved out years ago when the council placed her in a high-rise block of flats in Bethnal Green, overlooking the flower market on Columbia Road. Loves it there, particularly after one of her neighbours got a small part in *EastEnders*.

'What you doing here, love? Shouldn't you be at work?' She pulls the duvet off me and stares down. Her floral tabard clashes dreadfully in my feng shui kingdom.

'I'm getting up,' I croak. 'Could you iron me a blouse?' Lily's an absolute wonder at getting the creases out of my Equipment shirts. 'And put the espresso machine on. I'll just take a shower.'

By the time I'm dressed, Lily has set the breakfast table, ironed eight shirts and is replenishing my Shaker kitchen cupboards. She's probably my lifesaver – all five foot nothing of her – although I'd never tell her. But she must realise I value her by the little things I do. Like allowing her to leave her fluffy slippers in my wardrobe. It saves her carrying them on the bus.

'I saw this three-for-two offer,' she says, cramming three bottles into one of my cupboards. 'I know you use this stuff for your fancy dressings.'

I look over, noticing that she hasn't taken her headscarf off yet. She must be popping into Dino, her hairdresser, after she leaves here. Come to think of it, she's been seeing him a lot recently. And she's started wearing make-up. There's two stripes of blue over her eyelids.

'No, Lily. I use balsamic vinegar, not malt. I never use malt vinegar. Does this body look like a chip even gets close?' I thrust my hands towards my twenty-four-inch waist, shown to great advantage in N Peal cashmere and Armani suit. I decided against the shirt in the end.

Lily looks quite crestfallen as she starts to pack the bottles back into her wheelie basket. She is so keen on special offers. Just sees the magic words 'Three-for-two', 'Try-me-free' or 'Buy one, get 100 points' and it's in her shopping basket. She once saw a special offer on condoms and bought me six packets. Unfortunately the expiry date was within six weeks – it was a busy time!

17

Shit. She looks miserable. 'Look, Lily, put the bottles back. I'm sure I can use them. Delia must have a recipe with vinegar in one of her books. Anyway, didn't you say once that it was good for cleaning windows?'

She looks pleased. 'Good idea. I'll make a start on your sashes later. Was it a late night?' She sits down at the table and hands me a small cup of wake-up-and-go coffee.

'Went out with Julie. Had a lot to discuss.' I down my espresso in one and start dashing around grabbing keys, handbag and credit cards from where I dropped them in the early hours.

'And a lot to drink, I bet. You girls. What are you like? What's this?'

She hands me a paper napkin with the words *Battle Strategy* scribbled on it. At least I think that's what it says. Could be *Bottle Strathspey*, but that would make no sense at all. Well, we did write it after the second bottle. I vaguely recall that Julie insisted I set myself a strategy and adopt a five-point plan. 'Act like a general planning a military attack,' was her advice. I read the planned attack with sinking heart. It doesn't seem so easy in the sober light of day.

BATTLE STRATEGY
Make friends with colleagues
Ditto clients
Ignore Sam
Ditto Ciaran
Win deal

I must have been very drunk to have allowed number one to be included. 'It's nothing, Lily. Honest,' I say, as I crumple up the napkin and shove it into my handbag. 'Thanks for the vinegar. I've left a list of what I want done on the computer. See you soon.' I swing my bag on to my shoulder with an air of finality, and bounce on to Theberton Street to hail a cab before Lily can ask any more questions. This is day one of the attack. D (for Deal) Day is only 41 days away.

Twenty minutes later – London traffic! – who should I bump into when I first arrive? Sam! The man of my dreams, who had dreams about other women. Including his fiancée in Hong Kong. I think she owes me one. If I hadn't called to tell her that Sam was a two-faced lying scumbag, she would be married to him by now. Instead we're both single and that makes us quits.

I view it now as a lucky escape. Sam has become a lecherous monster, with so many notches on his bedpost that I'm surprised it hasn't turned into a futon. He now pursues all new female recruits, and after bedding them, hangs a flag on a small pole above his trading desk. I just can't avoid talking to him this morning. He stands there – a tall, dark, handsome bastard. What did I ever see in him? And why does his desk have to be near the lifts?

'Hmm. I see the flag's at half-mast. Is your old trouble back?' I point at the Irish tricolour. His colleagues who sit with him on the foreign exchange desk look up with some amusement. They know our history. That's the trouble with open-plan offices: everybody knows everyone else's history.

'Nope, only had those problems when I was with you, babe. I'm going through a steady period now.' He gives me two thumbs up, and then turns to wink at his colleagues on the desk. Get their approval. Prove he's a big man.

'Oh, Battersea Dogs' Home let you take one of their strays, did they?' I respond sharply, ignoring the giggles behind him.

'Ah. Come on, Trixie. You can do better than that!' Hate him. Hate him. I abruptly turn away from his desk. 'You've still got a great butt, Trixie, even though your head is up it half the time.' His colleagues snigger again. I want to tell them that he's not such a big man. Believe me. But that would be vindictive and cruel. Hmm. Like it. Perhaps I'll send them a drawing. To scale. Somebody must have a cigarette paper around.

Why does he have to work here? A constant reminder of what I once thought I had – love and a future with someone. No wonder my career has suffered over the past year, since we split. Every day I watch him chat up the latest recruits, see them fall for his charm – which he can turn on when he tries –

and I want to tell them to run away. He hasn't got it in him to be faithful. His mother even told me that when Sam was a child, he adopted a neighbour and christened her 'Mummy Two'. I wonder, for the thousandth time, what did I ever see in him?

I move across the trading floor, nodding at various colleagues on the way to my desk, where I find Bloodhound, who has sat next to me for the past six years, back from his holidays and engrossed in his screen.

'Are you and Sam talking again?' He looks over expectantly.

'Nope. We're insulting again.' I throw my bag on to the floor and switch on my trading screens.

'Glad to see me back?' The break has agreed with him. He has some colour in his face, and a sprinkling of freckles on his nose that weren't there a fortnight ago. The effect has diminished the prominence of his dark, sorrowful eyes, which turn down at the corners. He looks healthy and refreshed.

'No, you got that wrong. I was glad to see the back of you.' He sighs.

Bloodhound and I were once really good friends. I used to think his unfortunate tics and unusual features were endearing. In fact, we used to double-date. Sam and I, Bloodhound and Cocker Spaniel. Okay. That wasn't really her name, but she had wavy brown hair that hung down in two curtains, like spaniel's ears. They could have walked away with a prize or two at Cruft's.

That was back in the days before I knew about the fiancée. But Bloodhound knew, along with half my colleagues, and nobody thought it their business to mention anything. For eighteen months I was going out with a man who was engaged to another woman. Admittedly, he travelled frequently to the Far East, but I just thought he had a lot of clients in the region. Plus the Air Miles came in handy. And I truly believed his sister's second name was Chang. Unusual, I grant you, but I'm a fine one to talk. She, on the other hand, thought Trixie was his housekeeper.

It came to a head about a year ago when I discovered the

truth. The Hong Kong office was full of gossip about two members of staff who had returned to the trading floor after a night on the tiles and been caught by a video camera in the reception area as they fumbled around on the black leather sofas. And they weren't looking for pennies down the sides of the cushions.

Bloodhound and I pleaded with them to see what all the fuss was about, so they e-mailed the edited highlights to us. And there, screwing up his face like an orang-utan, was Sam. Talk about a knock to the solar plexus. I virtually retched up my lunch, and when I turned to Bloodhound, tears streaming down my face, I could see immediately that he had known. Guilt was etched across his features. Not shock.

Relations between us have been strained since, although I have noticed that he is not as friendly with Sam any more. I think he's embarrassed by the Office Lothario tag that Sam has snagged. Me? I'm humiliated by it.

'Where did you go for your holiday?' I ask, remembering Jim's words yesterday. 'You look well.'

'Thanks.' Bloodhound looks surprised. 'Sharm El Sheikh.' I look blank. 'In Egypt, a resort just by the Red Sea. It's one of the most amazing places in the world to go diving. You would not believe the different fish I saw.' Hmm. Time to draw this conversation to a close. I turn back to my screens.

'Afternoon, Trixie.'

I spin around to find Ciaran standing behind me, the sleeves of his shirt rolled up, and his Rolex watch sparkling under the office lights. He looks gorgeous. Even better than Liam Neeson, but as Julie said last night: 'Now ish not the time for dish-trakshuns.'

'No. It's a hologram,' I retort, hoping that my stern exterior will throw out the wrong signals.

'Could be. The other one was better-looking.' Ouch. I must be looking worse than I thought.

'Ciaran. Ciaran Ryan. How are you, mate? Haven't seen you since uni.' Bloodhound is advancing towards my Liam, hand outstretched. 'When did you get back from the States?'

'Would you look at that! Chris Tyler.' They start slapping each other on the backs, preppy boy style. 'I didn't know you were working here. You're looking great. Are you still with . . .' He clicks his fingers as if to spark his memory into action.

'No. Ended soon after university. She's now married to an interior designer. Well, you remember how she had our university rooms all swagged and dragged. She got into a minimalist phase and pared down her living arrangements, including me.'

'Shame. I left New York three months ago. Had a bit of gardening leave, you know how it is, so I travelled around the Far East. Joined yesterday. UK head of bond sales. You're on the coverage desk, right? I'm desperate to sell, so just lead me to those deals.' Who does he think he is, Moses? 'Listen, why don't the three of us go out for a drink, maybe tonight? You and I can catch up, Chris, and you and I can make up,' he adds, looking towards me. 'We met yesterday in most unfortunate circumstances,' he tells Bloodhound.

'Anyone meeting Trixie is in an unfortunate circumstance,' Bloodhound mutters under his breath – but just loud enough for me to hear. I shoot him daggers. Pity they weren't Wilkinson Sword.

'You do have the matter of a dry-cleaning bill to sort out.' I turn to Ciaran. He's cute but I sternly remind myself of point four of the Battle Strategy. 'I went for the top-quality service at thirty-five pounds. The lady wasn't sure that the coffee would actually come out, but said she'd try her best.'

'Shall we wait until the result? I mean, I still might have to take you shopping. Anyway, what says you both for that drink? Chris?'

'Bloodhound,' I interrupt, flicking my fingers through my hair. Drives men wild.

'Sorry?' Ciaran turns back to me, with a confused look on his face.

'His name's Bloodhound here.' I nod towards my neighbour. 'Everyone calls him it. You wouldn't like to be different.'

'No. *You* call me Bloodhound,' interrupts the subject of our conversation. 'Everyone else calls me Chris. You're the one that's different. In more ways than one.'

'So, it's a pet name? How sweet,' adds Ciaran. Pet? Is he blind? King Kong looked more like a pet than Bloodhound does. 'Anyway, what about that drink? Chris?'

'Sure. I could do with a pint tonight.' He pats his belly and leans back in his ergonomic chair. Sadly it doesn't topple over, although the castors are looking decidedly tired. I catch myself imagining Bloodhound in a wetsuit swimming after tropical fish. God, the stress of Jim's ultimatum is already getting to me.

'I was thinking more of champagne. After all, this is a kind of celebration. Trixie?'

Champagne? With Bloodhound? He'll make it go flat. But I have to get on better with him. Battle Strategy – point one. Julie said he's a master of persuading clients to do bond deals, and I need the support of the whole department if I'm to succeed. And Ciaran is new and senior. He doesn't know my history. I might be able to persuade him to work on a special bond issue just for my clients.

'Sure. Why not?' I say. Bloodhound looks confused – or is it frightened? 'Shall we go to Coq d'Argent?' Ciaran looks blank, so I explain. 'It's the new Conran restaurant on the site of the old Mappin and Webb building. A modern building, with orange and pink striped brickwork. The bar is right at the top. It's got great views, and if it's warm enough we can sit outside.'

'Sounds lovely,' he laughs.

'And you really *can't* see the colour scheme once you're inside. What about six thirty?' I smile at Bloodhound. Now he looks petrified.

'Er, Trixie. You normally finish at five, or sometimes even lunchtime,' he retorts. 'Are you turning over a new leaf?'

'I don't know what you're talking about. I arrived late this morning – after an unforeseen family crisis.' I adopt a ma-tronly, don't-mess-with-me tone.

'Your granny again?'

'After an unforeseen family crisis,' I repeat. 'And unfortu-nately I'll be unable to give my clients the service they require

23

within a shortened day. I am therefore staying later to make it up to them.' Bloodhound almost falls off his chair now in surprise, but I'm sure that Ciaran is impressed by my dedication to duty.

'Six thirty it is then. Wouldn't like your clients to miss out,' Ciaran says, in his lovely Irish lilt. 'I'll come by your desk to collect you both. See you.' He flicks his fringe back, and walks off towards the sales desk, where about twenty young men in shirtsleeves are shouting down their phones. A couple have feet up on their desks, relaxing as they chat up potential clients. A few dinosaurs from the eighties strut about in their red braces, believing they are Masters of the Universe. I watch as Ciaran sits down at the head of the desk, his personal assistant at his side, and then abruptly turn back to my screens. Bloodhound looks over at me.

'He's a good man.'

'Sorry?' I look at him as if I didn't understand his comment.

'He's a good man.' He jerks his head towards Ciaran. 'Could do worse.'

'I've done worse. And I seem to recall that was your recommendation as well. Now if you'll excuse me, I've got work to do.' I turn back to my screen. An internal message is flashing. It's from Jim, asking why I missed this morning's meeting. Decide an answer about a heady cocktail of stress and alcohol is not really a good idea in current circumstances, so I respond that I was giving myself a serious pep talk this morning. Seems to work. No response.

I've got to start wooing back my clients. As Julie said last night, Sandra and Moira are a waste of time, although I might just give Moira a call about that cute Georges Rech suit that I saw at the weekend. I know. I'll try Mark Benjamin. He was always a good laugh and a useful client. As I recall, my 1993 bonus was mainly due to his business. I search his name out on my Palm Pilot. I dial the number. It rings. Good sign. The company must still be in business.

'Benjamin Industries. Can I help you?' The switchboard operator cuts in after just two rings.

'Could I speak to Mark Benjamin, please,' I ask in the most pleasant voice in my repertoire.

'I'm sorry. He doesn't work here.' The operator seems terse.

'He must do. Short, fat guy with something really disgusting going on with his eyebrows. He can't have left. It's a family business.'

'I know. I'm his sister.' Her voice sounds icy. Oh God. I remember. Mark said the eyebrows ran in the family.

'Do you know where he's gone to?' I add, hopefully. He could be working for a multi-billion-pound conglomerate now. Needing to do lots of bond deals, and desperate to talk to his old buddy Trixie.

'Yes. The Douai Monastery in Kent.'

'Sorry?' That doesn't sound hopeful. Has he gone into religious artefacts?

'He's training to become a priest.'

'Well, he always did like his wine.' Ah! The line's dead.

Thankfully I have no more clients in the B section of my Palm Pilot, but Cs and Ds prove equally useless. What's happened to loyalty in the City? It's only been about a year since I last called, and half the people have moved on to new jobs. No wonder the headhunting business is making a fortune.

My luck was in with E. Caroline Edwards was still employed but she couldn't remember me. I don't think we actually did any business together. There is a note by her name saying 'prospective'. Good sign.

'Trixie, you say. It doesn't ring a bell. When would we last have spoken?' I remember those clipped tones, the velvet headbands and Ferragamo shoes.

'You might remember me as Trixie Trader. It's not really my name, of course, but my boss Jim was taking a creative writing class soon after I arrived, and he thought that it worked better on an alliterative level than my real name – Trixie Thompson-Smythe. We last spoke about a year ago when . . .' Oh my God. I've just remembered the missing part. Details which I should have put into my Palm Pilot. '. . . We bumped into each other at a freebie at Ascot.'

25

The penny drops for Miss Edwards. It hurtles like a grenade into any chances I may have of working for this woman.

'You!' I would be able to hear the explosion even without the phone connection. After all, our offices must only be ten miles apart. 'You were the strumpet with her tongue down my boyfriend's throat!' I move the phone away from my ear.

'He told me that he was single,' I mutter defensively. It was an awful day, shortly after the split with Sam, when I was going through a wild period. Julie called it my 'discovering the fish' phase. Caroline's boyfriend (although I didn't know he was at the time) and I were both guests of some fund manager, and had overindulged on the champagne. Caroline was also there on another corporate freebie, and unfortunately decided to pop down from her box to visit her beloved boyfriend. I vaguely remember an engagement ring catching the sunlight as she socked him one.

'He was from that moment,' she retorts. 'What do you want?'

'Just wondered how you were,' I explain lamely.

'Well, why don't you ask Chris?' the voice at the other end of the phone barks. 'I do my business through him.' Strangely, the connection breaks.

Bloodhound? Has he been looking after my clients? Stealing the goodwill that I spent years building up? No wonder he's Jim's golden boy. He's been getting all the business that should have come to me.

'Have you been stealing my clients?' Bloodhound looks up alarmed as I thrust my face into his 'personal space', as our American colleagues like to call it.

'Course not,' he exclaims. 'But when you stopped ringing them, somebody had to look after them. The bank couldn't lose their custom. I just stepped into the breach. Told them that you'd had a family crisis . . . I think I mentioned your granny.'

'My granny. How dare you use her name in vain? What a despicable person you are – using my sweet, ninety-three year-old grandmother as an excuse. How could anybody stoop so low?' People are looking over now. Jim even glances up from his glass office.

'Well, the poor woman always seems to be having a stroke or something. I thought you wouldn't mind. I was only trying to help,' Bloodhound continues, in a soothing, let's-not-make-a-fuss voice. Too late. 'You're welcome to them back, anyway. Call Frederick Kane. He's always asking about you. Says you should enter your granny into the *Guinness Book of Records*. Think he's in Frankfurt today, but he should be back in his office next week.'

'Does he want to borrow any money?' Beggars can't be choosers. Frederick was always quite friendly. Loved Sam. Asked a lot about him.

'Oh, yeah. He's expressed an interest. Haven't been able to find something suitable just yet, though. Here's his new number.' Bloodhound hands me a business card. 'And, word of friendly advice, listen to what your clients want. The customer is always right – even if it doesn't bring in much in the way of fees.'

Advice from Bloodhound. I'd rather take singing lessons from Cilla Black, or make-up lessons from a pantomime dame. Or Cilla Black, come to think of it. Before I can retort, Ciaran arrives. He looks even better in his suit, his Hermès tie loosened and the top button of his shirt open. Yes. I think I can see chest hair. Not too much, not too little – just the way I like it.

'Can I drag you two away early? Would your clients really mind, Trixie, if you don't give them the full service today? Tell them it's a special occasion.'

'Special occasion?'

'It seems special to me.' He smiles, a silly lop-sided smile that reveals a few of his perfect teeth. I'm there! Let me grab my coat! No need to explain! 'I know it's only a quarter past five but I think I'm still in Asian time. I'm parched and really need a nice chilled bottle of Krug. What say you?'

Krug? 'I say "lead the way".' I make to lift my coat from the stand behind me, but he grabs it and helps me into it. Is it my imagination, or are his hands really lingering a little too long on my shoulders? Down, girl! 'On second thoughts, I'll lead. You're the new boy in town. Wait till you see some of the new places to eat and drink . . . you'll soon end up looking like Bloodhound. Only joking,' I add quickly, when a concerned look spreads over his face. I glance back at my colleague, who is chatting on the phone. He indicates that he'll catch us up, so I stride off across the trading floor with Ciaran towards the lifts.

Thursday, October 5
(D Day minus 40 – another day wasted at the bar, and I'm not even a lawyer)

I am still three desks away when I hear Sam's dulcet tones echoing through the office intercom on Bloodhound's cluttered desk, recounting tales of his latest conquest to my neighbour.

'Honestly, Chris, she was hot. Couldn't keep her hands off me.' I can hear the childish excitement in his voice. The voices of his colleagues in the foreign exchange market can be heard in the background shouting 'mine' and 'yours' as they buy and sell currencies. Sam obviously is not busy. He just wants to tell Chris all about his personal trading.

'There was nothing she wouldn't do. Well, apart from make a cup of tea afterwards.' He cackles. 'She was more of a "grind her own beans" sort of girl. Typical Bubble.'

'Bubble?'

'Yeah. Bubble and Squeak, mate. Greek, you know. I can now add a Greek flag to my collection! You any idea what it looks like?'

'Is that Stud-U-Like?' Bloodhound jumps at the sound of my voice. 'Don't stop on account of me,' I instruct, as I pull my chair out and sit down facing my trading screens. The bank recently installed flat screens, no thicker than a tissue box. The old bulky screens generated too much heat, and not everybody in this place is conscientious about bodily hygiene. 'I just love hearing about Sam's latest conquests. Besides, I've plenty to keep me occupied.' I pretend to examine the morning's price data from the world's financial markets, but find it rather hard to concentrate with the throbbing in my head.

'Sam. I've got to go,' Bloodhound bawls into the intercom. 'Got a desk conference.' He swings round to face me. 'Where have you been? Jim was looking for you at the early meeting.

I told him you were visiting someone. Made a client name up.'

'Careful, Bloodhound. You almost sound like you care,' I bite back. 'Why don't you go over to Sam's desk? I'm sure he would draw you a diagram to illustrate his latest moves. The *Karma Sutra* has nothing on him. Believe me. I know. Move eighty-four was always a winner, but he could never get enough friends for his number fifty-five special.'

Bloodhound has the grace to look embarrassed.

'Look, Trixie. What can I do? He fills me in on his escapades most mornings – whether I want to hear or not – and you're not usually here. I'm sorry you overheard but, well, it wasn't my fault.' He shrugs, dons his headset and turns to answer one of the phone lines flashing on the screen in front of him. I settle into my chair, get out the *Daily Telegraph* to read, and open the emergency bottle of Lucozade that I keep in my desk drawer. Ten minutes later and only the obituaries read – well, I was just checking I wasn't there, I feel like the living dead – Bloodhound looks at me, whilst tapping a few buttons on the keyboard in front of him.

'You must be in trouble. That Lucozade is not even low-calorie. Is Trixie feeling the worse for wear?'

'I'm fine. Admittedly I may have drunk one or two more glasses than my limit last night but I feel fine,' I lie, hoping that those little dwarfs with hammers will move on soon. I have already let one day slide without achieving anything. I can't afford to lose any more time. In forty days I will be out on my cute little ear, unless I can get that deal together.

'Four or five more like, Trixie.' Bloodhound smiles. 'You weren't yourself last night. You told me, and I quote: "You're my best friend, you are. I really respect you." I know.' He pauses to laugh at the horror on my face. 'I was as shocked as you. And as for Ciaran, you told *him* that you loved him.'

I don't know which is worse. Telling Bloodhound that I like him or Ciaran that I love him. Neither statement is true. 'What did Ciaran say?' I ask, feeling sick and not really wanting to know the answer. How could I be so stupid? Drinking when you're stressed and emotional on an empty stomach, it's a recipe for disaster. I try to focus on my screens, but there seems to be a problem this morning. Everything appears to be written in duplicate.

'He was – how can I put it? – taken aback. I think that's the right phrase.' Bloodhound laughs, as if recalling an event from last night. 'When he kindly suggested that perhaps it was time for you to go home to bed, well . . .' He pauses for effect. Bastard! 'You don't really want to know what you said then. But I bet it would shock your mother and her friends at the Women's Institute.'

My head sinks into my hands as I ask Bloodhound through the open fingers, 'I didn't. Did I?' I can sense Bloodhound is enjoying this. So much for the ice queen image that I have perfected since I discovered Sam's infidelity.

'I told Ciaran that I haven't seen you so drunk since that night at Phoebe's when the waiters politely asked, "Top-up?" and you obligingly lifted your cashmere jumper.' Oh no. How could he tell that story? Ciaran will think that I'm a drunken slag. He won't want to help somebody like me to salvage her job. I might as well leave now. 'Although I did tell him that you were going through an emotional crisis at the time. PST – Post-Sam Trauma,' Bloodhound adds. Oh! So that makes it all right. I now look like a drunken slag *loser!*

'Don't tell me any more,' I say, putting my hand up in surrender. 'I don't think I could take it.' I'm completely humiliated. Telling Bloodhound that I like him is bad enough, but propositioning Ciaran! How on earth can I face him again? He'll think that I'm one of Sam's young strumpets. Perhaps I can apply for a transfer. To Australia. Oh shit. Can't do that. They don't generally transfer people just before they are made redundant.

'Morning, Trixie, and how are we this bright and sunny day?' My stomach lurches at the sound of the Irish accent behind me. I grab my phone, praying that he doesn't realise that it hasn't rung, and pretend that I've immediately become engrossed in a serious conversation.

'Sorry,' I mouth at him, clamping my hand over the mouthpiece. 'Got to take this call. Catch you later!' I turn back to face my screens, chattering away to a dialling tone about the vagaries of the French bond market.

'Sure, business takes precedence. But are you sure that you're not just trying to avoid me. Me. The man you love. The man whose babies would look like—'

I swivel around to face him, all pretence of a phone conversation over, as I drop the handset and stammer, 'Okay. You've made your point.' I am sure that my face has transmogrified into a plum tomato. 'I was drunk. I admit it. I don't remember anything from about the fourth bottle. Can we just be professional and put it all behind us?' I adopt my pleading expression.

'Well, I don't know. I was quite touched, in more ways than one,' he stops for effect, 'by your interest. Do you mean you don't think of me in that light?'

'No!' I bark. 'Certainly not. I only met you two days ago. This is a purely professional relationship. I don't think of you in any light, and particularly not today.' I pause for breath. 'What light?'

'Really?' Ciaran moves his face closer to mine and lowers his voice so that only I can hear. 'But I was sure. I mean, drunken people always speak the truth, don't they? Their inner feelings? They tell you things that they only dream of saying when they're sober. I thought that maybe—'

'No. That's certainly not the case here.' I don't think I can take much more of this. I push my chair back, establishing a respectable distance. My stomach is heaving, my head is banging and my ego is dented. 'Look. You're cute, but—'

Suddenly Ciaran and Bloodhound erupt into peals of laughter, and start slapping their hands in high-five gestures. 'Gotcha,' they shout in unison.

'What?' The two of them can barely keep themselves together. People are beginning to look over. 'Sit down, Ciaran,' I hiss, pushing a seat towards him. 'Now would you and Bloodhound tell me what's going on? Please!'

I ignore the lights flashing on the dealer board in front of me. Julie's phone number is lit up. I'll have to call her back later, along with Lily, who has left a message about special-offer rubber gloves, and one or two clients who weren't in yesterday when I rang. Bloodhound composes himself first.

'We made it up,' he tells me.

'What?' My head is pounding. When did we take on so many staff? No wonder they want redundancies. There must be twice as many people here as we need. I look at Bloodhound. He isn't making sense.

'Everything we just said. We made it up.'

'You mean, I didn't say I liked you?' I point a finger at his chest.

'No.' He actually looks quite disappointed. I almost feel guilty, but I just feel sick instead. Still, the facial expression pretty much looks the same.

'And you?' I look at Ciaran. 'I didn't say that I loved you, or anything about babies?'

'Ah, no. Regrettably not,' he answers, his eyes twinkling under the stark fluorescent lights. 'But I wish you had!'

'So you didn't mention Phoebe's party?' I ask Bloodhound hopefully, as I twist open a second bottle of Lucozade.

'Oh no. He did that, so he did,' interrupts Ciaran. 'And he's promised to bring the photos in one day.'

'He does, he dies,' I say. 'So what actually happened after the fourth bottle?' I'm not quite sure that I want to hear the answer, but it can't be worse than the prank they just played on me.

'You fell asleep. We woke you, phoned for a cab, wrote down your name and address on a yellow Post-It, stuck it on your forehead, and sent you on your way,' explains Bloodhound. 'And then we planned this morning. It was an old trick we used to play at university, but I think we're out of practice. We used to be able to keep it going for days.'

Relief surges through my body, but I'm still one bottle short of a full memory. 'Did anything really happen?' I ask, cautiously. One of Bloodhound's phones rings and he turns away to take it.

'Well,' hesitates Ciaran, 'you told us not to tell anybody, but . . .' He leans forward again, conspiratorially. 'You explained about Jim, and the ultimatum he set you two days ago.' I'm appalled. It will be all over the dealing floor by lunchtime. Everybody will look at me sympathetically. I don't think I can stand it. It will be as bad as facing everyone after the truth about Sam came out. 'Don't worry,' adds Ciaran. 'We aren't going to say anything. We're concerned. Honestly. Look at me. I arrive in a new post on the very day that you're told the bank's cutting jobs. I wouldn't blame you for resenting me.'

I hadn't quite thought of it like that, but somehow that makes it worse. It makes me seem even more dispensable. I'm never going to keep this job. So much for the Battle Strategy.

'If you want my advice,' Bloodhound says, as he hangs up the phone, 'I'd try to win the support of your colleagues. How many people here could you really call your friends?' He gestures towards the hundreds of dealers who inhabit the floor. 'Make friends. You said that Jim was concerned that you weren't part of the team. Make yourself part of it again.' God. Did I keep nothing to myself?

'Have a dinner party,' suggests Ciaran. 'It would be a good way for me to meet people at the bank.' Typical man. Thinking of himself in my crisis.

'Who said you were invited?' I bark, before adding: 'Who would I ask?'

'How many people sit on this desk, Trixie? Here.' Bloodhound draws a circle in the air, indicating the people in the immediate vicinity. 'These are the people in your team. And how many do you speak to?'

'Ten and, em, two.'

'Are you suggesting that the abuse you give me passes for polite speech?' I nod, feeling rather guilty. Somehow Bloodhound's droopy eyes look sadder than usual. 'And who's the other lucky person?'

I stand up and look over the bank of trading screens to the five people facing me. Their names are a blur. How could I not know them? One or two smile shyly, but the others remain engrossed in their phone calls and screens. Suddenly I see somebody that I recognise.

'I speak to him.' I point at the young man walking towards me wheeling a wire trolley. 'He works on this desk, doesn't he?' I stop as the trolley draws to a halt in front of me, and the young man passes me four letters.

'Hi, Fred,' says Bloodhound. 'How's life in the post room? Busy?' I watch as Fred walks away, dropping off his packages into the tangle of in-trays that perch precariously on top of each screen.

'Okay, okay, I get the point,' I say. 'I don't know as many people as I used to. Can you blame me, Bloodhound? They were all snakes in the grass when it came down to it.' He looks embarrassed. 'But what good will it do getting to know people? They can't get me a deal. They want them for themselves.'

'Well, it can't do any harm, can it? Just think how impressed Jim would be if he knew you were making an effort. Things have moved on over the past year or so. Getting a deal is more of a team effort. And take up smoking.'

'What? Sue the tobacco companies for smoking-related illness and live on the proceeds?' Stupid idea, Bloodhound!

'Everybody knows that the smoking room is where all the gossip takes place,' Ciaran chips in. 'Get involved. Listen to what's going on. You might learn something.' I feel uncomfortable that he has met me at such a vulnerable point. He must pity me.

'But I don't smoke, and what about the dangers of passive smoking?' I whinge.

'Trixie, at this moment in time, what is the worst thing that could happen to you?' asks the ever-logical Bloodhound. 'And anyway, doesn't Julie smoke? And you spend enough time in her company.'

An irate voice suddenly barks down the intercom on Bloodhound's desk. 'Could one of you tell Ciaran that it's getting busy back here? We need some direction. The bloody economic figures are due any moment.'

'Right.' Ciaran gets up from his seat. 'Better get back to work.

Glad we've got that sorted. Just tell me what date to put in my diary and I'll be there.' He starts to walk back towards his desk, where his team are jumping around, frantically ringing their clients with new sales ideas.

'Ciaran,' I shout out.

He turns and smiles.

'Yes?'

'What about the dry-cleaning bill?'

He winks at me, and carries on walking to his desk. And somehow I feel better.

Friday, October 6

It's over twenty-four hours since Ciaran and Bloodhound gave me that pep talk but I still can't bring myself to follow their advice. It's lunchtime and Bloodhound and I are sitting in the bar of Corney & Barrow in the Broadgate Centre, overlooking the ice-rink below, grabbing a sandwich and a bottle of Chablis. This is the best development in the City. Tucked behind Liverpool Street station, granite and glass buildings are arranged around a circular piazza, which in winter is converted into an ice rink and in summer becomes the hottest venue for exhibitions and sports tournaments, like five-a-side football, between different financial institutions. It's a magnet for City staff, attracted by the bars, restaurants and shops.

'I can't do it.'

Bloodhound turns away from the window. He's been watching a broomball tournament. A team from our bank is on the ice at the moment, distinguishable by their burgundy and green rugby shirts.

'I don't think "can't" comes into this, do you? I'm not being rude, but there's a clock ticking over you, and only you can stop it.'

'Yes, but—' I'm about to ask if there's some other way when a cry comes from down below. Bloodhound glances out.

'We've scored.' He turns back, refills our glasses and then waves the empty bottle at the waiter, looking for a replacement.

'So that makes us . . .'

'Yep! Ten–one down.' We laugh as he grabs the last sandwich from the plate in front of us. 'You were saying?'

'Oh my God,' I lift the wine list in front of my face as a colleague enters the wine bar. 'That's exactly what I mean. I'll never get her on my side. Too much water under the bridge and all that.'

'What? Marian?' Bloodhound takes the wine list from my hands and places it back on the table. 'Bit pointless that, Trix. After all, she sits ten foot away from you on the trading floor.' I feign a sulky look.

'She won't give me any breaks, unless it's my neck.'

'Don't be stupid. What happened?'

'Oh, last year, just after Sam and I split up, she came over and gave me one of those "plenty more fish in the sea" speeches. It really irritated me.'

'She probably meant it nicely, and why would that stop her helping you now?'

'Well, I didn't take it very well. I thought she was being all superior, and then I got her name in that raffle draw you organised last Christmas for the desk. You know the one where we had to buy the person we drew an appropriate present for under a fiver.'

'Yeah, so?'

'I bought her Head and Shoulders.'

There's a stunned silence, then Bloodhound, ever the optimist, says: 'Well, I'm sure she's forgiven that. Everybody knew you were going through a bad patch.'

'Hmm, she might have, but then I blew it last month.'

'How?'

'Well, I hadn't seen her for a while.' I take a gulp of wine to anaesthetise the impact of what I'm about to say. 'And I was feeling a bit guilty about how I had treated her, so when I bumped into her in the ladies', I wanted to make amends. I'd heard rumours that she was pregnant, so I asked her when it was due.'

'That was nice,' Bloodhound says encouragingly, as the waiter changes the wine bottles over.

'Yeah, I thought so, but then she told me that she'd had it two months before.' I sense he's worked out the import of this own goal as he downs his glass in one.

'Put it behind you. Write Marian off to experience, but make an effort with the others. You used to get on quite well with a few of them, and they were all a bit embarrassed by what happened with Sam. They probably want a chance to make up with you too.'

If Bloodhound were Pinocchio, he'd be pushing me off my chair by now. Still, I know he's only trying to help. Couldn't he just get the deal for me? That would be a perfect help. He hails the waiter as he takes his corporate card out of his wallet.

'Jim can pay for this,' he says, handing it to the waiter. A cheer from outside makes him look out the window. 'Sam's scored.'

'Wouldn't you know it!'

We are barely back at our desks ten minutes later when Bloodhound nods towards the smoking room.

'Go on. They're all in there now.'

'Aren't you coming too?'

'I think this is something you've got to do alone.' He turns back to his screen and starts dialling. I take a deep breath and make my way towards the room, feeling like a condemned man on his way to the gallows. I hesitate for one brief moment outside the door, glance back at Bloodhound, who does a thumbs-up, and step right in.

People are gathered in small groups, smoking and chatting. Two women, who I take to be secretaries, are sitting just by the doorway with Jim's PA Mary. I start as I overhear the word 'redundancies', and glare at Mary, but she's engrossed in her conversation, apparently oblivious to my entrance. I move further into the room, slump casually on to one of the comfy red leather sofas near my colleagues, flick the ash from its arm on to the dusty carpet, and turn to face them.

'What are you all doing next Friday evening?' I wave my unlit cigarette in a sweeping gesture designed to include them all. No response. The four carry on with their conversation as if I'd never spoken. How rude. I persevere.

'Excuse me.' I flash a dazzling smile, as I hold both hands up to gain their attention. Perhaps I should light the cigarette, but I'm not going to inhale. 'I just wondered what you were all doing next Friday?' Again, nothing. In fact, they don't even flinch. Other people in the smoking room are looking over at me, quizzically. The two secretaries are nudging each other. Mary is whispering to them. Probably explaining about my menstrual cycle. I take a deep breath. Last chance.

'Hi, don't mean to disturb, but what are you all doing on Friday? Today week?' I move forward, my head into their space, and burst out coughing at the fug. It catches their attention. Manfred, a German colleague who greases his hair into a quiff and grows a rather wispy goatee beard, looks at me.

'Sorry, are you speaking to us?' he asks, pushing his tortoise-shell glasses back up the bridge of his nose. He swipes some ash off his trouser leg. I always think green is a colour that should be left to leprechauns, but it seems to suit him.

'Yes, of course, Manfred. Who did you think I was speaking to?' I smile pleasantly.

'I wasn't sure. It's been so long since we've spoken.' Manfred looks confused. No wonder he's a smoker if he's this nervous.

'Don't be silly. It's not been that long.'

'I remember. We last spoke about nine months ago.' Another push of the glasses, and a quick puff on his cigarette.

'There you go.' What a fuss about nothing! Before I can repeat my invitation to dinner, Manfred continues.

'Yep, you came back from a very long lunch in a filthy mood and asked me if you could rub your fingers through my hair because you needed some oil to stop your desk drawer sticking.' Please, floor. Please swallow me up. How could he? I notice that he doesn't mention to the others that I'd over-heard him on the phone asking Sam about my expertise in bed. But now is not the time for recriminations. Now is the time to make friends.

'Oh, that was a joke! Ha! Ha!' I burst out laughing to make the point, but realise I'm flying solo. I notice Mary and the secretaries watching me. I persevere. 'Are you on for dinner?'

I can sense that Manfred is just about to make some snide excuse, when Ciaran walks in. He must have spotted me through the glass walls and decided to come in to mock. Only here four days and already he's stalking me. He's looking good in a grey pin-striped suit, cream shirt and that tie with frogs on that I spotted in Hermès' window in Royal Exchange.

'Trixie,' he says loudly. 'Is that dinner party still on next week?' He looks at Manfred. 'You're coming, aren't you? Give us a chance to chat about some ideas that I have.' Manfred shrugs his shoulders, before nodding. The sudden movement causes his greased hair to part like the Red Sea, revealing a small bald patch on the top of his head. It almost feels like justice.

A rather attractive brunette is regarding Ciaran with an expression that I'm sure her mother would be shocked by. I don't know her name. She's a recent recruit.

'Count me in. I've been meaning to introduce myself. It's Liz.' She offers her hand to me, gives a perfunctory shake and then pushes it towards Ciaran. 'Actually, Trixie,' she says, without taking her eyes off him, 'we have something in common. Sam! I was the French flag! About a month ago.' She winks lasciviously at Ciaran, her hand still firmly gripping his. 'I believe in good office relationships!'

I want to punch her. We do not have Sam in common. I was more than a one-night stand. Otherwise I wouldn't have experienced the hurt caused by the abrupt ending. But if I had known then what I now know about Sam, I wouldn't have wasted the energy.

'It would be lovely to have you,' I say graciously. Count to ten, Trixie. I mean, she won't be able to.

'That's what Sam said!' Liz bursts out laughing. An annoying braying cackle.

'Now, now.' Ciaran comes to the rescue. 'Ladies don't kiss and tell, do they? What about you two?' He turns to the remaining members of this smoking clique. 'It's Leon and Nancy, right?' They nod, and agree to come.

'Right,' I say. 'I'll give you all my address later. What about eight thirty?' There is a murmur of agreement. I am just about to leave when I hear a yelp.

'Trixie, can't I come?' It's Kate. She works on the foreign exchange desk, sitting just three seats down from Sam. The archetypal barrow girl made good. She's made it in a world of MBAs and Oxbridge graduates, a girl from Leytonstone who learned about trading working on her dad's fruit and vegetable market stall at weekends. She is one of the sharpest traders on the desk, instinctively knowing which way the currencies will react to snippets of news or economic data. But she has never really fitted into this world of driven people because she's fat. It's viewed as a massive failing amongst her contemporaries. Alcohol and drug abuse may be tolerated, but weight problems are not. Somehow, though, this has never been a barrier between the two of us. I think, on my part, it's due to the memory of the little fat schoolgirl I used to be. I empathise, but I'd never tell her!

Kate's way of dealing with this bigotry is to joke about her size. Today she is standing by a machine in the smoking room, a Mars bar, Twix and packet of Rolos in her hand, wearing a kaftan emblazoned with the words 'My mother went to Bali and all she bought me was this bloody marquee' emblazoned over her ample bosom. Now I happen to know that her mother has never been to Bali, and that her outfit was purchased in Camden Market.

'I don't know,' I say, teasing. 'I'm not sure I can afford the extra portions.'

'It's not my fault. It's my glands.'

'Well, I wish those glands would stop putting coins into that machine. They'll bankrupt you.'

'I'd give you my last Rolo.'

I pretend to give the matter some thought. 'Okay then. You know my address, but could you arrive at ten? Give us ninety minutes' start?' She laughs, but her expression soon changes when I add: 'And could you leave the Rolo on my desk?' I take pity on her. 'Only joking.'

I leave the room, thankful to get into the fresh air, and walk back to my desk. Sam is flying a flag I don't recognise. Must be one of the new girls on the Eastern European desk. He waves at me from the distance. I respond with a gesture of my own. It uses fewer fingers. Bloodhound turns as I sit down.

'Well?'

'Ciaran got Liz, Leon, Nancy and Manfred to agree to come. Are they house-trained?' He raises his eyebrows in frustration. 'Oh, Kate and Julie are coming as well. Should I invite another man? Balance the numbers out?'

'I'll bring a friend,' offers Bloodhound. Gosh, that makes two. 'Another university buddy. Ciaran knows him. You might be interested to meet him.' I want to ask if he's tall, dark, handsome and rich but fear it may look pushy. Besides, I've got to stay focused on the task in hand. Remember the Battle Strategy, I repeat to myself, over and over, as I watch Ciaran return to his desk. Nice butt!

'By the way,' adds Bloodhound, as he hands me a yellow Post-It note, 'Lily rang for you. Said something about getting three chickens for the price of two in Sainsbury's. Wanted to know if you wanted one, as she hasn't got room in her freezer for them all. I said I'd get you to call back. It's really nice of her to think of you, isn't it?'

'Hmm,' I grunt, as I press the speed-dial button that links my state-of-the-art desk with Lily's stuck-in-the-sixties tower-block flat.

'Hello,' echoes an extremely upper-class voice through the earpiece. 'Who's speaking, please?'

'It's me, Trixie,' I reply. Her voice immediately loses its affected tones and she reverts back to her working-class roots. 'You called.'

'That's right, love. Wondered if you wanted a chicken? They're free range. Those chefs on *Ready Steady Cook* are always saying they're the best. They're only small, mind – so you probably won't get more than one dinner out of them. Make a nice change from all that pasta stuff you keep cooking. I could drop it round tomorrow morning.'

'Fine,' I say. It is always best to concede defeat with Lily. I'll never hear the end of it if I don't. Little digs about the price of chickens over the next few months. And God help me if I ever mention that I've been to a rôtisserie. 'Julie is coming over tomorrow night, so we could have it then.'

'Lovely,' she says. 'I tell you what, there was a lovely little recipe for chicken in the *Mail* last week. I'll drop that round too.'

Monday, October 9
(D Day minus 36 – today I mean business)

Six days after my warning and I finally make it to the morning meeting. Not that I had much to contribute. When it came to my turn to stand up and explain what I expected to happen with my clients today, I faltered and said 'lunch'. Still, it was a start, and our business can, after all, be built over the restaurant table.

I have Julie to thank for my early appearance this morning. She came to my flat for the weekend and gave me another serious pep talk. We met on Saturday morning for brunch at Lola's in Upper Street, then spent hours browsing around the antique stalls and shops in Camden Passage. I'm not really a fan of old things, but Julie was looking for a chandelier to fit into her new flat off Brompton Road. We saw a few but Julie saw the price tags and decided she might have to wait until bonus time.

We spent the rest of the weekend watching old black-and-white films, vegging out in front of the coal fire and eating Lily's special offers. I suppose Julie could have gone home on Saturday night but, with the amount of red wine we'd consumed, I'm not sure that she would have remembered her address. And besides, we had loads more food to get through on the Sunday.

And, best of all, Lily is coming today to clear it all up. She's a marvel. Who needs a dishwasher when you can have a Lily? Perhaps I could clone her if ever the technology became available. Julie is always saying she needs one. Be a great Christmas present.

Julie gave me lots of useful tips on dealing with clients and persuading them to do deals, even when they don't feel that they need to do anything. She has really missed her vocation. She should work in the insurance industry.

45

Today I am empowered – I will not take no for an answer. And, unfortunately, neither will Julie. She rang me at six this morning to check that I was getting ready for work. I don't think she realised that I could say 'no' in quite so many languages. One day I might even show her the universal two-finger hand signals that go with some of them.

Anyway, I'm here now and I've got lots to get through. I've got theatre tickets to reserve (clients love culture) and impossible-to-get-for-six-weeks restaurant tables to book for immediate possession. Plus I've got to chat up Ciaran about deals that his team could help me with. And then there are the preparations for Dr Noriko. The Mr Big of Japan.

On Friday afternoon, after I had fought my way out of the stale smoking room atmosphere, Bloodhound told me that he had heard that Dr Noriko is arriving from Tokyo on Wednesday. The man whose company needs to borrow so much money that he could do a deal for breakfast, lunch and dinner – and still have room for supper.

This could be my chance. I met Dr Noriko when I was still with Sam. He was one of the clients Sam used to visit on his regular trips to the Far East, and once when he was in London we had to host a dinner for Dr Noriko at Le Caprice. He was a short, fat man whose hand developed an unnatural attachment to my bottom. I politely ignored it for the first course, but by dessert he was wearing a sling. I don't think it spoiled his relationship with Sam though, and mine was ending anyway. I just hadn't realised it.

Bloodhound says he's arriving at three in the afternoon on the British Airways flight from Tokyo, and as far as he knows requires his usual accessories. This is going to be the sticking point. In these days of political correctness, how on earth am I going to get girls on expenses? And, more to the point, what has the world come to when I'm actually considering the problem?

'Where's Ciaran today?' I ask Bloodhound as we walk back to our adjoining desks. 'Morning, Manfred. Morning, Marian.' This being-nice-to-my-colleagues is starting to grate. 'Leon,

Nancy, Eiffel Tower.' I nod at the others as I take my seat. They look over in surprise.

'He's on a three-day training course,' replies Bloodhound, suspiciously. 'Why? You missing him?'

'Course not. I wanted to ask him about what investors demand these days. Find out what's in favour – organise a deal around it. And I want him to prime his team about selling the latest deal for Dr Noriko's company. Anyway, I'm glad that he's not in. Don't want him to know that the coffee stains came out of this suit, now, do we?' I stand and do a twirl for Bloodhound, revealing a good-as-new Prada suit. Hmm. Don't think he quite appreciates good quality, or taste for that matter. His tie looks like a chicken with diarrhoea has sat on it. 'Not when there's still a chance he might buy me a replacement. Besides, he hasn't paid for the dry-cleaning yet.' I lean across to Bloodhound, conspiratorially. I don't want to alert too many people that Dr Noriko is arriving. 'Back to business. Where do you get them?'

'Get what?'

'You know.' I lower my voice another octave. 'Girls. Ladies of the night. How does one recruit them?'

Bloodhound looks at me with such a shocked expression that for one moment I think he's got a problem with his zipper. Then in an extremely uptight manner, he replies:

'Trixie. I know you're not going to believe this, but the closest that I have ever got to a kept woman is when I hugged my mother. I don't know where you hire prostitutes.' His voice is getting high-pitched. Better check out my zipper theory, just in case. 'Why would you think I would? And would you mind focusing on me?' He points at his face. 'Didn't your mother teach you anything?'

'Don't bring my mother into this. She'd just die of shame if she knew what I was up to. Her friends in the Women's Institute would probably expel her. Anyway, she's quite naïve about that kind of thing. She once saw a girl on Commercial Road late at night, and was so concerned that she was lost that she got the mini-cab to pull up and offer her a lift. Don't know who was more embarrassed.' I giggle at the story.

'Your mum was a bit out of her way.'

'Sorry?'

'I thought she lived in Gloucestershire.'

'What is this? A bloody inquisition?' I steer the conversation back. 'Look, I'm sorry I thought you would know anything about hiring girls. I just assumed. You're a man. Sort of.' He grimaces at me. 'And you're a friend of Sam's. They're for Dr Noriko,' I add.

'Really?' Bloodhound responds. 'What about Yellow Pages?'

'Don't tell me. They'll be under Flagellation Services.'

'Didn't think Dr Noriko was into that. What about trying one of those cards in the phone boxes? Some of them even have photos, so you can examine their wares.'

'I don't want to examine any wares,' I exclaim. 'I just want to keep a client happy.'

'I think that's their motto,' he laughs. Infuriating man. 'Seriously, the phone boxes are filled with them. I imagine you get a better class of girl if you check the booths in the City, though. Probably all called Clarissa or Melissa, rather than Betty from Bootle with the amazing bouncing boobs.'

'See! You *have* looked at them.'

'Sometimes you can't avoid it,' he admits. 'Have you seen the phone boxes in Moorgate? I had to bring a dictionary to understand what some of the cards said.'

'Could you go and look again, for me?' I put on my 'please-help-me-I'm-just-a-female' face but I sense Bloodhound is not going to fall for it. 'Perhaps ring one of the numbers . . . make an appointment, check them out?'

'No!' A couple of heads turn, but in the fevered activity of the trading floor a few extra cries go mostly unnoticed. 'I will not. Imagine if anyone saw me. How would I explain it? "Oh, I'm sorry, Jim. Trixie fancied hiring a prostitute but was too embarrassed to do it herself, so I offered to help her out." And what if I knew the girl?' I shrug my shoulders as if to say 'you must be joking'. He carries on full throttle. 'You do it. You're the one who wants to impress Dr Noriko. Anyway, you know the bank's rules on things like this. There is an ethical issue here, and you can hardly put them through on expenses.' Ooh, I don't believe it. Bloodhound has found his backbone. He sounds quite strict, and threatening.

'I know. I'll cross that bridge when I come to it.' Bloodhound doesn't have to mention that I could lose my job over this. Hell, I'll lose my job if I don't do this. The bank takes a rather prurient attitude towards sex, and the purchase thereof. I mean, there's not even a space for it on the expenses forms. They just say Food, Drink, Travel. Nothing about Client Entertainment.

'Look, Dr Noriko's hardly going to say anything to Jim, is he? And I guarantee that Jim will be pleased with the end result. But you're definitely certain that he's arriving on Wednesday?' I can't make any mistakes. Dr Noriko could save my career for me – I can see the spring collection in my wardrobe, and the convertible in the driveway.

'Yeah, that's what I heard. He's your best bet, Trixie. His company needs to borrow billions every year so he should be willing to move quickly. And he's known to be extremely grateful to those bankers who look after his needs.' He looks pointedly at me.

'Hmm. Not sure I want his gratitude. Right. I'm off to the phone boxes. I may be some time.' I stand, grab my handbag, and turn to move off, only to find Sam blocking my way.

'Trixie, darling. Just wondered if you fancied sharing a tipple tonight?' In his shirtsleeves he still looks gorgeous; the only difference is that now I know that looks really are skin deep. 'Is that a new suit? Looks good.' He seems to be staring in the direction of my chest, so I fold my arms, causing Sam to laugh out loud.

'I'd rather watch *Star Trek*, Sam. The characters are more realistic.' I spin on my Jimmy Choos and stride towards the bank of eight lifts at the edge of the trading floor. A woman on a mission. I remember the days when an invitation from Sam could make my heart race. Before we started going out. When I was scared to sit near him in a wine bar in case he felt the electricity. Then, as with all electric surges, I came to earth with a bang.

Sam was truly remorseful. I think he really did want to save our relationship, but I wasn't having any of it. Woman scorned and all that. And anyway, he was engaged to his Hong Kong amour. I wasn't going to be second best. For four weeks he tried to make amends. I was bombarded with bouquets of long-stemmed red roses, invitations to Paris for the weekend, members of his foreign exchange team telling me how wonderful he was. Even his mother rang me to persuade me to change my mind, citing 'a terrible misunderstanding'. He had told her that he was getting something out of the eye of a colleague in Hong Kong. Funny. I never realised that there was such a difference between Asian and Western anatomies.

Funny how Sam stopped begging, though, after I altered all the screen-savers on the trading floor to say 'Sam has three nipples' with a little holiday snap. It's strange what the cold weather can do to some body parts.

He also wasn't too happy when I returned his dinner suit, which he'd left in my wardrobe. The tailor had very kindly taken three inches off the trousers and sleeves. Did a marvellous job – invisible tailoring, he called it – couldn't even notice it. Sam was very grateful that I returned the suit without taking a pair of pinking shears to it. At least, he was until the evening that he changed in the office for a black-tie dinner with clients. It was a case of 'Norman Wisdom, eat your heart out'.

Since then Sam and I have enjoyed what could be described as frosty relations. He has slept with everything and everyone to dispel the rumours. Me, I've slept with a teddy bear, although the other night I did have a rather worrying dream about Ciaran and a dry-cleaning machine. I keep reciting my Battle Strategy. No distractions, even if they are good-looking.

I'm sure the security guards know that I am up to something unethical. They don't seem to take their eyes off me as I move through the electronic barriers out into the reception area. Okay. Be calm. They can't know anything. Walk through the doors, on to the street. Don't look back. Keep walking to the phone box. Slowly. No sudden movements. Act normally. Hmm, perhaps it's just as well that Bloodhound isn't doing this. Only a few more metres to walk . . . Oh my God, there's a queue. This really must be where the best girls hang out.

'Trixie. What are you doing here?' I jump at the sound of Jim's voice. He's standing right in front of me. Waiting in the queue. Wonder what his type is? 'Are you calling your head-hunters? Ha, ha. There's still another five weeks.' He bursts out laughing.

'What? You talking about my deadline for a deal?' I smile confidently at him. 'No worries there. Everything is under control. May have some news for you shortly, in fact. No, Jim, actually I was just walking past and spotted you in the queue, and wondered if you would like to borrow my mobile phone. It's a brand-new model, just out. First saw it early last week and just had to have it.'

Wednesday, October 11
(D Day minus 34 – two faux pas don't please a wife)

It is three o'clock and I'm standing in the middle of the
Terminal Four arrivals lounge at Heathrow Airport with a sign
hailing Dr Noriko. I had to tell Jim that I was off today with
women's problems – luckily the biscuit barrel had just been
replenished, so he bought the excuse. It is not really considered
the done thing to welcome clients personally at the airport
with transport – particularly when they haven't actually agreed
to do a deal with you as yet. Some old jobsworth in the
compliance department might actually consider such a gesture
akin to bribery. And as for the extra accoutrements for the
journey back to London, well, my career would definitely be
finished if Jim, or anybody else, found out about them. Bring
back the old days of brown envelopes stuffed with cash. That's
what I say.

Jim claimed that he wasn't standing in the queue for the
telephone box, but had merely stopped to help somebody out
with change. It didn't prevent him from borrowing my phone,
though, but I suppose it really was the last chance that day to
make contact with the Japanese office. And the one in Hong
Kong. I just hope I can claim the calls back on expenses. I am,
after all, nearly unemployed.

I'm so pleased with my choice of escorts. Victoria ('voluptuous Virgo with a voracious appetite') and Wanda ('sleek, dark
and wild – the nearest thing to a human panther') sound just
perfect for Dr Noriko. Unfortunately, neither girl accepts
American Express or provides receipts, but I'm not really sure
how I would get them past old Eagle-Eyes Brenda in the
expenses department anyway. Once she caught me out when
I tried to claim lunch for four people when there were only
three of us.

Sometimes I just don't understand Brenda. She rang last

week to query a bill for a lunch I had enjoyed with an old friend. She wanted to know why on earth I had paid £70 for a bottle of Chateau Firan 1985. I told her that she was quite right, and that really I should have gone for the 1989 Beychevelle at £150. From her full and frank response, I sensed that was not quite the point she was making. And I thought she was a wine buff.

A white stretch limousine is waiting in the short-stay car park. Parker the chauffeur was so mesmerised by Victoria and Wanda that I had to remind him to turn off the air-conditioning. They'd catch their death otherwise. I equipped the fridge with three bottles of champagne (thank goodness for Lily's bargains), chocolate truffles and one packet of condoms. Well, it's only an hour's journey to the Tower Hotel.

The announcements board says that the flight has landed and that the baggage is in the hall, so I suppose that Dr Noriko must now be collecting his luggage from the carousel. I push right to the front of the barriers opposite the Arrivals door, clasping a large white board in front of my bosom stating his name. Want to be certain he sees me first, just in case any other City banker is here to woo him. I have left a copy of my proposal for the deal, along with a fact file on the bank plus a biography of myself and the deals I have worked on, in the limousine. Somehow, though, I don't think Dr Noriko will have time to read it during the journey, so I sent another copy on to his hotel. It will arrive with his breakfast tomorrow morning. I'm sure it will prove more fascinating reading than the *Financial Times*. Well, wouldn't be hard.

The automatic doors swing open, and people start coming through. I can see the tags on a few suitcases. Yes. This is the Japanese flight. I mean, look at all the golf clubs! I spot Dr Noriko, looking somewhat sleepy, following a small crowd of businessmen out through the automatic doors. I hold my board up and wave.

'Dr Noriko. Welcome to London.' He turns and examines my board, before pushing his luggage trolley in my direction. Goodness, he doesn't travel light for an international businessman. 'It's me. Trixie Trader. I have arranged transport for you into London.'

Dr Noriko reaches me. I remember my Japanese etiquette, drop my head in a respectful bow, take my business card out of its sterling silver holder and offer it to him, mindful to hold the top of it with one hand. Dr Noriko quickly remembers his manners, takes out one of his cards and proffers it to me. I smile, bow and accept it by taking hold of the bottom two corners. Now how long did Bloodhound say that I had to examine it? One minute? Two? I opt for ninety seconds, and stand there studying Dr Noriko's card as I mentally count down the time. I then place it in my cardholder, and smile. This man could be my career saver.

'Miss Trader?' Dr Noriko looks at me with a confused expression on his face. 'I am surprised to see you.' He rubs his elbow with a pointed movement that suggests he hasn't forgotten our last meeting. 'What are you doing here?' he adds, as he clasps both hands behind his back. Out of danger. 'Whom are you waiting for?'

'You! I heard you were in town and I decided to organise transport and entertainment.' I open my eyes very wide at him, 'for you. A small gesture from my humble bank. I have some suggestions for a deal to raise funds for your company and have taken the liberty of sending the proposal on to your hotel.' I smile, and add conspiratorially, 'I doubt you'll have much time to read it in the limousine, though.'

'You have organised a limousine?' Dr Noriko is a bit slow today. Must be jet-lag.

'Yes, Noriko-San. I have equipped it with your usual require-ments. It's waiting in the short-lay car park. Sorry!' I shake my head and wink at him. 'Short-stay car park.' I indicate towards the exit as I take hold of Dr Noriko's trolley. 'I'll show you the way.'

'No! Wait!' Dr Noriko grabs the trolley out of my hands. 'I am not here on business. I do not need any entertainment.' He spits the word out. 'I am here on a family holiday. The children have just stopped to use the restroom. They'll be through the doors any moment. Go away.' He starts to push me away from his trolley as a small Japanese woman in a Burberry raincoat reaches him, a baby in arms and two small children in tow. They look fractious and tired.

'Good afternoon.' She smiles at me. 'Are you with the airline? I see you have my husband's name on your board. Have you organised transport into London? The children are so tired; they are just desperate to get to their beds. Come along. Show us the way.' She gestures to me to take the trolley, and hands the baby to her husband. 'Is there any food or drink in the car?'

She can't seriously mean this? What on earth shall I do? Think.

'Well, er, I did include, er, something to satisfy your husband's appetite.' My job is doomed. Dr Noriko is looking distinctly uneasy. 'But I didn't know he was bringing his family, and I'm afraid there's nothing really suitable for children in the car. Perhaps a London taxi would be more appropriate? No visitor to London should miss out on a trip in a real London cab.'

'Nonsense.' Mrs Noriko puts a firm hand on the trolley, and pushes it and me towards the exit. 'I'm sure everything will be in order. We can stop if the children need anything.' What? Like blindfolds? Dr Noriko is looking at me in horror. I can tell his whole life is flashing in front of his eyes.

I walk slowly towards the short-stay car park, pushing the trolley, pretending it keeps getting stuck on the uneven paving. The Noriko family follows behind. Mrs Noriko rattles on to her husband in Japanese but he's remarkably silent. If panic were a noise then an eruption would be coming out of him. And me! I can see the limousine in the distance. Parker is standing by the bonnet waiting for Dr Noriko. His eyes nearly jump out of their sockets at the sight of Mrs Noriko and her flock.

Dr Noriko catches up with me as I pause for the fourth time pretending the wheels have got stuck in a rut, and hisses out of the corner of his mouth:

'I just hope that nothing is going to embarrass me, or my family, in the limousine. It is their first time in London.

Nothing, I repeat nothing, must go wrong. Perhaps you didn't know, but I am playing a round of golf with your chairman at the weekend. He is an old family friend. We were at Harvard together.' Oh. They would have been, wouldn't they? I can kiss goodbye to this job. Perhaps I should just take the next flight out. I always wanted to visit Nepal, or perhaps the Galapagos Islands. I could start up an offshore banking centre.

Parker is walking very slowly around to the passenger door. He has pulled his peaked cap low over his eyes. He doesn't want to be party to this disaster. He stops, his hand on the door handle, as I catch up with him.

'Just a moment, Parker. I want to, er, check that everything is satisfactory for the journey back to London.' I open the door slowly, careful not to allow Mrs Noriko to see inside. Victoria and Wanda are stretched out on two of the seats, legs splayed, holding up their glasses of champagne in salutation. I mouth to them to sit up straight and close their legs. Wanda smiles, a cube of ice glistening between her teeth, before contorting her body into a shape that I never knew panthers could achieve. I withdraw from the car and turn to face Mrs Niroko.

'I don't know. There's a terrible smell in the car. I think the last passenger left a kipper in the exhaust pipe or something. It might make the children travel-sick. Perhaps a taxi?' I swivel the trolley around, in the direction of the cab rank in the distance.

'Do not be so silly. What is a kipper? And why would somebody put one in the exhaust pipe? I am sure it is just the smell of unleaded fuel. Anyway, we can open the windows. We have been travelling for hours and we just want to get to our hotel. Momoko, Takumi, come here. Stop running around, and I have told you before about picking your nose, Momoko. It is dirty.' She slaps the little girl on her arm, reiterating the point. 'Dirty.'

'What about a child seat? For the baby? The limousine doesn't have that facility. It could be dangerous. I am not sure that it is insured to carry small children.' Dr Noriko is nodding. He knows a Get-Out-Of-Jail card when he sees one.

'Perhaps a London cab,' he volunteers. 'London traffic can be so dangerous, and I would hate for anything to happen to the children.'

'My dear husband, what is sitting on top of our luggage?' Mrs Noriko points at the stack of Louis Vuitton suitcases, and there – like the king of the castle – is a child seat. 'You told me to bring it. Don't you remember?' Why, oh why, didn't I notice it earlier? 'Momoko, come here. I have called you once already.' She leans into her handbag and pulls out a bag of tissues, takes one out and grabs her daughter's nose with it and twists.

'Wait,' I tell Mrs Noriko, as she instructs the nervous Parker to load the luggage into the car and set up the child seat. 'There's something I must warn you. The, er, tour guides that I arranged were rather hot in the car – the air-conditioning is not working. They've put on their summer outfits. Personally I think they're a bit skimpy but apparently business has trebled since they've started wearing them, though some of the limo company's clients have complained. They think the summer outfits make the girls look like, well, ladies of the night. A woman of the world like yourself wouldn't fall into such an obvious trap.'

'That is very kind of you.' Mrs Noriko acknowledges my compliment. 'Unfortunately, although my English may be fluent, I am no woman of the world. I was just lucky enough to have a Norland nanny. In fact, this is my first trip outside Japan, although I feel like I know England so well. *Brief Encounter* is my favourite film and I've seen it thirty times. And then my husband has told me so much about his adventures overseas that I was desperate to experience for myself some of the pleasures that he has enjoyed.' I think she may live to regret that wish.

I hear the pop of a cork as Victoria and Wanda open another bottle of champagne. 'Ah, champagne!' says Mrs Noriko. 'I just love champagne – it's too expensive in Tokyo to buy for anything but the most special of occasions.' This will be special all right. 'What a lovely gesture.'

She leans into the limousine with the baby now back in her

arms, and makes to strap him into his child seat. Run, Trixie. Run like the wind. Get out of here. But I can't. I'm transfixed with horror and trepidation. Suddenly I hear a yelp, and Mrs Noriko jumps out of the limousine, nearly knocking her head on the door frame.

'Have you seen,' she pauses, 'what,' another pause, 'they are wearing?' She is pointing into the limousine. Her two children come up to look but she shoves them roughly away.

'I did warn you that not everyone approves of the tour guides' uniforms,' I splutter weakly.

'Tour guides! Tour guides!! Those tramps are not tour guides.' Mrs Noriko is shrieking, which is making it hard to hear what she is saying. 'Your company will pay for this.' She waves her finger at her husband. 'Did you know anything about this?' Dr Noriko looks in the limousine, and as he withdraws his head I can sense a mood of regret at what might have been. But quickly he changes into the loyal-husband-who-is-shocked-that-such-women-exist.

'No!' He is shaking his head manically. He points at me. 'I didn't even know she was going to be here. I've only met her once before. She was the girlfriend of that chap Sam I told you about. I don't know what she is doing here.' He tries to console his wife, patting her arm. 'But you are right. Somebody will pay for this.' He looks darkly at me. Oh, God. What have I done?

Thursday, October 12
(D Day minus 33 – there will be one less head for the bank to cut as I'm going to do it for them)

Even the security guards look surprised to see me when I arrive this morning at a quarter to seven. One of them, rather irritatingly, lifts his watch to his ear and shakes it to make sure that it is still ticking. I flash my security pass at them, and march through. I'm in no mind for social niceties today.

I want to catch Bloodhound before the morning meeting and give him a piece of my mind. I had Mrs Noriko ranting at me in the short-stay car park for what seemed like hours – and I thought the children were meant to be tired – whilst Dr Noriko has said he will file an official complaint with the chairman. I might just as well pack my belongings in a black bin liner and leave now.

And, to add insult to injury, Victoria and Wanda charged me travel expenses for their journey back to London after Mrs Noriko threw them out of the limousine.

Bloodhound is going to pay for this. He knows how much I prepared for my meeting with Dr Noriko. I stayed in the office until late in the evening on both Monday and Tuesday, and for what? To write a proposal for a deal that Dr Noriko is just going to throw in the bin – along with my career.

I storm out of the lift and march towards my desk, barely acknowledging the greetings of various colleagues on the way. Bloodhound looks startled to see me, as well he might. I'm sure that guilt is written all over his face.

'Trixie. What are you doing . . . ?'

He is unable to finish the question before I slap him – hard – across his cheek. The outline of my hand blazes out from his face. As he grasps his hand to his cheek the treacherous bastard looks shocked. People are looking over at us, attracted by the noise of flesh hitting flesh.

'What on earth . . . That hurt. What's got into you?'

'Good. I'm glad. It was meant to.' My blood is boiling now. I ignore the furtive glances from colleagues, peeking over their screens at the two of us. 'What's got into me? What's got into me? What do you think? Did you perhaps neglect to tell me one vital detail regarding Dr Noriko's trip?'

Bloodhound looks puzzled. Such an actor. He's missed his vocation.

'Like what? I told you. Terminal Four. British Airways. Arriving at three p.m. What more did you need to know?'

'Well, perhaps that he had his wife *and children* travelling with him?'

Shock registers on his face. 'Oh . . . my . . . God.' He says the words slowly, pausing between each one as the full horror of his betrayal dawns on him. 'But you sent a limousine with . . .'

'Yes!'

'No! What did he say?'

'Great, Trixie. Thanks a lot. My wife loves surprises, and threesomes. Can you find something to occupy the other girl whilst we just get started?' My hand is itching to slap him again.

'No? He didn't?'

'Of course he didn't! What do you think he said?'

'God. This is awful. It doesn't bear thinking about. What did his wife say?' Bloodhound continues, with a careful eye on my hand, which I am screwing up into a fist, ready for the second round.

'You are looking at the spawn of the devil.' Make him squirm. 'I have corrupted young minds and abused my position to inveigle poor desperate women into a career from which there is no salvation. Why?' I shout at him. 'Why did you do this to me? You know how much depended on me making a good impression. I'm ruined. Dr Noriko's going to file an official complaint with the chairman. And there's another fact you omitted to mention. Did you know they were close friends?'

'No. Of course not. But he won't complain. Don't be silly.

What would he say?' Bloodhound looks at me, ignoring the lights flashing on his dealer board alerting him to incoming telephone calls. ' "By the way, Robert. Just want to complain about a member of your staff. She sent a limousine to meet me with prostitutes in it. What's that you say? Why would she do something like that? Search me. I don't know why she would think I would want such a surprise. I'm a married man, after all." '

'He doesn't speak like that. He's Japanese! A Japanese businessman on a private family holiday, whose life has been turned upside down by an unexpected gift from a banker desperate to do business with him.'

'Exactly. He won't say anything.' Bloodhound holds his hands out in a placatory fashion. 'Have you not read about all those Japanese civil servants losing their jobs because they accepted hospitality in those No-Knickers bars? He'd lose his job if he complained, because there would have to be an official investigation here, and I, for one, would mention all the small tokens that I know he has requested on previous trips. He has some strange tastes.'

'I'm not bothered about previous trips! You don't seem to get it. This was the only trip I cared about and you, you have ruined my career. Why did you do it?'

I notice colleagues reluctantly leaving their desks to join the morning meeting, shooting glances back over their shoulders as they enter the glass-walled room at the edge of the floor. Bloodhound makes to stand up, but then seems to think better of it. So, I miss another morning meeting. What's new? And why should I bother anyway? I've lost this job now. I see Sam looking at us as he enters the meeting room.

'What's this? A lovers' tiff?' he shouts over. 'Why don't you kiss and make up?' He puckers up, and I feel like slapping him too.

'Get lost, arsehole.' I gesture at him. 'Crawl back under your duvet.' He laughs and closes the door of the meeting room behind him.

'Why did you do it? Why, Bloodhound? How could you set

me up?' I feel like crying. All my hopes and energies – wasted. I know that Bloodhound and I haven't been the closest of friends since my break-up with Sam, but I thought that I could at least *trust* him. After all, he saw what his last betrayal did to me.

'I didn't know, Trixie, believe me.'

'What? Like you didn't know about Miss Chang in Hong Kong?' I know I'm raking up history, but I cannot let Bloodhound get away with this.

'Look, you know that I knew about that. I confessed that to you at the time.'

'But you didn't tell me until you were found out. Just like you didn't tell me that Dr Noriko was travelling *en famille*.'

'I genuinely didn't know, Trixie. I heard that Dr Noriko was coming to London, and immediately all I could think was that this was an opportunity for you.'

'I've wondered about that. Why didn't you think there was an opportunity for *you*?'

'My job isn't under threat. I saw this as an opportunity to make amends. For not,' he hesitates, 'for not telling you about Sam. A year too late, admittedly, but I thought you might appreciate the gesture.'

'Appreciate it! Your gesture, as you so politely put it, has ruined me. Don't you get it?'

'Look. Calm down. Let's think through this logically. Shouting and hitting me isn't going to help.' Well, I don't know. I'm feeling slightly better. 'Irrespective of what happened yesterday, you put a good proposal together for Dr Noriko's company. He's a canny businessman and he has to consider it.'

'Don't be silly. He's probably spent an awkward evening trying to explain to his wife why a City banker would want to supply a limousine and two prostitutes for him! I don't think he will be looking kindly at anything else that I've supplied. So, you really didn't know?' I look at Bloodhound's face carefully, searching for any signs of guilt. He shakes his head ruefully.

'I really didn't. I don't blame you for not believing me, but I honestly did not know that he was coming to London on a family holiday. Truly.'

'But how *did* you find out he was coming?'

Bloodhound shifts uneasily in his chair. He hesitates.

'Sam told me.'

'What? You told Sam about my predicament?' The snake. Rat. Through the glass walls, I can see Sam holding court in the morning meeting. Probably telling them all about his wonderful clients, and how well he's judged the currency markets. He is dead meat!

'Of course not. But that morning when you interrupted us talking via the internal intercom, well, I,' he pauses, 'I forgot to turn off the connection. He heard our whole conversation, including the part where we discussed your situation.'

'And I suppose he then casually called you up and said he wanted to help.'

'Something like that. Yes.'

'And you bought that? When over the past year has he ever done anything nice for me? He makes lewd comments as he walks past, beds half the female staff on the trading floor and then rubs my nose in it by hanging flags over his desk. And suddenly, one day out of the blue, he decides to help. Were you not suspicious?'

'Obviously not. Look, Trixie, I just thought that maybe he was trying to make amends, particularly when he said that I wasn't to tell you about his efforts.' Why did God make Bloodhound so stupid? Alarm bells should have been ringing as far away as Australia. The morning meeting is over. People are traipsing out of the room, coffee cups in one hand, croissants and Danish pastries in the other. I'm going to confront Sam. He's going to pay. Look at him. Arrogant sod. He thinks he's so funny.

I start walking towards Sam, when I hear Jim call my name.

'Trixie.' He's standing in the doorway of his office. 'Can I have a word?'

This is it. My stomach churns. Bloodhound looks nervously at me, and then holds up his hands, revealing crossed fingers. I take a deep breath and move towards the office. Has Mary got the black bags ready? How many will I need?

'Come in. Sit down.' Jim ushers me in, points at a chair in front of his desk and closes the door. An ominous sign. He takes his seat, glances quickly at the screens to check on the markets, and begins.

'I've just had a call from the chairman.'

'I can explain. It was a genuine mistake.'

'Mistake? I hope not. Dr Noriko has been on to the chairman. He arrived yesterday on a family holiday – but you know that, don't you?' Spit it out, Jim. Call the security guards to escort me off the premises. 'Well, apparently, there's some sort of family emergency in Tokyo and his wife and children are catching the midday flight back today.' Emergency! She came to London to experience some of the pleasures that he'd enjoyed and then discovered that they didn't share the same tastes. 'Anyway, that's besides the point. His family went out last night, leaving him alone in the hotel room – apparently he was jet-lagged – and the upshot is that he read a proposal that you had biked over to his hotel. Great show of initiative, that. He loves it.' What? Is this a wind-up? 'Thinks it will be a great deal and wonders if you would like dinner to discuss it further. Suggested to the chairman that you might want to bring along two friends, some people that he's already met? You can sort those details out between you. He'll be at the hotel all afternoon.' The shock must be registering on my face.

'Come now, Trixie, don't look surprised. I always knew you had it in you. Just needed a friendly kick. But a word of warning.' He leans towards me. 'I've heard some rumours about Dr Noriko. It seems he makes some – how can I put it? – strange demands of people that he does business with. Be careful. Maybe you should take Chris along. Don't want to get into any problems with the regulators about unethical behaviour, do we?'

Certainly not. Anyway, I'm not sure that I'm going to accept his invitation to dinner. I can't afford the dessert course.

Bloodhound looks at me nervously as I walk back to my desk following the meeting with Jim. He tries to shelter his screen from me but is a minute too late. As I sit down I can see that he's e-mailing Julie, probably warning her to be ready to drop everything at a moment's notice and come over to pick up my pieces. He swings his chair round to face me and drops his voice.

'Well, how did it go? I've been crossing my fingers here for you.'

'And that's not easy when you have cloven hooves, is it?'

'Come on, Trixie. Drop the sarcasm. I feel partly responsible.'

'Oh no,' I say. 'I know who's entirely responsible.' I glance over to Sam's desk but he's not there. Just the Star and Stripes flying over it. I scan the football-pitch-sized trading floor and soon spot him. He's standing by the coffee machine, deep in conversation with one of the latest female recruits. She's twisting her blonde hair in her fingers, playing the coquette for all she's worth. Oh God. I don't believe it. They're clinking their Styrofoam cups. To think that once was me. I must have been a mug – no pun intended.

I can remember Sam's first line, as he fixed his brown eyes on me: 'I think you've lost something.' I did a quick check of all the buttons on my blouse before he added: 'Sorry, my mistake. I thought you'd lost your inhibitions.' Not a classic chat-up line, admittedly, but I was just so relieved that I wasn't Nell Gwyn-ing at the trading floor that I burst out laughing. We ended up going for a drink that evening. Unsurprisingly, my inhibitions went two days later – although they returned the next morning when Lily walked in on us, with her feather duster in hand, braced to attack the cobwebs. It was quite funny watching her pointedly keeping her eyes averted as she scanned the coving.

'I'm going over there!' I point towards the coffee machine and Sam. 'He's going to pay.'

'Wait.' Bloodhound places a restraining hand on my arm. 'Take a deep breath. Anyway, don't leave me in suspense. Fill me in. Come on. What did Jim say? Has Dr Noriko rung?'

'Oh yes.' I nod slowly. 'He was on the phone first thing.'

'I'm so sorry. Was Jim really angry?' Bloodhound looks wretched. 'Do you want me to go in to him and explain? I'll do it if you think it will make things better.'

'No, don't bother. Nothing will make things better.' I shrug my shoulders at him. 'The chairman is involved now.'

'You mean . . . Oh no! What about a tribunal?'

'What? Is that a new lap-dancing club?'

Bloodhound looks truly flustered. 'Lap-dancing? Trixie, I wasn't suggesting that you should, you know,' he hesitates, 'sell your body. I wouldn't think such a thing. I mean, I'm sure that you'll get another job soon. These things blow over. People will forget that you procured prostitutes. Oh God.' He spots my glacial expression. 'Can this day get any worse?'

'Now you've lost me.' I'm going to milk this one. Bloodhound may not be ultimately responsible but, really, talk about gullible. Trusting Sam of all people. 'How did we get on to a conversation about me selling my body? What sort of a girl do you think I am? My mother's in the Women's Institute. *Me* procuring prostitutes? I did no such thing. They were escorts.'

'I don't think anything. I just, I just worried when you mentioned lap-dancing clubs. Not that you wouldn't make a lot of money at it,' he adds quickly. 'You have a great figure. I've often admired it.'

'What?' I shriek at him. Throw the bait and reel him in. 'You peeping Tom! How can I sit beside you now, knowing that you have sexual fantasies about me? I could report you to Human Resources.'

'I don't.' Bloodhound's face is crimson.

'Why? What's wrong with me?'

Bloodhound looks as if he is about to cry. He's dug a hole the size of a canyon. 'Absolutely nothing. You're perfect, well, apart from your sharp tongue, but even that's quite endearing, when you get to know you.' He stops abruptly. Beads of sweat have gathered on his forehead. I'm getting slightly worried about his blood pressure. Time to put him out of his misery. If only I had a double-barrelled shotgun.

'Bloodhound.'

'Yes?'

'Shut up! Don't you recognise a wind-up? Although thanks for the compliments. You've got perfect judgement for one so flawed.'

'But . . .'

'I said shut up! Jim called me in to congratulate me.'

'Eh?'

'That's what I thought. Apparently Mrs Noriko and the children are returning to Tokyo today – Dr Noriko told the chairman there was a family emergency back home.'

'More like an emergency meeting with the divorce lawyers. I think she should take him for every yen that she can.'

'I warned you. Don't you want me to finish my story?' Got to be firm with these people. Let them know who's boss. Bloodhound nods. 'Anyway, the short version is that Dr Noriko had some unexpected time on his hands last night, examined my proposal and likes it.'

'What?' Bloodhound yelps, like an animal in pain. I spot colleagues looking over at him, just to check that I haven't socked him another one. 'I don't believe it.'

'Well, you should. Dr Noriko wants me to call him to organise,' I pause for emphasis, and indicate quote marks with my fingers, 'dinner. And he'd like me to bring my two friends,' another quote marks sign, 'along. Jim is thrilled at my initiative – although thankfully he doesn't know about all of them. Says that he always knew I had it in me. But, get this.' I lean closer to Bloodhound and drop my voice. 'He warned me that Dr Noriko has strange tastes and I should be careful. Suggested I might take you along – but I don't think his tastes are that strange!'

'What are you going to do?' Bloodhound pointedly ignores

my last comment. 'This could be the answer to your prayers. Think of the spring collections!' How well he knows me.

'I am. And the summer, autumn and winter ones. I'm going to have to organise dinner. Maybe I'll take him to Nobu – that was one of the tables I booked in advance, just in case one of my clients suddenly decided that they were desperate to meet me.' I check my Palm Pilot. 'Yep. Got a booking next Tuesday. I'll ring him. See if he can make it.'

'What are you going to do about,' he hesitates, 'you know.' His voice is so low that I can hardly hear him. 'His request to meet your friends?'

Bloodhound has hit the nail on my dilemma's head. What should I do? The booking is only for two, but I'm sure I could change that. I just don't think that I want to. If Dr Noriko is keen to do this deal then he will just have to do it without the frills. I feel different from yesterday. I'm now empowered. Yesterday I would have done a deal at any cost. Today I am just as keen to do the deal – more so, perhaps – but I want Dr Noriko to do business with me because my proposal was the best. Not because the girls I chose were the best – although I must say that I do have spectacular taste. No, if I lose this job it will be because I couldn't pull off the deal.

'I'm going to ignore it,' I tell Bloodhound. 'Dr Noriko will now play by my rules. Anyway, now that's sorted and you know the score, I have something else to sort out.' I look around for Sam. He's going to get it. Big time.

'Careful, Trixie.' Bloodhound's warning follows me as I walk over to the foreign exchange division. I notice that Sam has crossed off twelve stars on the American flag that's flying over his desk today.

'Where is he?' I enquire of Justin, the junior trader on the desk. He joined as a graduate recruit two months ago, but seems to be a quick learner. I notice he has an alphabet board on top of his screen. A and B are crossed out. 'I'll warn all the women on the floor whose names begin with C to watch out,' I add. 'Or would you prefer me to mention it to the men?' He blushes, before stammering that Sam has left for the weekend.

Apparently he is taking some clients off for a golfing weekend at Wentworth and was only in this morning to sort out some last-minute details. Blast. Damn. Shit. I was just in the mood to crucify him. It will have to keep. What's that phrase? Revenge is a dish best served cold. His will be freezing!

I return to my desk, and see that Julie has sent me an e-mail. Better respond to let her know that all is well.

To: JulieJ @ Wbank.co.uk

Dear Julie
Noriko loved the proposal – and has a few proposals of his own. Not quite so tasteful though. Job appears safe for now. Jim quite impressed with my initiative.
Trix

PS Have you seen the latest jokes about Charles and Camilla? I'll send them on to you.

I have just finished typing the reply when a light flashes up on the dealer-board screen in front of me indicating that somebody is calling on my direct line. I press the light on the screen to answer and lift my handset.

'Trixie here.'

'Trixie, darling. Lovely to speak to you.' The male voice sounds vaguely familiar but I can't quite place it. 'Chris said I should give you a ring. Says you are in the market for doing business. Keen to meet all those clients who want to raise some money.'

'Yes, that's right.' My mental Rolodex flicks through the voices of all potential clients. 'I'm rejuvenated and eager to do business. Are you in the market for borrowing?'

'Oh yes. But enough about me. I was sorry to hear that you split up with that delightful young man Sam.' Got it. Frederick Kane. Bloodhound said that he was looking to raise funds. I was meant to ring him this week, after he returned from Frankfurt.

'That was ages ago, Frederick.' I feel smug that I have now placed the voice.

'Actually, that's something I meant to mention, but,' he hesitates, 'it will keep until we meet. So when can we? Are you free for lunch next week? I can tell you about my financial needs and you can tell me how you can solve them. I used to like doing business with you.'

'Sounds good.' I press a few buttons to check my existing reservations. 'What about Wednesday? Number One Lombard Street? About twelve thirty?' I hear the flick of pages as Frederick checks in his diary. Isn't he computerised yet?

'Perfect. Look forward to it. Ciao.' He hangs up. It's like the buses. Nothing for years then two clients come along at once.

'That was Frederick Kane,' I mouth at Bloodhound, who is engrossed in a telephone call. 'We're meeting for lunch next week.' He gives me a thumbs-up sign. Right, back to work. Clients to call. Lunches to book. E-mails to respond to. I ring Dr Noriko and he confirms that he can make dinner on Tuesday. Luckily he doesn't mention Wanda and Victoria. Well, the calls are taped and could be taken down in evidence against him! I get so engrossed in my work that I don't even notice the time flying by. It is only when I feel a tap on my shoulder that I spot that it says 5 p.m. on my screen. I swing round to see Ciaran standing behind me, a big smile on his face and two cups of latté in his hands. Wow! He really could be Liam Neeson's body double. And perhaps I could be Natasha Richardson's.

'Hi,' I say as casually as is possible when temperatures are rising in parts of the body where they shouldn't be, considering the money this bank spends on state-of-the-art air-conditioning.

'Hi yourself. Just thought I would come over and see how you're doing. Have a coffee.' He hands one over and drops his voice. 'Any luck with you-know-what? I've been worried.' I don't allow myself to consider the fact that he's actually been thinking about me – *outside* office hours!

'Two possibilities. Pitching to both clients next week, so

fingers crossed.' I hold up my hands to reveal four fingers in perfect crosses. Oh, and my new manicure.

'I'll be crossing everything for you too.' I like his smile. It's warm and open, and causes little wrinkles to gather around his eyes. I feel myself blush. God, don't do this to me. Remember my Battle Strategy. 'Anyway, could you write down your address. I won't be here tomorrow – an off-site meeting – but just want to finalise details for dinner.'

Dinner. Have we got a date? I try to keep the excitement out of my voice.

'Dinner?'

'Your dinner party. Don't tell me you've forgotten.' Oh, that. Blast. How stupid. I feel slightly disappointed.

'No, don't be silly,' I lie. 'That's all in hand. My housekeeper Lily is catering – I think she was getting the food today, actually.' I scribble down my address on one of the bank's 'With Compliments' slips and hand it over. He looks down at it.

'Right. And you said about eight thirty?' I nod. 'Should I bring anything?' Yes. What about condoms? Lots of them.

'No. Just yourself. I've got loads of drink in the flat. Anyway, how was the training course?' He pulls a face, and shakes his head.

'Deadly dull. The self-development part of the course just took the biscuit. At the end of that day we had to form two lines, known as an Admiration Aisle, and then each of us had to walk through it one by one. Every person we passed had to say something nice about us. It was frightful. I felt like a complete idiot.'

'So go on, spill the beans. What nice things did they say?'

A red bloom is blossoming up his face. 'You don't want to know.'

'Try me. Come on.'

'Well, about five of them said that I looked like – God, this is embarrassing – that I looked like Liam Neeson. I mean, did you ever? I look nothing like him. What do you think?'

'No! Never noticed it myself.'

Friday, October 13
(D Day minus 32 – never work with children or housekeepers)

The guests are arriving in half an hour and Lily is calmly standing at the oven in my Shaker kitchen, wooden spoon in hand, stirring a Le Creuset saucepan on the hob, dressed only in bra, black skirt and a plastic apron with Donald Duck on the front.

'What are you doing?' I shriek.

'Making some gravy.' She carefully dips her finger into the wooden spoon. 'Hmm.' Her face screws up as she contemplates her culinary efforts. 'Think it needs more salt.' She grinds the cellar over the pot.

'Not that. Where's your blouse?'

'Hanging up on the back of the dining room door. Why?' She looks distractedly towards me as she begins to cut up small squares of bread to fry in a pan. 'Thought croutons would be nice.'

'Well, why aren't you wearing it?' I cannot stand this. Nine of the City's weirdest individuals coming for dinner at my flat, and Lily has decided to serve them in a half-naked state. Why didn't I just invite David Attenborough as well? There's going to be plenty of material for a telly series on wildlife.

'I didn't want to splash it,' responds Lily in a soothing tone. 'It's a real devil trying to get olive oil out of viscose. I don't care what they say in the adverts about washing powders and tablets, as far as I'm concerned nothing gets my whites the way I want them. I'll put it on, dear, just as soon as I've finished this. I even bought a new white lace tabard for this evening, so I'll look the part.' She stares at me. 'And, love, so do you.' She moves forward to examine my new outfit – a taupe silk shell top and matching cigarette pants from Nicole Farhi – but I step back quickly just in case she gets any greasy fingerprints on it. 'You look absolutely lovely. Your friends are going to be so impressed.'

'Are those new earrings?' I ask, catching a glint of light.

'Yes. A friend gave me them. They're pretty, aren't they?' She pushes her hair behind her ears to show me.

'They look like Tiffany's.'

'Well they're not. They're mine.' She turns back to her frying, and I pour myself a relaxing glass of pink champagne before moving into the dining room to check the table. The plain white porcelain, topped with scarlet linen napkins folded into gold tassels, and crystal glassware looks lovely against my new glass and pewter dining table and chairs. Wonder if I should tone it down, though. Perhaps the arum lilies should go. Don't want my colleagues to think I'm too affluent – I am trying to win their sympathy after all. Oh, and 'friendship'.

I check on the bowls of Kettle chips and Japanese crackers in the sitting room, and spend ages deciding which CD to put on the Bang & Olufsen before opting for Sade. I then return to the kitchen, where Lily is struggling to do up the buttons on her blouse. Perhaps it would be better if she took the oven gloves off first.

'By the way, what's the menu for tonight? Did you visit the organic butcher that I told you about?'

'Course I did, and I picked up a nice loin of pork. It's in the oven. Very lean, although it should be for the price. I don't know why Asda's not good enough for you and your friends.' She shakes her head in despair. 'Anyway, I've stuffed it with prunes – got the recipe from that nice book you have by that Raymond Blanc chap. Strange, though, on the back it says that he's a Leonardo da Vinci of chefs. I always thought that bloke was an artist.' She pauses to muse over the quandary. 'I'm going to serve it with roast potatoes, red cabbage and French beans, and a nice rich gravy. Listen to me.' She giggles. 'I sound like one of the contestants on *Master Chef*. And I thought your friends might also like some soup to start with. It's so chilly out there at the moment. I'm sure we'll have a frost tonight. That reminds me, I bought you some de-icer for your car. I said you'd run out. So I've prepared some potato and leek soup to warm them up.'

'Vichyssoise.'

'I didn't do any fish. Was I meant to?'

'No. Vichyssoise is the correct name for potato and leek soup. You will remember that when you serve it, won't you?'

'Course.' She flashes a smile at me as she fastens her new tabard over her white blouse. 'Fishy arse. I could hardly forget that. And for dessert—'

'Pudding,' I interrupt.

'Sorry, for *pudding* . . .' She stops, building up the anticipation. I hope she's made her wondrous profiteroles or even a fruit Pavlova. 'I've got ice cream.'

'Ice cream!' This is hardly the image I want to portray.

'Yes. We've raspberry ripple and Neapolitan.'

'Is that Ben and Jerry? I didn't know they did those flavours.'

'Ben and Jerry? Haven't seen their van around.'

'They don't have vans.' I cannot believe this. 'They're one of the world's top ice cream producers. From America. Like Häagen Dazs.'

'I couldn't get my ice cream from America. Think of the cost! No, I got this locally from one of north London's top ice cream producers,' she adds, proudly. Tell me this is a dream. Please! I look desperately around the kitchen work surfaces searching out any telltale signs of icing sugar or eggshells to prove that Lily is joking.

'Is that really all, Lily? Ice cream?'

'No.' She smiles at me as I greedily top up my champagne glass. I think I'm going to need it. 'Of course not. I've made some raspberry sauce, and I've even got some Flakes. You can all make 99s.' I down my champagne in one as the doorbell rings.

'Would you get that, Lily, please?' Why did I ever trust her with the catering? I should have hired a professional chef, or just gone to good old Harvey Nicks food hall.

'It's Julie.' Lily's voice echoes down the hallway. 'And one, two, three young men.' She directs them into the sitting room, muttering under her breath about Julie being a promiscuous girl, before returning to the kitchen.

74

'Who's that?' Ciaran looks so sexy in his civvies. He's standing over the coffee table, picking at the Kettle chips, in a black woollen suit, which I'm sure is Nicole Farhi, and a cream turtleneck cashmere sweater. God, what I wouldn't give to see him in his birthday suit. Steady.

'Lily, my housekeeper,' I reply, ignoring the look from Julie. 'Would you all like a drink – Julie?' I exchange air kisses with my dearest friend. She's looking cool in a little black dress, which she mutters in my ear is Emporio Armani, and Jimmy Choo sandals. 'Ciaran?' He moves forward to kiss me, and I have to concentrate hard not to pucker up and swallow his lips. 'Bloodhound?' I shift my head as he advances to kiss me. I want to get my colleagues' trust – not their diseases. Anyway, he could have dressed up. Levi jeans are so passé these days. 'And?' I stop mid-sentence as I look in horror at the fourth guest. Bloodhound's friend is a nerd. He has brought a nerd into my house. Into my nerd-free zone.

'This is Nathan, Trixie,' says Bloodhound. 'I told you about him. The three of us were at university together.' I stare at the tall, gawky individual standing in front of me. His hair is sitting in greasy curls, but it is his glasses that distract me. The lenses are so thick that for one fleeting moment I think he has four eyes. Nathan the Visually Challenged Nerd extends his hand towards me.

'Pleased to meet you,' he says. I feel his clammy hand in mine and inwardly cringe. 'I've heard so much about you from Chris.' I smile graciously, and quickly withdraw my hand.

'Right. Champagne all round!' I move towards the kitchen, as Ciaran shouts after me.

'Madam, you are spoiling us!'

I have just finished pouring the champagne when the bell rings again. Kate is standing on my doorstep, four bags of nachos in hand.

'You said not to bring wine, but I think you can never have too many nachos in the house. Here you are.' She pushes them into my hand and begins taking her coat off. 'What's for dinner?'

75

My God. She is wearing a long velvet skirt (marks out of ten? six) and an extremely clingy Lurex T-shirt with a ladybird embroidered over her bosom (marks? minus four). If they ever want to produce another Liberty Bell, I am looking at two perfect moulds.

'Wow. What is that fantastic smell?' Kate sniffs at the aromas drifting out of the kitchen. 'Mind if I have a look?' She then follows the direction of her nose, in a manner reminiscent of Hansel and Gretel and the trail of crumbs.

As I serve drinks to the first arrivals, the rest of my guests turn up. Manfred has overdone the Brylcreem. He is just oozing. I want to cover his chair in the dining room with a towel but decide it is not the best course of action to win Brownie points. Besides, being a German, he would probably think somebody else had been in before and reserved it. Liz is bursting with enthusiasm and almost knocks Ciaran over in her keenness to greet him. I thought they always kissed on the cheeks in France? And then I suddenly remember why I don't have much to do with Nancy and Leon. They're monosyllabic and boring. Nancy is wearing a pink anorak, and Leon's wearing brown suede shoes! I introduce Julie and Nathan to my colleagues.

'Love your outfit, Trixie,' says Liz, clinking glasses with me. 'I used to have something like that years ago. What about me? Do you like the dress?' She does a twirl to show off her figure-hugging silk cheongsam. I check her slim calves. God, I hate her! 'Sam bought it for me. He said I'd earned it. What a man! Don't know how you let him slip through your fingers.' Hmm, wish I'd had my hand over a steep cliff at the time. She looks around the room. 'You've done wonders here in such a small space.'

Kate returns from the kitchen, a bowl of nachos in one hand. 'Lily says that we can go through to the dining room at any time. She's ready to serve some sort of fish soup. I had a little taster' – probably with a ladle – 'and it's very nice. A bit like leek and potato soup. Couldn't taste the fish at all.' She glances around the room. 'Julie. Haven't seen you for ages. Where've you been hiding? What's it like working for an American bank?' She links arms with Julie and directs her towards the dining room, shovelling a handful of nachos into her mouth en route. Those glands!

I show the rest of my guests through before running into the kitchen to check on Lily, who's serving the soup out of a tureen into the bone-china soup bowls.

'It's vichyssoise. Remember. And what are they?' I point at a plate of gold-foil-covered chocolates.

'Ferrero Rocher. My friend Elsie says they serve them in all the best places. Even the embassies. Do you want me to bring the soup bowls through on a tray, or serve them separately?'

'It's up to you. Don't worry about what I think,' I mutter under my breath. 'You haven't done so far.' I grab three bottles of Fleurie.

'This looks delicious,' says Ciaran, as Lily places a bowl of soup in front of him. 'What is it?'

'Vichyssoise,' replies Lily. Thank you, God.

'Oh, it's nothing to do with fish then,' says Kate, in a confused voice. She smiles at Leon, who is sitting on her right-hand side. Julie is on her other side, beside Nerd Features.

'Lily, is it?' Liz looks with disdain at her tabard. 'I don't mean to be a nuisance but I'm vegan. Didn't Trixie say?'

'No,' replies Lily. 'That wasn't the word she used.' Good woman. 'Venal? Was that what she said?' Okay, Lily, that's enough. 'Or was it venereal?' Or maybe not. Liz is looking distinctly annoyed. 'What does vegan mean?'

'I eat no animal products.' Liz looks at Ciaran whom she has sat down beside, totally ignoring the name cards, and indicates her figure. 'Can't you tell?'

'And what about pork?' asks Lily. Liz shakes her head.

'Pork?' pipes up Leon. 'I can't eat that.'

'Why?' demands Lily, all indignant. 'What's wrong with it? I've stuffed it with prunes. I marinated them in cognac for six hours, just like the recipe said. It smells lovely, even if I do say so myself.'

'But I'm Jewish.'

'You can't be Jewish,' insists Lily. 'You're blond, for a start!' I decide it is time for me to intervene.

'Sorry, Leon. I didn't know you were Jewish. You've never mentioned it. How embarrassing.'

'Well, this is *only* the third time that you've talked to me.' Damn! This is not creating quite the impression that I wanted. Bloodhound and Ciaran are giggling on the other side of the table. Kate has finished her soup, and is tearing a second bread roll apart. 'But,' Leon continues, 'as my surname is Liebowitz, I thought you might've guessed.' Oh, is that what it is?

'Can I get you something else, Leon? We might be able to scrape together an omelette for you. What's in the fridge, Lily?'

'Ham.' Leon looks at her like she's the devil incarnate. It's an easy mistake to make. 'Or there's some sausages.'

'And what about me?' pipes up Liz. 'I'm truly sorry but I can't eat this soup. It's got cream in it. Nor the main course. What's for dessert?'

'Ice cream,' Lily replies. I can hear Kate muttering: 'Yummy, yummy. My favourite.'

'What about a green salad to start?' I ask Liz. 'And I'm sure we can find something else.' Leon is standing up. 'I think I should go,' he says. 'I can't watch a man eat pig. Thanks for the champagne.' He takes his jacket from the back of his chair, and walks from the room towards the front door. 'Goodbye. See you next week.' He slams the door behind him. *Quelle horreur!* What else can go wrong tonight? Well, I suppose it is Friday the thirteenth.

'I'll stay and just muck in then.' Liz smiles longingly at Ciaran, who seems amused by the events, and pushes her soup bowl over towards Kate. 'Don't worry. I'll just pick at my plate. I won't desert you.' Blast! 'A salad would be lovely.'

'With mayonnaise?' asks Lily, as she disappears into the kitchen to sort it out.

'Is everything all right for the rest of you?' I ask, crossing my fingers as I speak. 'Manfred?' He nods. 'Nancy?'

'It's fine. Thank you.'

'I do like your outfit,' I lie, taking in Nancy's black trousers and maroon velvet shirt, which went out with Dallas. 'Where did you get it?'

'Oxfam. Do you ever go there?'

'No. Not for a while, but after seeing your outfit, I might be tempted.' Gosh. This being-nice-to-people stuff isn't as hard as I thought. 'And Nathan.' I turn to the nerd sitting on my right. 'What line of business are you in?'

'Computers.'

'Come now, Nathan,' says Ciaran. 'Don't be coy. He was in computers but he's now into the Internet business. Set it up himself and has just floated the company on the Aim market. The last time I saw this man he hadn't two ha'pennies to rub together, and now he's a multi-millionaire. Can you imagine?' I notice that Liz has also turned her attention towards Nathan. What a shallow girl. He looks at me.

'You'll have to excuse my appearance. I literally only just got off the flight from Hong Kong. Didn't even have a chance to put my contact lenses in.' Excuse it? I barely noticed. 'I was negotiating a large acquisition.'

'Really?' My ears prick up. 'Can you give us any insights?'

'I'm sorry. It's all still top secret. It'll really catapult my company into the big time. I just need to raise some finance and it'll be all systems go.'

'Would you all excuse me? I'll be back in a moment.' I dash into my bedroom, grab my Palm Pilot from the bedside table and lock myself in the en-suite bathroom. I scribble down the words *Nathan needs money. Find out more from Bloodhound about the situation*, just in case any of this evening is a blur when I wake tomorrow.

I return to the room. 'More wine?' Lily has cleared the soup bowls away and served the pork, and is bringing in plates of steaming vegetables. Liz is picking at her salad. Skinny bitch. 'And you, Manfred, how are you getting on these days?'

He pushes his glasses up the bridge of his nose before replying.

'Fine. Yes. You know I was in Frankfurt for the past few days?' I didn't, but smile in acknowledgement. 'The German companies are just so desperate to borrow money on the bond markets. I think your team will be very busy in the coming months selling all the bonds to clients.' He smiles at Ciaran. 'Still, bonuses should be good this year.'

Liz looks up from her watercress and rocket. 'Sam was telling me that there are rumours of job cuts. Apparently some people have already been warned that they're on the way out.' I look nervously at Bloodhound and Ciaran, but both maintain absolutely straight faces.

'I heard that too,' adds Kate. 'Lily, could I have another slice, do you think?' She pushes her plate out for some more pork. 'I'll have Leon's share. Looks delicious. What about you, Trixie?'

'I'll stick with what I've got.'

'No. I meant about the job cuts. Have you heard about them? You usually pick up all the gossip.'

'No!' Everyone looks at me as I shout the word out. I'm sure that my face is blazing. 'Nothing at all. Too busy to listen to gossip these days.' I fill up the glasses in an attempt to deflect attention. 'Turned over a new leaf and all that.'

'I've heard,' says Nancy. 'But I think my job is safe. I have lots of deals to do in France.' What? Who with? Spit the names out!

'What sorts of companies are looking to raise money?' I ask Manfred, my mental Palm Pilot springing into action.

'Oh, you know. The usual. This pork is delicious, and I just love the red cabbage. It reminds me of sauerkraut. You must give me the recipe.' He smiles at Lily, who beams back proudly as she hands Liz a plate of baked beans on toast.

'It's the cumin, you know. Don't care what Delia says about coriander, I think cumin is the best-kept secret.' She flicks an imaginary speck of dust off her tabard.

'Ah, yes. The usual.' I interrupt her preening. 'Those engineering companies are always so keen. They must eat money.'

'I'm not talking about engineering companies. I mean the multi-media companies, like Nathan here runs, and the telecom industry. They all need so much.'

'Will you excuse me?' I dash back to my en suite, throw the

80

hand towel around to make it look like it has been used, and jot down the latest insider gossip. It's going to be a busy few weeks, but just think of the Air Miles.

As I return to the room, I hear Ciaran changing the subject away from work. Blast! I haven't heard enough inside stuff yet. He's talking about some local football team that he just joined. Apparently he's playing his second match tomorrow. Julie is asking about the offside rule. Perhaps I should have told her about the off-limits rule. She's such a flirt.

'Anybody for the last roast potato?' Kate queries. Everyone shakes their head. Liz hasn't touched her dish. I think Lily buttered the toast. 'Well, waste not, want not. That's always been my motto.' She spoons the survivor on to her plate, before scraping on the remains of the cabbage. 'Delicious.'

Three hours later and I know all there is to know about Bloodhound's secret passion for tropical fish. Apparently he had a disaster last week when he put two angelfish with voracious appetites in the tank. Manfred's membership of a morris-dancing club is a revelation. Imagine! Tight-lipped investment banker by day, and arm-waving idiot at the week-end. Not sure I'm winning him round, though. I mean, he didn't even respond when I jested: 'Pull the other one, it's got bells on.' Then Nancy suddenly remembers about a bell-making industry that needs to raise funds, causing me to dash to the loo again. My guests probably think I've got a bladder problem.

I know we've drunk too much when Kate decides to tell us her life story, and how to get rid of chilblains. Even Lily wouldn't have suggested the market traders' cure! However, old teetotal Nancy doesn't loosen up at all when I ask about her extra-curricular activities. She just replies, 'My cat', which if it had been anybody else could have caused some raised eye-brows. No wonder I have lost interest in my career. Just look at the colleagues I have to put up with.

And then there's Liz. When I suggest that we should move chairs for the dessert, I'm rather irked that she moves in tandem with Ciaran and remains seated beside him. I don't know why it bothers me so much. I mean, it's not as though Ciaran and I have spoken that much since he arrived, and he hasn't really been the life and soul of the party tonight. He just sits there with a pained expression on his face, although he appears to be getting on well with Julie. She also seems to be hitting it off with Nathan, but that's the thing about Julie, you can put her into any situation and she makes friends. She's smart, humorous and attractive – no wonder all the men keep referring questions to her. Not that I'm jealous, obviously.

Even the dessert is a success. Well, apart from for Liz. Lily brings her out a plate of cheese and biscuits as a replacement. I can't help thinking that she's playing the fool deliberately.

Lily beams with so much pride when Ciaran congratulates her on the Neapolitan ice cream that you'd have thought she'd made it herself. She actually gives him two Flakes as a reward.

I'm just starting to relax (dashing to the loo six times in one evening is quite stressful) when Liz suddenly jumps up, looking at her watch.

'It's two o'clock. I've got to go. Sam was meant to be ringing me at midnight to wish me good night. He'll worry that I wasn't in. You know how he is, Trixie, so thoughtful.' She smiles at me.

'Hmm,' I reply through gritted teeth. 'By the way, if you two are still an item, how come he's flying the Stars and Stripes?'

'Oh, he doesn't like people to think we are too serious. He doesn't want the other women on the floor to feel intimidated by the depth of our relationship. He wants them to feel that they can come to him any time.' She can say that again.

The others start to rise from their seats. Julie kisses me good night, and then reminds me about our shopping expedition later today. 'Meet you at one in Joe's in Fenwick's,' she says, before shouting out her farewell to Lily, who is sitting patiently in the kitchen reading a magazine, waiting to load the final glasses into the dishwasher.

'Bye, dear. Remember what I said about the quilted toilet paper. It really is better for you,' she shouts out. 'It doesn't chafe.'

Julie shoots out the door. Manfred shakes my hand.

'Thanks very much. You've been a great host. It's been most enjoyable.' Why does he always sound as though somebody wound him up?

'Good night, Nancy,' I say politely. 'Kate, have you got that doggy bag? Ciaran, Nathan and Bloodhound, thank you all for coming. Hope to meet you again soon, Nathan,' I add, extending my hand. As Ciaran kisses me goodbye, he whispers that he thinks it went well. 'Keep at it. You're winning them over – and you know that you won me over the minute we bumped.' I quickly look up at him but his expression is hard to read.

'Good luck at the match,' I say. 'Hope you score.'

'Oh, I intend to.' He smiles, then gracefully kisses all the female guests good night. Liz sweeps towards the door, pauses in the frame, and turns to me.

'I hope you don't mind it when I mention Sam.'

'Why should I mind? He's part of my history.'

'Yes, but I've heard it was pretty acrimonious in the end. He told me about your man in Hong Kong, but I'm not judging you, honestly. I just wondered if you ever regretted the end of the affair.' She studies my face. 'Not still hankering after him?'

'No,' I respond truthfully, and then, oh hell, what's a little white lie between bitches? 'It wasn't anybody in Hong Kong that came between us. No,' I drop my voice to appear more conspiratorial, 'it was his gonorrhoea.' Gosh. Is that what it means when somebody blanches? I wave at her as she walks, cross-legged, towards the black cab, then quietly close my front door. One–nil, I think.

Saturday, October 14
(D Day minus 31 – who put the bell in my head?)

Why didn't I leave a bottle of water by my bed last night? I wake with a terrible thirst. Lily must have put too much salt in the vichyssoise. And I really don't think those prunes agreed with me. I grab my Egyptian cotton dressing gown from the back of the door and make my way into the kitchen. It is times like this that I really couldn't be parted from Lily. The fridge is stacked with bottles of Perrier, and on the marble worktop she has left out a packet of Resolve.

It almost makes worthwhile the hour that I was forced to sit with her in the kitchen after the guests were gone, whilst she cleared up all the debris from the dining room. Although I could have done without the lecture on the evils of alcohol as she counted four empty champagne bottles and ten wine bottles. What did she expect? You can't invite guests to dinner and then expect them to nurse two glasses all night. Whoever said 'less is more' must have been a terrible host.

And now it's nine thirty. Why did I wake so early? The sun is too bright this morning – and six and a half hours' sleep is not enough for any human being. Well, unless they happen to be Margaret Thatcher – but then that opens another huge debate about her origins.

I squeeze some oranges, put the coffee on, and pour out a bowl of Special K, being careful not to make any sudden movements with my head. There seems to be a clapper inside it, banging my skull at a frenetic pace. Is this it? Is this the lifestyle that I am desperate to save? Breakfast alone on a Saturday morning and an evening spent with colleagues, some of whom I wouldn't care if I never saw again? The only thing that Nancy and I have in common is that we both breathe, and as for Leon and Manfred . . . The only thing we share is a desk.

But I must save it. Okay, it's not perfect. One long-term

relationship and so many flings that I can't count them on the fingers of two hands were not quite what I dreamed of when I was a child. I had imagined that at the grand old age of twenty-eight I would be married with a few small children. I didn't think of working – most of the women I knew when I was growing up didn't. They brought up the children and the man was the breadwinner.

But when I went to university, I suddenly had friends who had mothers who were professional people. Julie's mother, for instance, was a lawyer. So I added a career into the equation. Trixie aged twenty-eight would balance a successful career with a happy marriage, a beautiful toddler and a baby in the cradle. And the more I heard about it, the more I wanted to have a career in the City. A chance for Cinderella to meet Prince Charming. Only when I met him, he forgot which fairy tale he was in and turned into a frog.

And yet, I had loved my job until then. It was tailor-made for me. Wining and dining clients, organising hospitality events and, at the end of it, persuading them that they needed to do deals with me. And they did. In their droves. There was something immensely satisfying about sitting down with a client who knew how much money he needed to raise but hadn't a clue either how to go about getting it or how much it would cost. I had to *think* about the problem. Analyse it. If, for example, the client needed to raise Swiss francs to build a factory in Switzerland, then I had to consider all the permutations. Would it be cheaper to borrow in Japanese yen; and then swap it into Swiss francs?

It was like playing swapsy with marbles in the school playground. I'd discover the ranking of the child owning the marble I desired, and then play a series of matches with other children until I had the requisite marble to challenge him or her. Now I would examine all the companies who needed to borrow money, and then work out a way of satisfying each of their requirements. I would make every company borrow where they had an advantage, then I would work behind the scenes to swap all the money around until everybody had what they really wanted. It was not easy. Timing was everything, and I was the queen of timing.

And then Sam came along, and working together, we managed to pull off some spectacular deals, drawing on his knowledge of the foreign exchange markets and mine of the clients' needs. We were a great double act, until I realised it was really a threesome.

But I could love my job again. The buzz of pulling off a deal – keeping it quiet from everybody else until it is time to press the button – is almost indescribable. I met a journalist once who told me that there was something amazing about working on an exclusive story, a scoop that would blow the minds of everybody when they read it. You would get a whisper of a story, then slowly and quietly work to put all the pieces of the puzzle together until suddenly you hit upon the one person who could fill the remaining gaps. And then the evening before it was published, you would fret about wording, the last-minute details, recheck the facts whilst adrenalin poured through your veins, and you knew that you would not sleep that night because the next morning something would have changed forever. Because of you. And I knew exactly what he meant.

I want to get that back. Correction. I'm going to get that back. I started to get those twinges of excitement even before I saw Dr Noriko at the airport. I could do something for him – although not perhaps in the way he wanted – and it felt good. That's why I want to keep my job. It's not really the money, although I would be a liar if I said that I did not love the trappings of success, but it's the buzz that drives me. Or used to. Jim could see that in me, but it's not something I would ever tell my colleagues. Wouldn't want them thinking I've gone soft. Let them think that Trixie is fighting to preserve her wardrobe and lifestyle.

I'm just clearing the dishwasher, in preparation for today's offering of dirty mugs and wine glasses, when the phone rings.

'Hello,' I say, slightly out of breath after a frantic search for the handset.

'Good morning, and how are we today?' It's Ciaran. What's he doing ringing at this time? Normal people should still be in their beds. 'I'm not disturbing anything, am I?'

'No! And I'm fine, thank you.' Great, Trixie. You sound like Nancy. 'And you?' Scintillating Trixie. He'll be ringing every day now.

'Fine.' Who says the art of conversation is dead? Go on. Bite the bullet. Or shoot it through your head, and put yourself out of this misery.

'Are you getting ready for your match? What time's kick-off?'

'Haven't you looked outside this morning? It's pouring.' Own goal. 'The match is off, and that's why I'm ringing you. It's rather embarrassing, but,' go on, profess your undying love, 'well, I haven't seen you wearing the Prada suit that I spilled that coffee on, and I wondered if the stain actually came out. I mean, I did say that I would pay for a new one.' Is he asking me shopping? That's quite romantic. Boyfriends and girlfriends do that. Not work colleagues. Better ring Julie and call off our day out. I'm sure that she'll understand. I mean, we are talking about a free suit here. 'And I heard you and Julie making arrangements last night to go shopping today and . . .' Yes, yes. No problem to cancel. What time shall we meet? Fancy lunch first and the pictures afterwards? If we could just include a drop of alcohol along the way, I'm sure things will get moving between us. 'I wanted to say that if you see something you like today, then, well, don't hesitate to buy it. I'll refund the money.' Oh!

I pause before answering. Don't want him to pick up on my disappointment. Though why I should feel let down when I've just spent the past twenty minutes telling myself the reasons that I love my job and should go all-out to save it, I don't know. Remember the Battle Strategy. Point four.

'Oh, that's very kind of you. But actually, well, I was going to tell you last week, but then you were on that course, it all came out. The coffee. After dry-cleaning. No problem. No need to buy a new suit.'

'Well, at least let me pay for the dry-cleaning. How much was it?'

'No, honestly, it doesn't matter. Forget it.' What's a girl to do? Ask for a cheque and look like a tight-wad? Anyway, the suit probably needed a clean. I think this is what they call an awkward pause. Ciaran seems to take ages before responding.

'Well, if you're sure?'

'I am.' Please don't hang up yet. Think of something to say. 'Thanks for coming last night. I hope you enjoyed it. I worried about you at one point because you had a very strange expression on your face.'

'Oh, that!' He bursts out laughing. 'You'll never guess what that man-eater Liz did.'

'What?'

'She put her hand under the table and started rubbing my thigh.'

'No!' How dare she? Isn't she meant to be dating Sam? What a pair!

'I know. I didn't know what to do, or where to look. I didn't like to say anything because I didn't want to embarrass her, and I was scared in case any sudden movement encouraged her. I had to concentrate on sitting upright and still, like a ramrod.'

'I think you could have thought of a better expression.' We both burst out laughing.

'Seriously, though, she's awful. So forward. I mean, did you see the way she swooned around Nathan when she found out he was a multi-millionaire?'

'No,' I lie. 'How shallow.'

'I think Sam's got his work cut out there, although from what I hear, they deserve each other. The more I hear about him the more I can't put the two of you together.' He pauses. 'I'm sorry. That was rude. For all I know, you may still have feelings for him.' Does his last comment sound like a question?

'Don't worry. Nothing you could say about Sam can upset me. I look at him now and shudder, and I constantly ask myself why I ever got involved with him.'

'Well, you know the old cliché about love being blind.'

'Sure do, but even the blind have Braille to guide them. Still, spurned love is spiteful.' I giggle at the memory of Liz's face as I fired my Exocet missile, and then confide in him my evil deed. I hear a sharp intake of breath on the other end of the phone, before he explodes into laughter. 'Sam's going to go ballistic with me. Perhaps I should call in sick on Monday. Wait till he's calmed down.'

'What! And miss all the fun! Anyway you can't,' warns the voice of reason at the other end. 'Don't forget Jim's ultimatum. The clock's ticking. You've what? Thirty-one days? And I've only just arrived. Can't have my buddies leaving shortly afterwards. How would that look to outsiders?'

'True. Actually, I've a busy week. Got to follow up lots of leads that I picked up—' I stop mid-sentence.

'Last night?'

'How did you know?'

'It's what I would have done. Besides, nobody goes to the loo that many times in one evening, unless they're shoving something up their nose.' He was counting!

'I wasn't.'

'I know.'

'You won't tell the others?'

'My lips are sealed. But,' he hesitates, 'if you're going to worry about going to work on Monday, how about some company on Sunday evening?'

'What?'

'I mean, what about supper? If you won't let me pay for dry-cleaning, the least I can do is to buy you supper. Nothing fancy. We could go somewhere local to you, if you'd like.'

I delay my response to make sure that I don't sound desperate.

'I'd like.'

'Fine. I'll pick you up about eight. Okay? There's nothing you don't eat, is there?' I wonder if he's alluding to my nightmare guests.

'Nothing. Although you remember that I don't touch alcohol,' I tease.

89

'How could I forget? Teetotal Trixie. See you tomorrow.' He hangs up. Damn. How can I lose a stone by tomorrow? I know. I'll ask Julie. She's always doing some Cabbage Diet or other.

Unfortunately, she doesn't seem quite so keen to help when I explain the situation over our flutes of champagne at Joe's. Okay, so I'm late. When I arrive she's staring at the black-and-white portrait of Jeremy Irons on the wall. I can tell from the entrance that the colours mirror her mood.

'What time do you call this?' she asks as I approach the table.

'I know. I know. It's just been one of those days, and then I spotted this darling jacket in the window of Armani and I just had to have it.' We air-kiss, and then I stop in surprise. 'What on earth is that?'

'Fresh fruit cocktail.'

'Why? Are you trying to get your vitamins up? Are you coming down with something?' I move to put my hand on her forehead but she pushes it away.

'No. I just didn't know how long you would be, and I wasn't going to drink alone. So show me the jacket.'

I reach into the Armani bag and pull out a bright red cashmere jacket. I don't think it's appropriate to show her the evening dress as well, particularly when I've been moaning all week about the need to get my debts down just in case I do lose my job.

'I think the jacket will go wonderfully with my black leather trousers. What do you think? With perhaps a black crewneck underneath?' I wait for her to voice her opinion, although I know instinctively that I am going to reject it. Julie's taste is sometimes dubious; she has been known to mix Oasis with Versace. I once explained this faux pas to Lily, who got terribly confused. Couldn't understand why anybody would want to mix those dreadful Gallagher brothers with that nice Mr Liberace.

'Why do you need another red jacket, Trixie? Didn't you buy one last month?' Mother? Are you here?

'But that was a different style. It was long and more formal. This is funkier. More fun. Come on. You must see the difference.'

90

'I suppose I do, but really.' She sighs. 'Shouldn't you be concentrating on rationalising your financial situation at the moment?' Mother? It is you.

'I suppose. But I need a new jacket for tomorrow night. I've got a date with Ciaran.'

'What?'

'Well, not really a date,' I add quickly. 'He's invited me for supper. What's wrong? I thought you'd be pleased. You did like him last night, didn't you?' I stop as I catch sight of Julie's stern expression.

'Yes, but that's not the point. I thought you'd decided to concentrate on your career at the moment. Won't he just be a distraction?' And Granny. When did you arrive?

'No. I won't let him be. It's nothing heavy, Julie. I just, I just like him. Actually, when he rang this morning, I thought he was inviting me shopping. I was just about to hang up to ring you to cancel—' I stop as I realise what I've said.

'You were going to cancel me! I thought we'd agreed that we'd never let men come between us. A date does not come before lunch with girlfriends in my alphabet.' Maybe not in yours, but it does actually in the real-world alphabet. Somehow I feel now is not the appropriate time to interject, as she reiterates: 'Friends come first.' Yes, but boyfriends come better.

She irritably waves the waiter aside as he approaches to tell us the specials of the day, although she permits me to order two glasses of champagne. Hmm. I must be paying then.

'I know. I'm sorry. I wasn't thinking. Come on, Julie.' I lean over and take her hand. 'How many men have I been interested in since Sam? None. I'm just enjoying myself. Nothing serious. I swear to you that I am going to keep my job and dedicate myself to my career.' I pause. 'I know you're just trying to look out for me, and I appreciate that, but I will be careful. Once bitten and all that.' I let go of her hand and grab my menu. 'Anyway, can we choose now? I'm ravenous after last night. I think we overdid it on the old drink front. What did you think of everyone?'

Julie examines her menu.

'Think I'll have the usual. And you?'

'I quite fancy one of the specials that he was going to tell us about. Luckily for you I can see it on the board. Pasta with pine nuts and rocket. You haven't answered the question.' I hail the waiter to take our order.

'Sorry.' She considers my query. 'You go first. Do you like them all? How do you think the evening went? After all, it was a meet-the-relatives sort of night.' Yeah, but if I had relatives like that I think I would shoot myself. And them. I screw my nose up and shake my head.

'In truth, the majority of them I wouldn't want to share my cold with, let alone another evening. They have no spark. No energy. And the irony is that I'm the one that Jim thinks is the weak link. They're just,' I stop as I search for the correct word, 'dull. Only word to describe them, but every time I think of Manfred as a morris dancer, I can't help imagining *The Sound of Music*. I can just see him in breeches made out of floral curtains, jumping up and down jingling his bells.'

'Or his enormous Alpine horn!'

'Manfred? No!' I shake my head to rid myself of the awful image. 'But do you know the weird thing?' I take a large gulp of my champagne before continuing, then lean over towards Julie, checking that the old grannies on the neighbouring table can't hear me. 'I'm sure that somebody went through my knicker drawer last night.'

'What?' Julie looks at me as if I'm mad.

'I know. Silly, isn't it? I mean, I always clear them out when I've got builders or decorators coming in, but I sort of thought that I could trust work colleagues. But I'm definite that somebody rifled through them. My La Perla underwear was mixed up with the Rigby and Peller stuff, and the manky knickers that—'

'Don't even go there,' interrupts Julie, holding her hand up. I persevere.

'The manky knickers that Lily is desperate to turn into dusters were all pushed from the back of the drawer to the front. I suppose Lily can have them now. She says they bring her brass knockers up a treat.' I sip on my champagne and giggle at Julie's bewildered expression. The two old dears on the neighbouring table also seem to be enjoying the revelation.

'Well, as I was about to say, your colleagues are strange. I really like Chris, though – sorry, Bloodhound.' She laughs at the face I pull. 'He's a nice bloke, not blessed with looks but nice, and he's very fond of you.'

'Yeah, and Winalot,' I mutter under my breath. 'And?'

'Don't be cruel about Chris. Give him a chance. You're always slagging him off. Anyway, Nancy, Leon and Manfred are dreadful. How their clients put up with them, I just don't know. They must be crying out to speak to a banker with a bit of spirit and long words in their vocabulary.' She butters a slice of ciabatta and starts chewing on it. Calories. Calories. I can't help it. I want to shout out 'a moment on the lips'. Painful memories of my tubby past make me so intolerant to people being careless about their diet.

'You noticed, then?'

'Couldn't fail to.' She stops, takes another mouthful of ciabatta and chews it, before adding: 'I'm not sure about Nathan. He's quite understated but there's something about him. Can't quite put my finger on it. Something strange. As for Liz? Well, condom producers will never have to issue profits warnings while she's around.'

I tell her about Liz's handling of Ciaran, and of my handling of Liz. Ciabatta makes such a mess when it's spluttered over a paper tablecloth. I wish Julie would learn some table manners.

'Ciaran seems like a nice guy,' she admits, as she tries to sweep the bits off the table before the waiter returns. 'So come on. What are you going to wear?'

Sunday, October 15
(D Day minus 30 – hang the Battle Strategy!)

It is eight and I have changed my outfit three times, checked for spinach in my teeth twice, despite the fact that I haven't eaten the awful green stuff for years, and am now sitting in one of my armchairs, which is placed strategically close to the window, watching out for the arrival of Ciaran. I feel like a teenager again. My stomach is churning, and when the phone rang earlier I was sure that it was Ciaran ringing to cancel. (Memories of unrequited teenage love came rushing back to the surface.) Instead it was Julie ringing to wish me luck, and a second call was from Lily telling me that she had left her bus pass round my flat and could I put it somewhere safe.

I just hope we don't go anywhere with leather seats because that could lead to some embarrassing noises when I sit down in these black leather trousers. Still, it's worth taking the chance, because even if I do say so myself, I look hot, with a capital H, in these trousers. The hundreds of lunges and crunches that my personal trainer has bullied me into doing over the past six months have finally paid off. Ciaran won't know where to look! (And they hide my calves.)

A quick check of my make-up in the mirror over the fireplace, and I'm ready. What should I do? Open a bottle of wine, listen to some music and look casual. Give no hint to the hours of preparation and one Bic razor that went into looking this good. I opt for the wine – well, I would, wouldn't I? – and lounge in the armchair by the window, trying desperately to follow *Ballykissangel* on the telly. I might pick up some tips on dealing with Irish people.

My God! A Jaguar XKR convertible has just pulled up outside. Those things cost the best part of £70,000. It couldn't be his, could it? It is! He's getting out of it. Wow, it's gorgeous. I'd love a car like that. My Toyota Celica Coupé looks somehow

94

dated, and it's less than a year old. Shit! The Jaguar will have leather seats. I'm doomed before I start. Oh! He's a bit casually dressed, isn't he? The black jeans and tan suede jacket look nice, but couldn't he have made more of an effort? Shit! He's seen me looking out and is waving at me. It's times like this when I wish that I had followed Lily's advice and put up 'some nice little nets' that would 'finish off the windows a treat'. I lift my wine glass to him, get up from the chair and start moving towards the front door. Deep breath. Oops. I run back to turn off the television – wouldn't want him to think that I was uncultured – and leave a copy of *Great Expectations* open on the arm of the chair.

'Hi there,' I say, as he steps into the hallway and greets me with a quick peck on my cheek. 'Sorry, couldn't remember what time you said.' Liar, liar, pants are on fire. 'Just having a quick glass of sauvignon. Would you like one?'

'Thanks, Trixie, but I always make a rule of not drinking on Sundays. Let the old liver have a weekly holiday.' Wow. How considerate. So tonight will be extra fun then. 'But don't let that stop you.' He smiles, his eyes twinkling. 'Anyway, shall we get going? I'm starving!' He turns around and opens the door again.

'Lead the way.' I grab my bag, keys and day-old jacket. 'Where are we going?'

'Surprise. I spotted somewhere on Upper Street and it seemed rather appropriate for this evening.' So we're not going in the car. Don't know whether I'm pleased or disappointed. 'Like the jacket,' he says admiringly, as I put it on. 'Is it new?'

'This old thing? Had it years.'

We stroll towards Upper Street chatting about what we've done today. I lie about how nice it was to meet Nathan, but Ciaran doesn't seem to want to chat about him. It only takes a few minutes before we reach the junction. Ciaran turns to the right. Hmm. So we're not going to Granita or Euphorium. We walk past Camden Passage, with its selection of antique shops and Fredericks, the long-established Islington restaurant which *Harden's Guide* describes as 'an ideal setting for a special occasion', and on towards Angel. I think Ciaran may have lost his sense of direction.

'We're here.' He beams at me.

'Where?' I look around frantically for the Michelin star that will signal our eatery.

He points at the plate-glass window beside him, through which I can see people sitting on lurid-coloured wooden chairs eating . . . *quelle horreur*! Pizza!

'Pizza Express!' Ciaran says triumphantly. 'I can't tell you how much I missed their Fiorentina pizzas when I was living in New York. I only spotted it when I drove past on the way to you.' He holds the door open. 'Come on. What are we waiting for?' The punch line? The bit where you say 'only joking' and redirect me to one of Islington's finest restaurants, perhaps? But no, he's opening the door.

'The only place that I ever eat pizza at is a darling little trattoria on the outskirts of Florence,' I lie, remembering the trio of ham and pineapple pizzas nestling in my freezer which Lily bought only last week. 'Such a bargain, dear. I got them all for the price of one because it was their sell-by date today, but I've popped them in the freezer and they'll be fine. And only four hundred calories each.'

'Really? Whereabouts in Florence?' Ciaran indicates to the waiter that he wants a table for two. 'I always thought pizza wasn't as popular there as in other Italian cities. Can't say I know any great pizzerias in Florence, although there is that one on Borgo San Lorenzo.' Eh? 'Did you mean Fiesole? Or there's that lovely trattoria at Maiano, just three kilometres down the road from Fiesole.' What! Next he'll be giving me the map coordinates.

'Oh, you wouldn't know it.' Something tells me that I shouldn't even go down this route. It's going to be a dead end.

'No? Try me. I spent three months working as a waiter in Florence when I was a student. I know it really well. Was it Trattoria Le Cave?' I get the feeling that Ciaran is rather enjoying this.

'Look, I can't tell you,' I bluff. 'Can't have everyone going there. I love it because it is so unspoiled. And non-touristic, as they say in Italy. Don't want to publicise it. Anyway, I must examine this menu.' I look down at the card in my hand, praying that by holding my breath I am preventing a red cloud from wafting across my face.

After ordering a Fiorentina, one salade Niçoise, without dough balls, a bottle of fizzy water and a large glass of Frascati for me (he should have ordered the bottle; it works out cheaper in the long run), Ciaran fixes his blue eyes on me and asks if I could tell him a little more about myself.

'What's there to tell? I'm twenty-eight. Joined the bank as a graduate trainee after studying anthropology at Birmingham University. I enjoy partying, designer clothes and champagne. My best friend is Julie. You met her on Friday. End of story.'

'Yeah, she's a grand girl. What about your family?' asks Ciaran. 'My mammy is very important to me, although I don't think she'll ever forgive me for leaving Ireland.'

Time to change the subject, quick. 'Why did you leave? I thought Ireland was the Celtic Tiger? The dynamo of the European Union, where everybody wants to live not leave.'

'Dunno. I love Ireland, it's my home, but when I moved to Bristol for university, I suddenly realised that I had to leave. I mean, the opportunities are there, but not really in finance. And I suppose, in truth, I couldn't stand the claustrophobia. Dublin, where I come from, can be extremely claustrophobic. You only have to walk down O'Connell Street or across the Ha'penny Bridge and you bump into so many people you know. Can never get away with anything.'

'What do you want to get away with?' Oh God, Trixie. Corny line! Next you'll be winking and licking your lips seductively. You've got to stop watching *EastEnders*.

'Now that would be telling. Anyway, what about you? Where did you find Lily? She's a treasure.' Too right. Should be buried. Why does he keep asking about my background? 'Do you know she gave me a tip on how to remove candle wax from carpets? And she was right! Brown paper and an iron, in case you're wondering.'

'That's Lily. I think she cuts out those helpful tips from the Sunday newspapers. Actually, I can't really remember how I met her.' I lift the anchovies from my bowl and place them on to a side plate. 'Seems like I've known her forever. She just runs my flat for me, pops in every morning to wash the breakfast dishes and make the bed. I leave her a list of things to do on the computer. I think she likes feeling useful, and it's a bit of pocket money for her. She's all alone, her husband ran away years ago.'

'Well, she seems very fond of you.' He tucks into his pizza with relish. Hope it doesn't have too much garlic in it.

'I suppose.'

'Bloodhound said your family live in Gloucestershire.' Talk about an inquisition. Next he'll be shining lights into my eyes. 'Destined to work in the City from birth, I bet.'

'Something like that,' I mutter.

'And I bet your mother is in the Women's Institute.'

'Yeah, she's quite involved, actually. I keep worrying that her group will opt to do one of those charity calendars; you know, where they pose naked but have their vital parts shielded by sunflowers.'

'I know the ones you mean. Why worry? It's in a good cause.' Ciaran shovels his pizza into his mouth and pats his stomach. 'Wonderful. Fancy another drink?' I nod, enthusiastically. I knew he should have ordered the bottle.

'She's allergic to sunflowers.'

'Sorry?' He looks confused as he calls the waiter over.

'Well, if she can't use a sunflower she'll have to find another flower to camouflage her. And there aren't that many quite big enough. She'd be flashing for the world and I don't think it's quite ready!'

'Ooh, put the claws away.' Ciaran gives the drinks order to the waiter. 'Why worry about something that might never happen? They could use conifers or bay trees, they're quite bushy, and I'm not trying to be rude there. It'd be a bit different from the norm. So I suppose it was all ponies, ballet classes and prep schools when you were growing up.'

'Something like that.'

'You're too highfaluting for me, a poor boy from Ringsend.' He looks slightly disappointed, although that's maybe at the spinach that has dropped on to his jacket.

'Don't be silly. What's Ringsend like?'

'It was the docks, although now, with all the changes going on in Ireland, they probably call it a harbour development. Still, it was a tough place to grow up. I think that's why I got on so well with your Lily. I felt we had lots in common.'

'If she was here now she'd tell you to dab your jacket with a bit of cold water to stop the staining.' I watch as he dips his napkin into his glass of fizzy water and dabs. Putty in my hands. 'How did you get to Bristol University?'

'All the fault of the Christian Brothers. They told me I had a mind for figures.' Tell me more! He pushes his plate to one side. Goodness, he even eats the crusts. He must be a real man. 'Anyway, now that we've finished eating, I have some news for you that I think you may find exciting.'

Yippee. He's in love with me. I smile at him as my stomach ties itself in double reef knots. He puts his hand into the inside pocket of his suede jacket – don't tell me he's bought an engagement ring already – and pulls out a . . . sheaf of papers. Oh.

'I've drawn up a list,' he scours the top sheets, 'of potential clients who might be interested in doing deals. Some of them I know from my days on Wall Street, and I hear they're looking to raise money.' He pauses, looks up at me and smiles.

I smile back, thinking that I should be grateful, yet feeling somewhat saddened. So this isn't a date. Instead he's just a mate, doing me a favour. Yet this is exactly as it should be at the moment. I have too much to worry about on the work front without spending sleepless nights fretting about 'will he, won't he' phone calls. The finger strain from dialling 1471, just in case he rang but didn't leave a message. And the constant checking of the answerphone.

'I think you should try to swing a business trip to New York,' he adds. 'You'll need to win these guys' trust and you can't beat a face-to-face meeting.' Suddenly my spirits lift. I see Barneys, Saks Fifth Avenue, Calvin Klein and Donna Karan. Who needs a man when you have a wardrobe and an empty suitcase?

He points to one name on the list. Some guy based at the Rockefeller Centre. Nope! Don't fancy going there. Too many flagpoles outside. Another in the World Trade Centre. Right, which shops are in that vicinity? Everybody knows that what costs a pound here only costs a dollar there. So the bank manager will be pleased with my parsimony. Winners all round.

'Are you listening?' Ciaran interrupts my mental arithmetic, still pointing at the name. 'He probably needs to borrow about half a billion dollars.' Don't we all. 'But he's scared of bankers. If you treat him kindly,' he winks, 'I'm sure you can do business together. Don't bother with him.' He crosses another name off the list. 'Got an e-mail this morning telling me that he's given it all up to join some commune. He's good for about three hundred million dollars.' He ticks another name. 'She's always open to new ideas.' She? What sort of ideas? What sort of people does he consort with? He hands the list over to me.

'This is really good of you.' I study the remaining names. Trying to find that wanton woman. 'I'll start calling them tomorrow.'

'It's a start. I've racked my brain, and I probably shouldn't really be helping you like this – Chinese walls and all that – but I can't let down a mate, can I?' I shake my head. Mate? Is that mate as in platonic friend, or mate as in copulating friend? 'The thing about these names,' he adds, 'is that they're not the big ones. Most of the banks don't even bother calling them. Not like the clients that Manfred was talking about on Friday. They've so many bankers courting them that they can be extremely selective, so you shouldn't be upset if you don't get anywhere with them.' Why should I be upset? I don't seem to be getting anywhere with anyone! I'm experienced at it. He looks at his watch.

'Shit! Is that the time? I have to get going. I always make it a rule to get at least one early night a week. I usually aim for Sunday.' Me too!

I fold the list and put it in my bag.

'Thanks ever so much.' I inject as much sincerity as I can into my voice. It's not that I'm not grateful, I'm just disappointed. Get a grip, Trixie. Concentrate. No distractions. Get the deal, and then get distracted. 'I'll approach Jim about a business trip tomorrow. He might well agree. I think he recognises that I've been making an effort recently.'

Ciaran throws some money on to the table, and waves off my efforts to go Dutch, muttering about dry-cleaning bills. We leave Pizza Express and walk back towards my flat. As we reach his car, he turns down my offer of coffee.

'Can I take a raincheck? I think it's an early night for me. Good luck with those names.' He kisses me on the cheek – exactly like I'd kiss a business client, all official and unromantic. 'See you tomorrow. I'll bring the coffee!' He gets into the car and drives away. Hooting the horn, with his arm waving out the window. Just like in the movies. And I suddenly feel really depressed even though I know that he may just have handed me the key to my future.

Monday, October 16

It may not have been the early night that I had been planning but, as Lily would say, it did me a power of good. Three Irish coffees (I was in the mood for a taste of the Emerald Isle) and I awake feeling rejuvenated. Who cares about Ciaran? I'm a woman, and we all know those jokes that God only created men because he needed something to practise on before creating perfection. I don't need him, and I actually now feel quite silly about those unexpected feelings of disappointment that I experienced last night. If I'm not careful, I'll turn into one of those softies that I profess to detest. So it's time that I put thoughts of romance out of my head and followed Julie's advice: the Battle Strategy is the only way forward!

When I arrive at work I find that strategic move three – putting Sam completely behind me – is actually going to be quite easy. His desk and screens have been moved to the perimeter of the trading floor. The man himself is nowhere to be seen, and the only way that I can be sure that it is his workstation is the flagpole attached to the side of the desk, currently flying an enormous skull and crossbones.

I grunt at Bloodhound as I take my coat off. I place my bag on my desk, settle in my chair and start turning on all my screens. I wonder if the local electricity board has a power surge every morning when City bankers arrive at their desks. Would it be equivalent to the surge that occurs during the commercial break of Coronation Street in the cliffhanger episodes? Or when England take a penalty shoot-out during an important match against Germany?

'Thanks for Friday.' Bloodhound smiles at me. I glance around to ensure that nobody who heard his comment could have possibly misconstrued its meaning.

'You're welcome,' I reply magnanimously. 'What's going

102

on?' I nod towards Sam's desk, and the bustle of activity around the gap where it used to stand. 'Is there some big foreign exchange scandal or something? Why is everyone milling around over there?'

'You haven't heard?' He looks at me, concerned. 'It's Sam.' He pauses.

'Yes?' Spit it out, man! Has there been an accident? I can feel my stomach spontaneously turn – after all, this is a man I once loved. Does he have a donor card? I must ring the hospital. No point in them taking his heart. It never functioned correctly.

'Liz has discovered that he's got . . .' Bloodhound leans very close and I can barely hear the next word, but I think he says 'gonorrhoea'. Oh, shit! I almost wish that he had had an accident now. He is going to kill me. 'Are you all right?' Bloodhound stares at me, but the look I give him leaves him in no doubt that I am fine. Worried about my little joke, or rather Sam's little joke, but quite healthy, thank you.

'Where is Liz?' I ask, nodding towards her empty desk.

'She's at the doctor's. Emergency appointment,' Bloodhound answers, still in hushed tones. 'Sam's returning from his golf weekend this afternoon. He doesn't know that we all know his secret. Apparently Liz ignored all his calls over the weekend.' I hope he doesn't bring his clubs into the bank with him. A putter across my head will not be a pretty sight. Particularly if it's a four iron.

'I don't mean to be funny, but why the relocation? It's hardly contagious – well, unless you've got up close and personal. What are his colleagues on the foreign exchange desk worried about? Is there something that they're not telling us; have the bonding sessions gone a bit too far?' I ask, searching desperately for something to lighten the situation.

'Oh, they're not bothered,' replies Bloodhound. 'They think it's quite funny. They were the ones who ran the skull and crossbones up his pole.' I do think he could have phrased that better. 'It's the girls on the floor who've insisted his desk be moved. Apparently the doctor on the fifth floor has been inundated with requests for appointments. There's even talk that he's run out of rubber gloves, and it's only nine. Which reminds me. Jim was looking for you at the morning meeting. I covered for you, but he wanted to know how your conversation with Dr Noriko went on Friday.'

I nod, and, after checking if Bloodhound wants one, move over to the coffee machine in the kitchenette at the side of the trading floor to get my morning dose of caffeine. I've barely got back to my desk and taken my first sip of stimulants' paradise when Jim appears by my side. I explain, in my most conscientious voice, that I was late this morning because I decided to finish my proposal for Dr Noriko and thought it would be more effective to do so at home, in the peace of my study (other people might call it a bed) rather than the bustle of the trading floor.

As if on cue, the traders on the bank of desks adjoining my section begin screaming into telephones and jumping up and down. They must have called the market wrong and are now desperately trying to save their jobs. I notice Ciaran joining them, trying to discover what has gone wrong.

'I'm meeting Dr Noriko tomorrow evening at Nobu,' I tell Jim. 'I'm following up a few other leads this week. Hope you'll pass the expenses,' I joke, remembering the stash of cab receipts in my top drawer. 'Could be a costly exercise. Oh, that reminds me, I was thinking of taking a trip to New York to visit some clients. What do you think?' I suddenly notice that Jim is not really listening, but is staring at the skull and crossbones flag. 'Jim,' I prompt, 'a trip to New York?'

'Hmm.' He turns back to me distractedly. 'Yeah. Anything. Go and visit some of your clients. Get that deal.' He swings on his heel and walks back towards his office. I'm sure that I heard him say I should travel Upper Class. Well, better follow instructions. They don't call me Toe-the-Line Trixie for nothing. And I'm not going to argue with Jim – if he says I have clients in New York, then I have clients in New York. Just blowed if I know them.

I ring the bank's travel agents and ask them to check Upper Class availability on Virgin for the following week, and then I discreetly remove my Palm Pilot from my handbag and search out details of the leads that I picked up on Friday evening. I am just about to ring Helmut, the head of one of the Frankfurt telecom companies Manfred was talking about, when Kate comes bounding over. She obviously hasn't any client meetings today as she's rather casually dressed in a clinging T-shirt proclaiming, *Of course I don't look busy . . . I did it right the first time*. One day I'll *have* to take her clothes-shopping.

'Hi. Just wanted to thank you for your hospitality on Friday. The food was first class, and I loved the doggy bag that Lily gave me to take away. Had it all for breakfast the next day. Her tip on cleaning the grouting in the bathroom worked so well that I can almost see myself in the tiles now.' Perish the thought! 'Have you heard about Sam?' I nod. 'Are you,' she looks at me, 'clear?'

'Oh yes. Never in any danger. I think Liz must have got hold of the wrong end of the stick.' Where do they come from, these dreadful double entendres?

'Right, well, I'll leave you. I can see you're busy.' She looks at the telephone headset in my hands. 'Just wanted to say thank you.' Kate wanders off, and I get back to dialling Helmut. He's not in. His secretary tells me that he's travelling on business and won't be back for two weeks. She doesn't sound friendly. I think I may have caught her at a bad moment. Perhaps she was polishing her claws.

'Is there any possibility that I could book an appointment to meet with him on his return?' I ask politely, fingers crossed.

'What would be the purpose of such a meeting?' Miss Frosty Knickers asks. No wonder Helmut has gone on such a long business trip. He probably wants to get away from her.

'I have some ideas on how the company could raise funds.' Well, I will by the time I meet him. I still have to do some research into the company. Not even sure what it does, really. All Manfred said was telecoms. Maybe I'll get one of those voice-activated telephones as a gift for my advice.

'Hmm, and your bank is?' The Ice Maiden almost cracks when I tell her. 'We only deal with Manfred there. Surely you know that. Can't you discuss your ideas with him and get him to ring us if he thinks they're any good?' Any good? Cheek. Anyway, that's not quite the plan I had in mind. If I work with him and we win the deal, which of us actually gets credited with it?

'Well, I thought that you might like some new insight into the company. A fresh pair of eyes and all that. I'm not attacking Manfred.' I take a deep breath. 'He's one of our finest bankers, but one can get stale if one continually deals with the same clients. I might spot something he's missed.' I sound so sincere that I almost convince myself.

'Manfred wouldn't miss anything. He's done some wonderful deals for this company. I'm sorry now, but I'm busy. We don't need your services.' And with that Miss Poker-Stuck-Up-Her-Bottom hangs up. How rude. Well, her loss.

I look up another of the clients that I heard about on Friday night. John Harrison. Runs an Internet company in the north of England. Liz said that his daughter went to Bedales. What was her name again? Oh yeah. Mary. Well, if Mary can go to Bedales, so can I.

I dial the number and ask the switchboard operator if I can be put through to Mr Harrison's office.

'Certainly. Putting you through.' The phone rings twice and I hear a broad northern accent answer.

'John Harrison.'

'Mr Harrison,' I gush. 'My name is Trixie Thompson-Smythe. I was at school with your daughter Mary. Anyway, I happened to bump into her last week and told her that I was now working in the City, helping clients to raise finance, and she said that I should give you a call.'

'She did, did she?'

'Oh yes. Said your company was looking to raise a few hundred million pounds and that I should give you a ring. So,' I pause, 'here I am. Didn't she mention it? Typical Mary. Mind like a sieve. I constantly lent her books at school because she forgot to bring her own to class. Oops. Shouldn't tell her dad that, should I? Please don't mention it to her.' I think that should be enough of an act to convince him.

'Miss Thompson-Smythe—'

'Trixie,' I interrupt. 'Actually, most people call me Trixie Trader. It's a kind of nickname. Only school teachers really call me Thompson-Smythe.' And the Inland Revenue, I nearly add.

'Hmm, whatever. You say that you went to school with my daughter? Well, you've come a long way. Very advanced.'

'You're too kind,' I say. 'About that meeting?'

'Incredible, because when I last saw Mary, this morning, she never even mentioned you. In fact, the only thing she spoke about this morning was La La.'

'I'm sorry?' Search for the emergency exit, Trixie. Eject.

'La La, one of the Teletubbies. It's her favourite programme, but then you'd know that, being her great friend. It's her passion in life. That and Miss Jones, the teacher at her Montessori school.' Too late. Crashed and burned.

'Oh!' I desperately look for another way out. They all appear blocked. Liz must have got it wrong. Shit.

'What bank did you say you worked for, Miss Thompson-Smythe?' I hang up quickly without answering, and glance across at Bloodhound, to check that he hasn't been listening in to my call. But he appears engrossed in a telephone discussion about angelfish. I spot Ciaran walking across the floor towards the lifts. He's looking good today. Oh, come on, be honest. He looks good every day. He sees me watching him and lifts his hand in a friendly wave. God, it's as if every movement of his fingers is tickling my heart, and some other parts of my body that even Heineken couldn't reach. I manage to nod casually, and turn back to my screen. Who should I call now? These leads are turning out to be as much use as a diet sheet for Kate.

'Trixie?' I look up and see Manfred towering above me, leaning over his screens, which back on to mine.

'Oh, hi, Manfred. Hope you enjoyed Friday.' I smile at him. 'It was so nice to get to know my colleagues in a more convivial atmosphere.'

'And to get to know our clients as well?' He suddenly looks very big and threatening.

'I'm sorry?' When in doubt, act stupid. I fix a blank expression on my face.

'I've just been speaking to my mother.'

'Your mother?' Uh-oh. The pfennig is beginning to drop.

'Yes. She works as personal assistant to the chief executive at a German telecom company, which, coincidentally, just happens to be one of the ones that I mentioned on Friday night. A company that I've been courting for years, with my mother's help.'

'I can explain.' I stand up in a vain attempt to balance out the odds. I feel quite intimidated by him towering above me.

'Don't bother,' Manfred snaps. 'But I'm warning you,' he shakes his finger in my face, 'if I find out that you have contacted any more of my clients, without my express permission, I shall report the matter to higher authorities. Do you understand?' I nod, and sit back down at my desk. I feel like a little schoolgirl who's been caught eating somebody else's chocolate bar. But then I think of Manfred with bells around his ankles, skipping along knocking poles with other men, and *somehow* I feel better.

I ring Julie but she's too busy to chat. She hesitates before admitting that she's working on a big deal, but didn't like to mention it before now. Thought it would feel like salt in a wound. Hmm. She's right. Especially as she doesn't even need to do another deal – she's done loads this year already.

I turn the Palm Pilot off and put it back into my bag. What a waste of a good joint of pork. When I look up, Ciaran is standing by my side with two Styrofoam cups of latté in his hands.

'Here, just popped out to Starbucks. Sorry it wasn't here any earlier, like I promised, but things have been a bit hectic this morning.' He perches on the edge of my desk. I take one of the cups from his hands. 'Is that your work?' He nods at the skull and crossbones.

'I think so,' I admit, shamefaced. 'He's going to kill me when he finds out that I lied to Liz. Talk about hook, line and sinker. Still, it was worth it just to see her face.'

Ciaran sips his coffee. 'How's it all going this morning? Any luck following up Friday's leads?' I shake my head and recount both confrontations. At least he has the grace not to laugh, although he does smile when I mention my method of dealing with Manfred. 'You will pursue the tips I gave you yesterday, won't you? They really are kosher – unlike the pork! Boom, boom!'

'Yep. Sure will. Jim has approved a trip to New York, and I've already been on the phone to the travel agent booking seats for next week. I'll ring them later this afternoon and set up some meetings. Then I've got dinner with Dr Noriko tomorrow night and lunch with another potential client on Wednesday. So fingers crossed.'

He smiles. 'So you're quite busy this week, are you?'

'Trying to be. The clock's ticking and I've nothing to show for all the calls I've made.' Ciaran's sleeves are rolled up and I can see the contours of his muscles. He definitely works out regularly.

'So you wouldn't have time for dinner with me one night?' I grasp the coffee cup tightly. 'Well, I had such a good time last night and I wondered if you'd like to repeat the experience.'

'You mean there's another Pizza Express you want to try out? The one on London Wall, perhaps?' Shut up, Trixie! You sound like a complete snob. He'll withdraw the invitation if you're not careful.

'Ah, I kind of sensed you weren't impressed by the venue. Your face was a picture when we turned up outside the door. Well, to make amends, what about The Ivy this time round?'

'What? Can you get a table? When?' I suddenly find that I'm available every single night. Dr Noriko can eat alone if necessary tomorrow.

'What about Friday? And yes, I can get a table. My name's in their little black book.' God, I hope my name is in his little black book. 'I'll confirm details nearer the time. And you . . . get on with your calls.' He touches my arm lightly, and walks back to his desk. I realise that now I have another deadline to meet. I have four days to make myself look sensational. I dial the Aveda salon in Harvey Nicks and set up a series of appointments. Would a bikini wax be tempting fate?

Tuesday, October 17
(D Day minus 28 – I think I'll get what I want but Dr Noriko won't be so lucky)

Dr Noriko is sitting at a wooden table when I arrive at just past eight. He does not look as fresh as he did at the airport, particularly after seeing the two beauties splayed across the back seat of the limousine. This evening he is unshaven and dark rings frame his brown eyes. He doesn't notice me as I approach, because he's engrossed in sipping sake from a frosted glass. From the gold leaf floating in it, I would say that it is Hokusetsu Honjozo Kinpaku-iri. Trust him to order the most expensive brand! Still, at least this time it's on expenses.

'Here you are.' The waiter pulls out the wooden chair for me, and Dr Noriko looks up in surprise. He politely stands as I lean across the table to shake hands with him – we've done the business cards thing once and I can't be bothered with it again. I can never be sure that I'm holding the card by the right fingers, or the right corners, and that I'm not unintentionally offending anybody. For a race that's so smart and advanced, they can be very sensitive about the silliest of issues. Anyway, this time Dr Noriko has approached me. He must have liked something about my proposal and he has requested this meeting. I'm in the driving seat. Call me Jenson Button.

I sit down and then wait while the waiter drops the linen napkin into my lap. I love that part of eating out. I always want to ask them to adjust it.

'How are you, Dr Noriko?' I say, after ordering a glass of champagne. I'm not tempted by sake. Gold leaf or not. 'I must say that I was surprised to hear from you after that terrible misunderstanding at the airport.'

'I'm afraid, Miss Trader, that there's been another misunderstanding tonight.' Dr Noriko sips slowly on his sake, a tiny

111

piece of gold leaf stuck to his lip, as he points to the table in front of him. 'This only seats two people. I thought there were going to be four of us this evening.' Some people. They never learn, do they?

'Did you? Oh, I'm afraid that would be quite impossible. For a start, neither of the young ladies was available tonight, and secondly, I've decided that I'm not going to go down that route again. I was almost out of my mind with worry after that débâcle. I was scared that I would lose my job. If you really do want that kind of service then I'm afraid you must take your business elsewhere.' I lift the napkin from my knees, place it on the table in front of me, and make to stand up.

'Sit down, Trixie, please.' Dr Noriko looks at me, or rather my bosom, as he points at my chair. 'You're right. I should have learned my lesson that day.' I fold my arms over my chest and sit down again.

'How are things with your wife? You said that she went back to Tokyo almost immediately.' He nods, holds up his empty frosted glass and shakes it at a passing waiter to indicate that he'd like another one.

'Yes, she's decided that her travelling days are over – before they've even started. And her departure was nothing like the one in *Brief Encounter*! I will return to Tokyo next week.'

I don't really want to know the answer to the question that I'm about to ask, but feel I have to make the enquiry. 'I hope that her unexpected departure was not related to my awful faux pas at the airport.' Stupid question. Of course it was.

'Not entirely,' admits Dr Noriko, 'although it certainly did not help. She now thinks that London is a city filled with prostitutes and no place for a decent woman and her children to visit.'

'I think that's a slight exaggeration,' I say, glancing down the menu. Reckon I'll have the black cod with miso and some sashimi.

'Unfortunately, as the cab drove through the City towards our hotel, my wife was convinced that she saw prostitutes on every street corner and outside every building. She was even

112

adamant that there were some outside the Tower Hotel. Nothing I could say would convince her otherwise.'

'So that's why she decided to return to Tokyo? I don't mean to be rude about your wife, but that's plain silly. There are no prostitutes in the City. Now if you'd driven around Spitalfields or Commercial Road, she might have had a point.'

'I know. She just wouldn't believe me that all the women outside the buildings were actually smoking, and were not standing there touting for business.'

'Don't ever take her to Amsterdam,' I tell him, 'unless I'm allowed to come too!' Even Dr Noriko is laughing now. His little eyes have crinkled into thin slits, and his bulbous nose is quivering. I'm winning him over – pretty soon he won't even remember that there should be four of us, and anyway, if he drinks enough sake he'll probably think that there are. 'Shall we order?' I ask him, as I spot a waiter approaching us. He nods, and launches into a conversation in Japanese with the waiter about various dishes. He looks towards me and asks what I am having. I give my order, check the wine list and suggest a rather crisp, dry Californian wine from Santa Barbara called Au Bon Climat. Dr Noriko appears pleased with my choice. Round one is mine, I think.

'So, Trixie, you've been prying into my personal affairs; now I'll return the favour. How are things between you and Sam?' Dr Noriko settles back into his seat. Through the window behind him I can see the lights flickering around Hyde Park Corner. London at night – there's no place quite like it. 'The last time we dined together, you were a couple. Is that over?'

I nod, drain my champagne glass and tell him about Sam's arrival at work yesterday afternoon, how he discovered that his desk had been moved and half the trading floor were treating him like a pariah. Of course, I didn't explain about my part in his downfall, which luckily enough Sam does not know about yet. Liz refused to listen to any of his explanations, or tell him where she got such a ridiculous idea.

Dr Noriko giggles over his enoki mushrooms and scallop tempura when I tell him about Sally, a female foreign exchange

113

trader, who jumped so high when Sam patted her on the shoulder on his way to his desk yesterday that she bit through her tongue. 'She's talking about suing Sam for harassment,' I tell him. But most of all he laughs when I describe the e-mail that Sam prepared for his colleagues, claiming that he had never contracted Gone Or Eah and that the only sexually transmitted disease that he had ever got was a case of crabs, which had responded well to treatment. Unfortunately for Sam he pressed the wrong buttons on his computer and the e-mail zoomed across the ether to his clients. His colleagues, on the other hand, received a rather interesting missive about the likely direction of the dollar over the next few days.

'Anyway,' I tell Dr Noriko, who is dipping his sushi into the tiny bowl of soy sauce, 'it's just as well that he didn't send that one outside the bank. He called the direction of the dollar wrong – his clients would all be out of pocket by now. Instead the phones have been ringing off the hook with clients asking for all the gory details about crabs. He's never been busier. Although I did hear that one female client was screaming down the phone at him about his irresponsible behaviour – think she might have experienced the love machine and its added attractions!' Come to think of it, that's probably why he flew the flag of the European Investment Bank for a week last year.

'So, sometimes you bankers do consort with clients?' Dr Noriko's eyes gleam as he sucks on his sushi and chopsticks in a highly suggestive manner.

'Thought we'd got past all that. Let's get this straight. This is a business relationship and it'll be totally above board. I'll not be providing any late-night entertainment for you – either personally or otherwise.' I hold up my hand to prevent him butting in. 'I'm here to discuss the proposal that I had delivered to your hotel last week.' Goodness, don't I sound assertive? I study his expression carefully. The Japanese are masters at making their faces unreadable, and I just cannot work out what Dr Noriko is thinking. Perhaps I should reconsider my stance on the hookers after all, if it saves my job. Suddenly I realise that Dr Noriko is not really looking at me, but at something just beyond my shoulder. I turn as a voluptuous blonde walks past, arm in arm with a spectacular example of the male species. Her cleavage is so deep that if she lay down I swear somebody could park a bicycle in there. Dr Noriko appears hypnotised. Luckily the position of his chair means that he is unable to see her when she reaches her table, just three down from us. She really *does* need a table for four!

'Dr Noriko? Can we return to the matter in hand?' I top up his wine glass and remove from my briefcase a copy of the proposal that he received earlier. I push some of the empty dishes to one side and make a space on the tabletop for it. 'You said on the telephone that you had some reservations about my bank's ability to pull off this deal. Would you like to talk about that?'

He shrugs. 'You're talking about a very ambitious deal, one that many other larger banks would be unable to pull off. What makes you so different? I want to believe in you, truly. The amount of funds that you are talking about, and the fact that you mean to raise them in dollars and then swap them back into yen at such attractive levels, it's all very appealing. My company needs this sort of transaction, but I can't allow a deal to go ahead if there is the slightest chance that it will go wrong.' I wince at the suggestion.

'I can assure you that nothing will go wrong.' I reach for my briefcase on the floor beside my shoes, and pull out some more papers. 'I have taken the liberty of preparing a document detailing my bank's success with other similar-sized transactions.' I pass it over to him. Dr Noriko glances down at it, turning the pages carefully while he considers the information.

'I don't see your name here.' Dr Noriko looks up at me.

'Sorry?'

'Which of these deals have you worked on? Your name is not linked with any of them.'

'I've been taking more of an administrative role in recent years,' I lie. 'A deal for your company would mark my return to the front line.'

'You're sure that you can do this? And these costs are achievable?'

'Absolutely. I've studied the markets carefully over the past few days, and if we move quickly, then I think there's a chance – and I can't put it more strongly than that at the moment – that we could even cut them.'

'Okay then.' Dr Noriko holds his hand out across the table, knocking an empty glass over in the process. 'You have yourself a deal.'

'Really? Oh, Dr Noriko, thank you.' I shake his hand vigorously. I've beaten the schedule. My job is safe. Somebody else's name will replace mine on the redundancy list. I would kiss Dr Noriko if I didn't think that he would get completely the wrong idea. 'Shall we have a couple of glasses of champagne to celebrate?'

'A couple of glasses,' he repeats, laughing as I hail a passing waiter. 'The last time we met for dinner I got the impression you were more of a couple of bottles sort of girl.'

'A bottle of your finest champagne,' I request. The fees on this deal will be absolutely huge. All the extra bits that Dr Noriko finds so attractive come at a price. I mentally tot up the sums – I could buy a car like Ciaran's just with the bonus from doing this deal. But hang on, Trixie. Enjoy the moment but don't get carried away. And definitely don't drink too much. Dr Noriko has a rather lustful look in his eyes.

Wednesday, October 18
(D Day minus 27 – I've got a deal and I don't care any more)

I couldn't sleep last night with excitement. I've got a deal – and I'm not even halfway through my allotted time. And not just any old deal. A big one. A complicated one, with all the additional fees that that brings. One that will make my competitors wince and convey to them that I have returned, and that they had better beware. I can just see my phone ringing off its hook as other companies queue to secure my services. The press department will spin into action to alert the relevant journalists about this groundbreaking deal. I will be fêted, maybe even on television; probably get a promotion. Jim will be delighted. And my bank manager will be ecstatic.

When I did eventually drift off, I dreamt about awards ceremonies. Me, dressed in a figure-hugging Donna Karan gown, stepping on to a dais in the middle of the Great Room at the Grosvenor House Hotel to collect my prize in front of hundreds of my City contemporaries. There would be no speeches, but the cavernous room would echo with whispered conversations: 'There goes Trixie Trader. She lost it a few years ago, over a man, wouldn't you know, and I really did think she should be written off. But look at her now. Marvellous deal. And she looks so good. How does she manage to balance her life so well? The original superwoman.' And I would walk back to my seat, careful not to catch my Jimmy Choo spike heels on the hem of my dress, graciously nodding and smiling at the audience, while my colleagues in their dinner jackets and bow ties would be on their feet clapping as I approached our table. And then the waiters would materialise with bottles of vintage Krug – courtesy of the chief executives of other investment banks desperate to lure me to join their staff. Actually I was really annoyed that I awoke when I did – because I was just discussing possible bonuses, and was extremely keen to discover what the American banks actually do pay.

And then I was even more annoyed because I couldn't believe the time. The digital numbers on the alarm clock on my bedside table say that it is just before six. I'm now making a habit of beating the clocks. If it carries on like this, I'll have to seriously consider joining the British 1,500-metre team. Still, it's amazing what a burst of adrenalin can do for you – pity they can't offer it on the National Health Service. I jump out of bed, pad through to the bathroom and indulge myself in an ecstasy of Jo Malone bubbles as I prepare to break the good news to Jim. I think I'll play it cool. Act like there was nothing to it – but then, knowing him, he'll probably pointedly ask why, if it was so easy, I haven't been doing it more. I dress carefully, flicking through the outfits in my walk-in wardrobe, before I decide on a red suit by Max Mara. It matches my buoyant mood, and, if I'm honest, my eyes after all that champagne last night.

Of course, Dr Noriko didn't want to go back to his hotel. He kept suggesting we could hit the nightspots, but I knew what he really meant was the G-spots. I finally loaded him into a black cab at one o'clock.

Jim is in his office, staring at some papers in preparation for the morning meeting, when I arrive at work. The trading floor is half-empty, but every few minutes the bank of lifts at the edge of the floor open their steel doors and disgorge members of staff arriving for a day of fun and frolics. Oh yes, and some work. I rush into his office without knocking, before his awful personal assistant Mary arrives and takes up her position outside the door.

'Jim. Jim. I've got it!' I exclaim, completely blowing my initial strategy. He looks at me in horror, dropping the sheaf of papers on to the desk before him.

'Oh my God, Trixie, when did you find out?'

'Last night. It took a while to pin it down but the doctor soon realised that I had what he was looking for.' I'm almost bouncing on my heels in excitement, but Jim just stares at me. 'I know. It was a shock for me too, but I really do think that I deserve this.'

'Deserve this,' he splutters. 'Nobody deserves this. Why weren't you careful?'

I look at Jim in confusion. He doesn't appear as happy as I had expected. Then the penny begins to drop.

'Jim,' I ask tentatively, 'what are we talking about?'

'You know.' He walks past me, closes the door and lowers his tone. 'Gonorrhoea. You just told me that you have it.'

'No, Jim. I didn't. I came in here to tell you that Dr Noriko is willing to sign on the dotted line for the deal that I presented to him last night.' I hand him a copy of the proposal for his perusal.

'What? Oh my God. What an appalling mistake to make – I have had a lot of things on my mind recently.' Jim looks horrified, but as he glances through the proposal his face begins to light up and he thrusts his hand out to give mine a vigorous shake. 'This is brilliant. Truly inspired. And in only three weeks. If I had known you would work this hard, I'd have given you a kick up the backside last year!'

'The markets weren't ready for this deal last year!'

'You need to show this proposal to the credit department, who'll need to conduct an in-depth study of Dr Noriko's business and other loans and borrowings that he may have outstanding.'

'Right.'

'And I'd sound out that Ciaran chappie, the new bond sales guy – I think you've met him – to gauge the appetite of investors for this sort of deal.'

I tell him that I'll get right to it. I leave the room quietly and make my way to my desk, where Bloodhound looks in amazement at me. I ignore his surreptitious glance at his wristwatch, and tell him the good news. He looks delighted, and suggests drinks at lunchtime to celebrate, but I remind him about my appointment with Frederick.

'Just think. I could end up winning Frederick's business too. Nothing for years and then two deals in one day. I should control London buses.' This day could not get any better, particularly when the next person I spot is Ciaran, who has walked across the trading floor to speak to me.

'Hi.' He perches on the side of my desk. 'You're nice and early this morning. Just wanted to say that I've booked the table on Friday for nine. We could have had an earlier sitting, but then we would have had to vacate it by nine, and I want to make a night of it.' I feel the blush rising up my face as he heads off in the direction of the morning meeting. I grab my papers, wave them in front of my face to cool it, seize the cup of coffee that Bloodhound has just placed in front of me, and follow him.

The meeting is boring. I stand in a crowded, stuffy room, listening to a stream of analysts discussing the major events of the day and how they are likely to affect the various market-places. Manfred stands up and spouts forth on a deal that he has just won. Unfortunately I missed the sweepstake this morning where we bet on how long Manfred will hold centre stage in the morning meeting. I once won with twenty-four minutes, but the idea of the sweepstake wasn't so funny when I heard that somebody had once won just by getting the time I turned up that day correct! Think it was Sam, and he had inside information. However, this morning Manfred's presentation is short and swift, and he keeps glancing over at me to check that I am not writing things down. Relax, Manfred, you old mummy's boy, I want to say, I've got my own deal now. And my one's bigger than your one. Stop it! I'm sounding like Sam.

I want to put my hand up, and prime the sales teams to get ready to sell hundreds of millions of pounds' worth of bonds issued by Dr Noriko's company. I want to tell the swaps guys to prepare for one of the biggest swapping transactions ever. And I want to tell the loans eggheads to be ready for some behind-the-scenes lending. I want to, but I don't. It would be a risk. The credit department has to approve the bank's involvement in this deal before I can say anything. And I don't want to tempt fate. Not this time.

The morning meeting lasts over half an hour. I return to my desk, and ring the credit department to discuss my proposed deal. They want to see a copy of the paperwork, so I put it into one of the internal mail envelopes and slip it into the post. Now there's nothing to do but wait, although Jim has insisted that I speak to Ciaran about the deal. The sacrifices I make for this bank!

Ciaran sounds slightly distracted when I call to tell him that it would be extremely helpful if he could test investor appetite for Dr Noriko's deal, which I explain in great depth to him. I even joke that it could work in his favour on Friday night. I might pay. He promises to get back to me with an assessment.

Imagine! He might tell me that investor appetite is voracious and that it's imperative that I increase the size of the deal, before it's even launched, to sate demand. I see cash registers ringing frantically with my future purchases. And now I can ignore the Battle Strategy. I've got the deal, so I can go for the man. And what a man he is, standing by his desk in his black double-breasted wool suit and lilac shirt and tie. This is a challenge that I'm going to enjoy.

I turn back to my screens with my new-found appetite for hard work. Okay, Trixie, don't overdo it! Correction. I turn back to my screens to check up on the markets. Everything's moving so fast. I hope that the credit department come back with the approval quickly; otherwise I might have to rework some of the mathematics of the deal. I make a few calls to check on some of the clients I recently reactivated. I quite enjoy chatting to them, listening to all the latest gossip, but unfortunately none of them actually wants to borrow anything. Frederick calls to check that we're still on for lunch, and in my enthusiasm to get a second deal, I agree to bring the time forward. We are now going to meet at the bar in One Lombard Street for a libation or three at noon, then take up our table in the restaurant at one.

I arrive just before twelve and seat my pert little bottom on one of the stools surrounding the circular bar, order a glass of champagne and examine my surroundings. There are only a few people at the bar, but the tables in the brasserie are rapidly filling up as bankers, who've been at their desks for more than five hours, answer the call of rumbling stomachs. I play spot-the-banker. Old-style City stockbrokers are easy. Their bulbous noses and the broken veins across their faces clash with the tranquil colours of the restaurant, but it's the way they sit that is the real giveaway. They're forced to push their seats way back from the table in order to fit their ample girths. American bankers are easy. They're either casually dressed or stuffing a green salad and mineral water into their mouths. Then there are my friends – they're the ones with three bottles on their table, none of which is water. I wave at a few of them, and then look in horror at what has just walked through the door. I'm not sure what sort of category that banker should be put in. Or even if it is a banker – or human.

It hands a fox fur to the waiter and heads for the bar. Quick! Look away! Grab a newspaper. I attract the bartender's attention. Sorry, he has no newspaper. Well, what about *War and Peace*? Surely a copy of that must be lying around amongst the mixers under the bar. Aren't bartenders usually students? *Vanity Fair*? *Ulysses*? He shakes his head. I don't think I'll be returning to this venue. What is he offering me now? Do I really look like the sort of person who reads *Hello!* magazine? Okay, hand it over, but is there a copy of the *Daily Telegraph* that I can slip it inside?

I furtively study the huge creature approaching the bar, in short skirt and open-necked blouse, with a Hermès scarf tied in a floppy bow. Its brown hair is cut into a short bob, and its face is covered in lashings of pan-stick make-up. A rather attractive Adam's apple bobs up and down as it teeters along in its high heels. (Don't recognise the brand but they must be specially made to take the weight of the six-footer.) I really have seen it all now. The bartender takes its order of a vodka and tonic, and suddenly it squeals:

'Trixie! Is it you?'

I look over my shoulder, praying desperately that somebody else's mother was stupid enough to name their daughter after their favourite aunt, who just happened to be a flapper girl. But no! Nobody else is registering. Well, at least they are registering, but not because it has called their name. There is only one thing for it. Pretend to be deaf. Lose yourself in the latest article about Calista Flockhart – dream about having calves that thin. Ignore the aberration in the corner.

'You naughty girl. You're pretending you don't recognise me. You tease. How are we going to enjoy our lunch if you keep up this charade?' Suddenly my champagne splutters out of my nostrils, and I feel as though I'm choking. The creature struggles down from its stool, grabs a napkin and starts patting my back. 'There, there. I suppose that I was being a teensy-weensy bit mischievous by not explaining the situation. I just thought it would be a pleasant surprise.' Pleasant?

'Frederick?' I splutter, as I ask the bartender to bring over a Scotch. A large one. 'What's happened? Where's your beard?' Oops. Now he's up close, I can see the shadow through the American tan pan-stick.

'It's Fredericka now, dear. I was going to correct you on the phone, but I find that it's not really the best way to tell people. It's so anonymous. They immediately jump to the conclusion that I will look like an over-made-up vaudeville queen, and, of course, you can see that's really not the case.' I almost choke on my Scotch, but miraculously manage to retain a straight face. 'But,' she touches my knee with a scarlet talon, 'I just knew that you would understand. We can have a nice girlie lunch and I can tell you all about it. By the way, what make-up are you wearing? It looks so subtle. You must give me some tips. I haven't really mastered the art of putting on eye shadow.' He can say that again – pandas look more subtle. 'And how do you cope with these panty girdles? They keep riding up.' Another Scotch on the rocks, please. Very large.

I spot the maître d' arriving. I could swear that he's stifling the giggles. As he helps me down from my stool, he mutters that he has reserved a corner table for us – where we won't be seen or disturbed. Too late! As we walk across the brasserie to the restaurant, I spot Sam sitting at a large table with members of his team. Unfortunately, he sees me.

'Yo, Trixie,' he shouts. 'How's your sister?' The others on the

123

table burst out laughing, but their smirks turn to cowardly grimaces as Fredericka approaches the table and, to Sam's total surprise, parks a large smacker on his face.

'Sam, darling, you are naughty. Don't you recognise me? All those evenings we spent drinking together in the West End?' Sam is shaking his head violently. Perhaps he's thinking of all those drunken nights out when he may not have returned with quite the memory he went out with. 'Come now. It's Frederick. But you, you wicked boy, can now call me Fredericka!' The painted lady, and I use that term loosely, then gives Sam a lustful wink, hands him her business card and follows me down the stairs, though not before shouting over her massive shoulder: 'Call me!'

A murmur greets us as we enter the restaurant and walk towards the corner table. It would be at the furthest end; there'll be no tip for the maître d'. I wait while he pulls out the cloth-covered chair, drops a linen napkin in my lap and then removes the empty plate, decorated with a ribbon, that marks the table setting. Why do restaurants have those plates? Is there a European Union ruling to employ more people to wash up? And then I watch with interest as he hesitates over Fredericka. Luckily the monster with the blue eye shadow takes pity on him and drops the napkin itself/herself/himself.

'Your face is a picture,' Fredericka tells me. Perhaps, but I've seen hers in works by Picasso. 'I was so pleased when Chris said to give you a ring. My secretary – marvellous woman, taken this all in her stride – says that you're extremely keen to do a deal. And I thought, I just *have* to see that woman.'

I smile. Perhaps it might even be worth the embarrassment of meeting this thing. I take a deep breath, careful not to swallow the cloying perfume that hovers around us.

'Extremely keen is not quite how I would put it.' I don't want Fredericka to think that I'm desperate. 'My bank is looking to expand its bond operations, and we have a number of very innovative ideas which obviously we want our long-standing and valuable clients to benefit from. I'd heard on the grapevine that you're looking to borrow money. Anyway, let's order first,'

I suggest as I spot a waiter approaching, 'before we get down to the nitty-gritty.'

I settle on sea bass, baked in sea salt and aromatic herbs and spices, while she opts for mignons of veal, with caramelised Jerusalem artichokes. Typical. You can dress them in frilly garments, paint lipstick on them, but a man always chooses the red meat. Next she'll be asking for tomato ketchup. I give the sommelier the wine order – a dry white Bordeaux – and settle back into my seat.

'So, Fredericka, what's new? I mean,' I add, scrambling to save face after the inappropriate question, 'apart from the obvious.'

'The obvious is, I'm afraid, all that I have been doing,' she explains, with a rueful shrug of her massive shoulders. 'I'm not quite, you know,' she whispers, indicating towards her lap with scarlet talons, 'quite finished.' My eyes inadvertently take her signal as an indication to examine for tell-tale bumps. 'But I've started a course of hormone treatment, and have to live like this for another year before the hospital will go for the final cut.' There is real pain in the eyes of the men on the next table, and I suddenly notice that they've both stopped eating their bangers and mash.

Our starters arrive, over which Fredericka tells me her life history. I can only nod in agreement at the shock that her mother must have felt when she arrived home with friends to find her seventeen-year-old son dressed in her baby-doll pyjamas. I mean, baby-dolls! They went out with the ark. But I truly do feel for her when she explains about the confusion she has felt throughout her life. Her nagging belief that there was another body within. I switch off as she goes over the details of the operation, and the requirement to live as a woman for one year before she can go through with it. Her company, she initially claims, has treated her well, but as we get halfway down the second bottle, I begin to hear a different story. One of bigotry, bitchiness and jealousy.

'Over the past few years my position within the company has altered. My bonuses have been cut back. I'm not as powerful as

I once was.' I expect it's the hormone treatment. 'Hmm, this veal is lovely, Trixie. Would you like to try a mouthful?' She holds a fork up before I shake my head and lie about not eating meat. 'Oh well, your loss. I think though it could probably do with a bit of ketchup.'

'That's all very interesting, Frederick . . .' I hesitate and immediately watch her arch her carefully plucked eyebrows at me, '. . . ka. But surely your power base is not so depleted, if you've called me here to discuss a deal.' I check that the two men seated next to us aren't listening in at this point, but instead they're urgently beckoning the waiter to bring the bill.

'Well,' she sweeps her hair back behind her jug ears, 'if I'm being honest, I thought it would help my career if I brought in a really good deal for the company. You don't think that's shallow and selfish, do you?' I shake my head vigorously. 'I thought it could work to my advantage too.' My ears prick up. The two men are now beating a hasty retreat, are almost sprinting towards the exit. 'As I've already told you, they've cut back on my bonuses, and I find myself financially embarrassed. My resources were drained by the costs of the clothes, and this,' she points towards her lap again, 'will have to wait unless I can raise the cash quickly.'

Fredericka sips gently at her Bordeaux, before coyly raising her eyes towards me. 'So I thought I would put my business out to tender.' What? Is she going on the streets? That would cause a few raised eyebrows, to say the least. She starts to fiddle nervously with her napkin. 'I heard you were extremely keen to do a deal, and I'm willing to give you my company's business, but I must get something in return.'

'Well, Fredericka, I can give you a few tips on make-up, and maybe show you how to sit at a bar stool without opening your legs.' This is easy. Two deals in two days. My job is more than safe; it is secure for years to come. 'And between us girls, I have a wonderful lady who sugar-waxes.' I nod slowly. 'She could do wonders with you. My treat, of course.'

The waiter arrives to clear away the dirty plates. The restaurant is emptying as people return to their screen-covered desks to check on what the American markets are doing. A Bloomberg screen, which provides a constant flow of financial information, sits at the bottom of the nearby stairs, and I consider excusing myself and going to it, just to give the effect of a hassled City banker. But then the waiter offers post-lunch drinks, and I decide a few quick Kummels and ice will prove more effective.

'I think that perhaps, Trixie, you're missing the point. I need money.'

'Yes, yes.' I wave my hand airily. 'We can discuss the finer details later. What sort of sum are we looking at?'

'About twenty thousand pounds.'

'What?' I almost drop my Kummel. 'I am not sure that I am the right banker for you, then. I usually do deals which are several million, if not hundreds of millions, pounds.'

'See what I mean about you missing the point? The deal I want to do for the company is worth about one hundred million pounds. The deal I want to cut for myself is worth twenty thousand. I want a payment, not a loan.' Suddenly Fredericka's face has a dark air to it, and it's not the six o'clock shadow. 'To enable me to go forward with the operation.' She sips her port, and relaxes back into her seat. 'It's not even a quarter of the fees that this deal will generate for your bank. I think it's a fair price to pay, particularly as it could be the first of many deals.'

'What? For you or the company?' I burst out, without thinking. 'What sort of a bank do you think we are? We don't offer back-handers or whatever you call it in this circumstance.'

'Really? Well, I think you should consider the matter a bit more carefully. Do you really have the authority to turn down this deal, which could open the floodgates to others?' She opens her snakeskin handbag, takes out a business card and hands it to me. 'This is my personal number and e-mail. No nasty tapes or traces; my company need never know. Let me know what you decide.' She downs her port and stands up. 'But do it quickly. I haven't got much time. When I look in the mirror when I'm naked, I feel like a freak in a circus.'

Not *just* when you're naked, dear. Fredericka holds her hand out, and in a daze, I shake it. The second deal has disappeared through my immaculately manicured fingertips. There is no way that Jim will sanction a payment like that. It amounts to a bribe – a bit like the two hookers I laid on (bad choice of words) for Dr Noriko, I think uncomfortably. Unfortunately, this means that I will be forced to concentrate solely on him and his needs. Business, that is. I call the waiter over, and order another large Kummel along with the bill. I think I deserve it after such a lunch.

Wednesday, October 18

(D Day minus 27 – I'sh got a deal and I don't care any more, cossh you're my bessht friend, you are)

A huge bouquet of sunflowers is resting on my chair when I arrive back at the office – at some time past four. This bloody watch. The little hand is definitely at four but the big hand seems to have split in two. Can't trust the Italians to make anything that works on time.

'Trixie,' hisses Bloodhound as I stumble past him on the way to my desk, and attempt to grab the card from the flowers, 'what time do you call this?'

'Good point! I dunno.' I shake my wrist beside my ear. 'Thish bloody watch is broken.' I wave my hand in the air. 'It's the last time I'm buying a Guushi. I don't know if it'sh half pasht four or quarter to five.' I turn to Bloodhound and shrug my shoulders.

'Are you drunk?' He looks around quickly to check nobody is watching. 'You're an idiot. For goodness' sake, this is all Jim needs as ammunition!'

'Shhhhhh,' I answer, patting my index finger on my lips. What a great sound. I could join a jazz band. I can see the billboards: *Trixie Trader and her amazing non-collagen-enhanced flexible lips – weddings, bar mitzvahs and funerals her speciality.* Bloodhound is looking at me like I'm a recalcitrant child, so I warn him: 'Don't shay anything. Don't want to attract any attention.' I begin to sway from side to side as the effect of four large Kummels and ice interacts with the cold air blasting down from the conditioning units overhead. 'I don't think I should eat shee bash again. Doeshn't agree with me.'

'Sit down,' Bloodhound orders as I nearly lose my footing.

'Can't,' I insist, wobbling on my spike heels.

'I'm not asking you, I'm telling you. Down, now. Stop slobbering.' He points at the chair. Who does he think he is?

Barbara Woodhouse? I may be slobbering now but in the morning, as Winston Churchill once said, I'll be sober. Well, as long as I don't go out again tonight.

'Can't,' I repeat, stamping my foot, causing a few people on nearby desks to look over.

'For God's sake, Trixie, people are watching,' he hisses at me. 'This is not the time to act like a spoiled Home Counties brat.' Bastard! I glare at him.

'I can't shit down, shorry, seet down, becosh there's a bunch of flowersh on my sheet.' The bright yellow of the sunflowers and palm leaves hurts my eyes, and I start rummaging in my handbag for my sunglasses.

'Oh, for goodness' sake!' Bloodhound glides his seat over to mine, and lifts the flowers on to the floor beside his feet. 'I'm not putting them anywhere near you in your present condition. Pull yourself together. Jim's been looking for you, the credit department has called and Dr Noriko has rung twice. I'm not your secretary. Now pull yourself together before Jim sees you.' He hands me a bottle of spring water from a cooler by his desk. 'Drink this. How did your lunch go with Frederick? Or is that a silly question?'

'Ka,' I retort.

'Bless you.' He searches in his jacket pocket for a clean handkerchief. Is he mad? I'd rather wipe my nose with sandpaper.

'I'm not schneezing,' I splutter. 'His name is Fredericka now. He ish now a woman. Well, almosht.' I point two fingers towards Bloodhound's groin – a place I never thought I'd want to look – and open and shut them in a scissors motion. 'He wants me to give him the money to get his bits chopped off.' I explode in peals of laughter, but Bloodhound retains a stony face, despite the tears that are forming in his eyes. 'If I give him ten bob to Bobbit then he'll award me the mandate for his company's deal. Man-date. I like that word, don't you?' I smile at Bloodhound but quickly look away. In my current state I'm seeing three of him, and my stomach really can't take it.

130

'I wishhh Sham had got rid of hish,' I confide in Blood-hound. 'But he was too attached to it. He called it Tonto, like the guy from *The Lone Ranger*, cosh he reckoned it was obedient, strong and a faithful friend – always there when he needed it. Hah! I called it Toto, like the dog from *The Wizard of Oz*, behind his back. Coshh it was shmall, messhy and never came when you wanted it to.' I could swear I can hear someone laughing. I attempt to stand up and search around for the guilty party, but Bloodhound places a restraining hand on my arm.

'I'm getting you some coffee,' he says. 'Now sit there. Do not move from that chair and do not, under any circumstances, answer any phone.'

I nod at him, but as he turns to go to the kitchen area, I wave my hand in the air. 'Shtop!'

'What?' He spins around, conscious of the heads that have turned in my direction. 'Keep quiet. That's all I've asked you to do.' He throws up his hands in exasperation.

'Jusht want to shee who sent me the flowersh. Pleesh pash it to me.' I point at the card. He hands it to me with an irritable expression. I wait until he has moved off, then rip open the envelope. The flowers are from Ciaran. Ciaran. Just the sight of that name in my present state makes me exhale a romantic sigh. I sit still for a moment, reading the message – his writing is terrible, can't make a word out, something about coagulation? – and enjoying my mood. I feel all warm and tingly. Or is that the Kummel? I slump back into my chair just as three lights on the dealer board flash in front of me. Somebody is calling. Since when have I done what Bloodhound asked? Better answer. I lift the handset and press a button – why do they put them so close together? Don't they know people in the City have liquid lunches? With transsexuals. And it's not in their job descriptions.

'Hello, Trixie Trader here. At your shervich.'

'At my cervix? I don't think so, darling,' Sam's voice bellows down the line. 'But if you would let me at yours.' Damn. I've pressed the wrong button.

'You'll be lucky,' I retort down the phone, before flicking the button to disconnect the line. Three lights are still flashing. Or is it six? I press the first two.

'Hello, is that you, Trixie?' I recognise the voice of Charlotte in the credit department. Sober up. Come on. Act natural.

'Tish me. Are you ringing up with my credit approval?' Good. Don't think she could suspect that I'm inebriated. Thank God these aren't smell-a-phones.

'Sort of.' Charlotte hesitates for a moment. 'It's not quite as cut and dried as we first thought. Might need a few more days to consider the matter.' A few more days? In credit and accounts departments-speak that means weeks. Or months. I might miss the deadline, all because some jobsworth is going strictly by the two-hundred-page book.

'Oh go on,' I urge. 'Be your friend for life.' How could she refuse such an offer? Actually, it's not quite as generous as it initially sounds. After all, Charlotte is in her late sixties. Still, I could end up feeding her mashed cabbage and carrots at some old people's home in years to come.

'That's very kind, Trixie. But—'

She can't get the words out before I interrupt, in my most gushing voice.

'Go on. Pretty pleash. Pretty, pretty pleash. Getting on my kneash.' I make to kneel down in front of my desk, when a firm hand grabs under my armpit and swings me back up into my seat. 'What are you doing?' I protest. Bloodhound takes the handset from me and mutters into it something about me being in a very funny mood. I hear the word 'premenstrual.' He turns to me, hands me the coffee and orders me to drink it slowly.

'I think, Trixie, that you should go home when you've finished it,' he instructs, as I inadvertently slurp the first mouthful. 'If Jim finds you in this state, he'll go mad. I'll cover for you. Say you're visiting a client or something.' He turns back to my dealer board and answers the remaining flashing lights. I hear him tell people that I've left the office for the afternoon to give a client presentation, but will return tomorrow morning. Early. He glares at me pointedly when he says that bit.

'Right.' Bloodhound turns to me as I drain the coffee cup. 'Is it one of Lily's days?' I nod. 'I'll ring and ask her to wait for you. She can put you to bed!'

'Tell her that I've seen some great six-for-four offers this afternoon,' I instruct. 'Oh, better call Julie. Shee's my besht friend, she ish. I'm meant to be meeting her tonight at the Met Bar.'

'I'll deal with that,' he says firmly. He helps me to my feet, gathers up my belongings and puts them in my bag. He lifts the bouquet. 'Will you be able to manage this?' We walk towards the bank of lifts, with me carefully trying to keep my balance. I don't think anybody suspects. Look, anybody could have stumbled over that piece of fax paper. It was dangerous to leave it on the floor by the machine. Perhaps I should enter it into the office injuries book. When we reach our destination, Bloodhound presses the button to call the lift.

'See you tomorrow. Look, don't do this again. You've only got, what, twenty seven days left? Don't blow this job for the wrong reasons. Put Frederick, or whatever the hell he calls himself these days, down to experience, and get on with getting that deal. After the initial fiasco with Dr Noriko, you don't want to get involved with any more potential bribe situations, do you?' I shake my head. Uh-oh. Stomach rising. Deep breaths. Bloodhound continues: 'You've got a few more aces up your sleeve, haven't you? Here's the lift. Go on, get straight home – and don't pop into any more bars on the way.' He gives me a friendly nudge. I enter the lift, which luckily is empty. 'I'll call Lily and Julie for you.'

'Thankssh, Bloodhound,' I say, pointing a finger towards him. 'You're my friend, you are. Not my besht one, though, but closhe.' The doors shut but I could swear that Bloodhound is blushing as he watches them glide together.

Thursday, October 19
(D Day minus 26 – and on the eighth day He created the HANGOVER!)

I am changing my mind about God. How can somebody who is meant to be all-knowing make two such obvious mistakes? The time zone thing is, of course, my real pet hate, being a career investment banker and forced to endure morning meetings. But to create hangovers as well! He was either having a bad day or He didn't understand the full implication of what He was doing. And it takes a real devious mind to create something that does not truly afflict you until your late twenties. You get lulled into a false sense of security in your teens, and then . . . Wham! Just when you can afford more than a bottle of cider or Lambrusco, the evils of drink make themselves felt. And seen.

Drink quality champagne, an older friend once recommended, and you will avoid hangovers. So I did. Unfortunately, he never alerted me to the recommended dosage, so I assumed it must be similar to that of aspirin. Take two bottles every four hours. Do not exceed eight bottles in any twenty-four-hour period. And if symptoms persist, contact your doctor.

The same friend also warned me never to mix my drinks. After a few months struggling to imbibe all alcohol neat, I realised my mistake. It was when I asked the waiter in the American Bar at the Savoy for a Manhattan, with each ingredient in separate glasses, that the penny dropped.

But yesterday I avoided all the advice. I overindulged, I mixed, and this morning I feel like SHIT! There is no other way to put it. It's the type of morning that would make the old Trixie ring in with some elaborate excuse about slippery leaves, train lines, women's problems or power cuts – the electricity grid is just riddled with gremlins – but not today. No. Today I'm suffering in semi-silence. I'm sitting at my desk, nibbling a scrambled egg and bacon muffin and guzzling Lucozade, while struggling to focus on the flashing screen in front of me. Bloodhound just grunts in disapproval each time I yelp as the glare of the screen burns my stinging eyes.

'You're so stupid,' he says finally, after I don my Chloe sunglasses. 'Talk about alerting everybody to the fact that you have a hangover. You might just as well borrow Sam's flagpole and hang out a white flag. Let Jim know that you are not taking his threat seriously, and that he should put you out of your misery today.' Does Jim have a supply of Resolve in his drawer?

'I *am* taking it seriously,' I snap back. 'Yesterday started so well, but then it just went horribly wrong when that big, ugly cross-dressing, willy-owning freak turned up. Can't you understand? I had hoped that I might be able to achieve even more than Jim expected. Two deals. Not one. Two. Let him know that I have changed. But all my plans just,' I throw my hands in the air, 'evaporated. And all because of you!'

'Me?' Bloodhound looks genuinely shocked, but slides his chair back from me, just in case I start exercising the old right hook again. 'You can't blame me for Frederick's penchant for a woman's body.'

'But *you* were the one who set it up.'

'Because I knew his company needed to borrow money. I didn't know anything about this snip-and-lose business,' protests Bloodhound. 'I won't pass on any more leads if I'm going to get blamed if they go wrong.' He turns to his screens with a flourish and extends his cold shoulder towards me.

I know he's right. Bloodhound may be irritating but he's not vindictive. It's just my hangover that is making me bitter and suspicious. I suspect Bloodhound knows that too, because after ignoring me for almost twenty minutes while he makes some calls, he turns and asks if I would like a coffee. He even offers to get two Danish pastries from the canteen in the basement. Bloodhound, the lapdog. How could I refuse? Ten minutes later we're sipping and nibbling amiably. Bloodhound breaks the silence.

'How was Lily when you got home? Did she wait on for you?'

135

'Fine. She's used to it.' I didn't tell him that she's so used to it that by the time I had arrived home she had donned a throwaway plastic apron, like the ones they use in hospital emergency rooms, and placed a bucket on either side of my bed, which was stripped of its Ralph Lauren Egyptian cotton sheets. (They were replaced by Woolworth specials – hope I don't come out in a rash.) In fact she was outside in the square when I arrived, chatting to an ice-cream man, who was leaning out of the little hatch in his van, which was ringing out 'Greensleeves'. That awful tune reverberated through my dreams last night, although it was played on a lute. I was Guinevere, my Titian curls cascading down my back, whilst Ciaran was Sir Lancelot, resplendent in armour, rescuing me from the drudgery of royal life.

'She made me a pot of strong coffee, and insisted that I drank it all before I went to bed. I think I finally passed out about eight. She left a note on the kitchen table that you rang last night – thanks – along with the news that the bread bin was filled with croissants because Sainsbury's was running a French offer. If I don't eat them, apparently she's going to make bread-and-butter pudding, using a Gary Rhodes recipe, for the local hospice.'

Bloodhound giggles. 'I called Julie for you. And I told Jim that you were meeting a client for afternoon tea at the Ritz.'

'Cheers.' I dampen the end of my finger and press on all the crumbs that have fallen on to my desk. 'Sorry about what I said earlier. Me and hangovers, huh!' He nods in agreement. 'Bloody Julie didn't ring last night, though. She must have found another playmate to go drinking with. Did she say anything on the phone?'

'No. Don't think so. I was sure she said she was going to ring you.' Bloodhound scrunches his nose up as if he's considering the matter, then turns back to his screen. 'Anyway, coffee break over. Next time the Danishes are on you.'

Julie's direct line is flashing, but she can wait. I'm going to sulk. Where were her words of comfort last night? I answer another line. It's Lily, checking that I got into work all right.

Has she no faith? Dr Noriko is next on the line. I assure him that the deal is going ahead as planned but there are some technical issues our end that need to be cleared up before I can press the Go button. Better not tell him about the delay at the credit department. He'll think we're all amateurs. I then touch base with a few clients who I have reactivated in recent weeks. Keeping it friendly.

Julie's light flashes at regular intervals. Eventually I give in.

'Hello,' I say, in my frostiest voice. 'Nice of you to call. Where were you last night when I needed you?'

'What do you mean? Where was I? I was at the Met Bar. I told you.' Julie sounds quite offended.

'And when did you tell me?' Gotcha!

'Last night when I rang you at about ten. You sounded half asleep – you were muttering some nonsense about trying to find the key to open the armour, and did I have a can-opener. Don't you remember?'

'Don't be so silly.' Better close up this hole before it swallows me. 'I was just joking. Anyway, who did you find at such short notice to go with you to the Met Bar? Have you got a secret friend that you haven't told me about?'

'Don't be so ridiculous,' Julie bellows down the phone. 'So, are you feeling better this morning?'

'A little. But I have a mother of a hangover. Every time I move my head to the side, it feels like a little man is beating a stick just above my eyebrow. It's like having your eyebrows plucked from the inside.'

'Don't be such a baby. Anyway, do you still want me to come around this evening to help you choose your outfit for the big date tomorrow night?'

'Yeah. And I wonder if you could bring over your beaded pashmina. I thought I might borrow it. Is that all right?'

'Sure. Gotta hop. My dealer board's lit up like Blackpool illuminations. See you about eight.' She hangs up. Then it strikes me. Julie never told me whom she went to the Met Bar with. Must ask Bloodhound if she mentioned anything to him. I'd ask him now but he's not at his desk. I survey the trading floor, and spot him by the flagpole. He's talking to Sam. Traitor.

He's almost as treacherous as these markets. Every time I look at my screen, I can see that the markets have moved a little further. They are very jittery and if the credit department doesn't come back with approval for Dr Noriko's deal soon, the mathematics of it just will not make sense. The deal will either go away, or need to be rethought. With a deadline looming, neither option looks attractive. I had better hope that New York brings in some new leads next week.

'Trixie.' I look up to see Jim at my side. He has obviously dressed in a hurry because his gold-patterned tie clashes terribly with his green-striped shirt. As for the red braces . . . 'Just checking up on how things are going. Is the American trip sorted?'

'Yep,' I answer. 'Fly out early Monday afternoon and return on the Wednesday red-eye. I was thinking of flying out Sunday, but family commitments . . .' I leave the sentence open.

'Indeed,' he answers, in a similarly oblique fashion. 'Mustn't neglect the family, even if we are on a deadline. Eh?' His red braces now match the horns that are sprouting from the top of his bald head. 'How many meetings have you got arranged? Are they worth the Upper Class fare?' I cringe at his penny-picking – it's not as if it's his money.

'I've eight meetings arranged, two dinners and one lunch,' I tell him, and then lie for good measure. 'My two breakfast meetings have both, unfortunately, been cancelled.' Adopt forlorn expression. And don't mention that two of the meetings are with personal shoppers. You can't always be good!

'And the afternoon tea yesterday? Any tips?' Hmm. This could be a trick question. Is he trying to catch me out? Does he suspect my true whereabouts?

'Sadly no.' I pretend to check up on the screens in front of me. 'The only tip yesterday was the service charge.'

'Well, well, I can see you're busy.' Jim makes to leave and return to his office. 'By the way, I heard from the credit department yesterday afternoon.'

'Oh yes,' I answer casually. 'Unfortunately they won't be able to give me a decision on Dr Noriko's deal for a few more days. Think they're short-staffed.'

'Hmm,' adds Jim. 'Charlotte said that you had been most persuasive, trying to get an early decision.' I could swear that his eyes are twinkling. 'Mosht pershwashive,' he shouts over his shoulder, as he marches across the floor back to his office. I think it's time for a hair of the dog.

Friday, October 20
(D Day minus 25 – Battle Strategy? What Battle Strategy?)

I arrive at The Ivy ten minutes late. I told Ciaran earlier in the day that I would meet him there. I couldn't have borne it if he had arrived at my flat to see me scurrying around, pulling rollers out of my hair and throwing every eye-shadow palette down in despair while I frantically searched for the correct shade.

As the waiter leads me to the table (discreetly placed at the outside perimeter of the restaurant) I surreptitiously study my host for the evening. There's not a trace of panic in his face. No anxious studying of his wristwatch, as he wonders if perhaps his beautiful date may stand him up. No! Ciaran is sitting, glass of champagne in hand, merrily chatting away to the two socialites on the adjoining table.

'Trixie,' he exclaims, shrugging his shoulders at the two blonde bimbos, who grudgingly turn back to chat to each other. Two airheads together. Perhaps we should move tables. There's bound to be some turbulence. 'Wow!' he adds, as he leans across the table to kiss me on the cheek. 'You look stunning.' And so I should. Three hours at the beautician's (but if Jim asks, the European Investment Bank), one at the hairdresser (Standard & Poor's) and Julie's make-up skills, plus a drop-dead-gorgeous Versace dress, Gina sandals and Julie's silver beaded pashmina. Total cost: £2,500. Response: Stunning. Analysis: Value for money.

'You scrub up well too,' I reply. And he has. Ciaran is wearing a black Dolce & Gabbana suit and a white open-neck shirt. Little silver hearts adorn his cuffs.

'A glass of champagne?' he asks, as he pours the amber nectar into the flute placed in front of me. A man after my own heart. None of these half-measures. The bubbles are popping at the brim. 'Cheers.' We clink glasses, before I turn to peruse my surroundings in search of the perennial celebrity.

140

'Have you been here before?' Ciaran asks casually. Oops! Must have appeared like a rubber-necker. I turn back to face him, blatantly ignoring those actors from that sitcom.

'Of course. Actually, I brought Lily here for her birthday, but only after I warned her that those tabards were not a fashion statement. She loved it. Tom and Nicole were sitting over there.' I point to a table in the corner. 'Mind you, I think she'd have preferred Richard and Judy. She thought Tom was an "insignificant little fellow" – well, he was going through his grunge look.'

He laughs, and the bimbos shoot me a daggers glance. I do a quick recce of the dining room. 'Nobody famous here tonight, though,' I add, although the name 'Liam Neeson' keeps being whispered around the restaurant, as diners fix their attention on my date.

Suddenly the stained-glass windows that top the opposite wall of the restaurant illuminate, as if the outside world has suddenly erupted into a tumultuous thunderstorm.

'Is it lightning?' I ask Ciaran.

'Sadly no. It's the paparazzi. Somebody big must be arriving.' As if on cue, Madonna walks into the restaurant. She strolls towards her table, which is three down from ours, sits down and suddenly notices us. The former virgin gets up from her seat and heads over in our direction.

'Liam.' She addresses Ciaran, without acknowledging me. 'Didn't know you were in town. Are you going to Elton's on Saturday?'

'Ah no,' he responds. 'Now, if you will excuse me.' He nods towards me. Madonna gives me the once-over, and returns to her seat. I can see the headlines tomorrow: *Liam Neeson out with mysterious Titian beauty*. And before I know it the tabloids will be splashing with the story *Liam Neeson to divorce*.

'Wow!' I exclaim. 'Does that often happen?'

'Only when Madonna's in town. Now, what are we going to eat?' He nudges the one-page menu in my hand. 'I can recommend the shepherd's pie.'

The waiter arrives to take our order. Caesar salad and fish

cakes for me. Mushroom and leek tart, with Gruyère cheese, and shepherd's pie for Ciaran. And a bottle of something fantastic. Sorry, two bottles. One to go with the entrées and one with the mains. This is *my* kind of man.

What can I say? We get on. The hours fly by as we chat about work, life and the universe. Actually I lied about the universe. Who wants to talk about that? But whenever I read highbrow magazines (i.e. not *Vogue*) they always mention it, so I thought I'd better put it in.

I tell him about the arrival of Liz at work that morning. She had been keeping a low profile since that débâcle with Sam and gonorrhoea, but today she was remarkably up-front. Those Wonderbras! Amazing what they can do with so little material. We laugh – much to the irritation of the bimbettes on the neighbouring table – about Liz. She was boasting about a new client who had rung her up out of the blue regarding a deal.

'What's his name?' I had asked, casually. You never know if it might have been a lead. And beggars can't be choosers. Ask Sam.

'It's not a he. It's a she,' Liz had protested.

'Okay. What's *her* name?'

'Fredericka.' Well, you could have knocked me down with one of the ostrich feathers that decorate Kate's headboard. She bought them as a reminder of a disastrous investment she'd made in an ostrich farm. (You'd have thought that Kate of all people would have realised that there isn't that much meat on the birds!)

'You know her?' Liz was all interested then; desperate to learn something that could give her an edge over the competition.

'Sort of.' Slowly. Come on, Trixie. Sucker her in. She deserves it. 'I've heard a bit about her. She has some strange,' I hesitated over the word, 'fetishes.'

'Really!' Liz was all agog now. Here was something that she could share with her client! 'Like what?'

'Well.' I ushered her closer to me, as if I didn't want anybody else to hear my indiscretion. 'She likes people to mention that she looks like a man in drag. It's a fantasy thing.'

Suddenly, Ciaran's Bordeaux is splattered all over the white linen cloth on my side of the table. He tries to catch his breath.

'My God, Trixie, you're priceless.' He contemplates the tablecloth in front of me with some consternation. 'I'm so sorry. I just couldn't,' he starts to giggle again, 'believe that you would be so cruel to that poor defenceless creature.' Defenceless? Has he gone near her recently? One too-close whiff of her perfume and you would swear that you had been hit in the eyes with pepper spray. 'Look at that tablecloth. I'll have to ask them to replace it. I'm so sorry.'

'No problem,' I reply magnanimously, as a rather cute waiter arrives and starts to fuss around my side of the table. The bimbettes are positively preening. 'Anyway, back to Liz and work. It's been a funny old week. Did I tell you that the credit department has delayed its decision on Dr Noriko's deal? By the way, what's the feedback on the investor demand for such a deal?'

'Come on now, Trixie. Can't we talk about something else? It's not very romantic if all you want to chat about is work, is it?' Romantic! Any lingering doubts about the nature of to-night are dispelled as I look across at Ciaran. His blue eyes are twinkling. I can tell that he enjoys throwing out these small pieces of bait. I just want him to reel me in. Quickly!

'Sorry. You're the boss,' I say. Of course he's not, but it appeals to the male ego to believe that they are. 'What shall we talk about now?' So we move our discussion on to music. Luckily not classical or opera, as I would be a bit out of my depth there. Unfortunately, Ciaran dislikes my comments about *Riverdance*. He thinks I'm taking the Michael when I say that it sent shivers down my spine when I watched forty ramrod dancers kick their legs in the air, wondering just what was injected into theirs to prevent them bending.

All too soon the awkward moment arrives. Standing on West Street, the big question is, how do I get home? Or how do *we* get home? I spot the yellow light of a free black cab in the distance. The end of a date – the only time in your life you can guarantee a cab will turn up too soon. 'I suppose I should hail that.' My heart sinks as Ciaran nods, and thrusts his arm out in front of the oncoming vehicle.

'To Islington,' he orders the driver, and then moves to the passenger door. 'Trixie, I hope you don't mind if I come with you. My mother wouldn't forgive me for not seeing a young lady to her door.' Bless you Mrs Ryan. And bless you again for considering me a lady! Particularly given the thoughts going through my mind at the moment.

We sit in silence in the back seat. Him pressed up against the left wall of the cab. Me against the right. Goodness, if we weren't such streetwise, young, wild things about town, people would think we were embarrassed and nervous. The driver is busy moaning about the traffic, and telling us that he used to work in the City. He was a trader on the floor of Liffe, the futures market, and turned to cabbing when the market went electronic. Apparently the hand signals come in handy. We both sit and smile, acting as if his conversation is the most fascinating we've ever heard.

'It was a lovely evening,' I say eventually, as the cab turns into Upper Street. 'I really enjoyed myself.'

'Me too,' he says, and then, before I can say, 'but I haven't brushed my teeth since the Caesar salad', he kisses me softly on the lips. Wow. As he moves back from me and looks into my eyes, I note with satisfaction that my lipstick really is long-lasting. 'I've been wanting to do that all night. But I was worried about the headlines,' he jokes.

'Luckily,' I say hesitantly, pressing the button that cuts the intercom connection with the driver, 'there are no reporters around.' I lean towards him, and he takes my hands in his. There's no awkward clatter of teeth hitting teeth. Our mouths fit perfectly, as somehow I always knew they would. I feel at home.

'Yo, lady.' The cab driver is flexing his larynx. Well, it's probably the only type of exercise it'll get all year. 'Are you getting out?' I pull away from Ciaran and look up. The cab has stopped parallel to my Toyota. Embarrassing moment number three. I see that Lily has left a light on in the hallway, but my flat suddenly seems empty. I don't want to be alone tonight.

'Yes. Sorry. This is my stop.' I sit up straight, pull Julie's pashmina around me and grab my beaded bag. 'Well, em, I guess this is good night, unless, of course, you want to come in for a nightcap.' Coffee sounds so passé.

'What have you got?' Bloody cheek. He's fussy. He really wants a nightcap. Perhaps I should just send him home and have done with it. Maybe it's just his polite way of letting me down gently.

'Port,' I retort. 'Vintage.'

'Brilliant.' Ciaran gently nudges me towards the door. 'So what are we waiting for?' He follows me out of the cab, slips the driver a ten-pound note and walks beside me to my front door. 'Now if it hadn't been vintage,' he murmurs as I search for my keys, 'well, I would just have gone on home.' But as he nuzzles my neck, I get a feeling in my bones that the last statement was a lie.

I move into my flat, turning on the table lamps in the living room, and lighting a hurricane lamp resting on the coffee table. Ciaran throws his jacket over the back of one of my armchairs and follows me into the dining room, where I fetch the port from the drinks cabinet.

'I meant to ask you at the dinner party about these pictures,' he says, pointing at the oil portraits that line the walls. 'They stand out. The rest of the décor is so modern.'

I take the bottle and two glasses and move beside him to consider the stern face of the gentleman staring down. The artist was so good that even the chafing from his stiff wing collar is visible.

'Oh, just some old ancestor,' I say vaguely. 'Come on through. The other room's more comfortable.'

'Really!' exclaims Ciaran. 'Is he on your mother's or your father's side? Do you know much about him? My granny used to spend hours telling us family tales. She said it was important for us to know where we came from.'

'Oh, I never paid any attention to any of that sort of stuff. This,' I point to a picture of a young girl in small bonnet and voluminous skirts, 'was his wife, I think.'

'Are you sure you've got that right?' asks Ciaran. 'I mean this picture looks like it's from a different generation from the last one. Was she much older than him?'

'Oh, I don't know. Look, do you want this port or not? I'm going to put some music on. Nina Simone all right?'

'Okay,' shrugs Ciaran, taking a full glass from me. He follows me back to the other room and then – to my alarm – he sits himself on the armchair that his jacket's resting on! In my shock I almost drop the mini-disc. His mother obviously didn't teach him that in situations like this it's impolite to leave a girl on her own on the sofa. It makes her look like a hussy when she asks you to join her. And I'm blowed if I'm going to appear forward.

'I meant to say the other night, you've got a lovely place here. I love the way it's decorated,' says Ciaran, surveying the room.

'Thanks. I got a designer in. I gave him the keys and a budget and, hey presto! He created this.'

'Did your designer advise you against flowers?' He sips his port, watching me carefully.

'Sorry?'

'The flowers I sent you, I don't actually see them anywhere.' A quick sweep of the room with his right hand.

'Oh my God! I'm so sorry. You must think me very rude. I had to give them to Julie. Lily's eyes just stream at sunflowers, and when I arrived in the cab with them, it was like sneeze-city in here. I kept some of the foliage, though.' I point at a few green, leafy sticks standing in a vase, but they look forlorn, missing their vibrant companions.

'Oh, okay. I just thought that maybe I'd misunderstood the situation.' The situation? How could you misunderstand it? I'm sitting here like a pathetic heroine from a romantic eighteenth-century novel just waiting for a smouldering look across the drawing room!

146

'Not at all,' I say, choosing my words carefully. 'They were the nicest thing that happened to me this week.'

'The nicest thing?' Ciaran puts his glass down and stands up. Don't go. Please! I'll try to improve my vocabulary.

'Yes.'

'Even nicer than what just happened in the cab?' He takes a few steps towards me.

'Well.' I'm getting flustered. I feel all hot and clammy. Ciaran is standing in front of me, and slowly leans down to pull me up. My hands are shaky.

'Even nicer than this?' He leans over and kisses me ever so gently on the nape of my neck. 'Or this?' My left ear. 'Or this?' My right ear. 'Or this?' He nuzzles behind my ear, moving his way towards the back of my neck. Rechristen him Columbus. He's just discovered a new erogenous zone! Then, when I'm getting really scared that my legs will give way, he gently takes my hand and leads me towards my bedroom.

'Let's take this slowly,' I whisper.

'As slowly as you like, darling,' he whispers back. 'After all, I'm a Catholic. We prefer the rhythm method.'

Saturday, October 21
(D Day minus 24 – normal service will be resumed shortly)

I wake to the sound of a door slamming. Sunlight is peeking through the curtains, which I hurriedly pulled last night, just after Ciaran and I came into this room. I open my eyes and look at the pillow beside me. He's not there. My stomach turns as I glance at the floor where he hastily threw his clothes. They're not there! I sit bolt upright and am just about to give in to the rising panic and scream when my bedroom door opens and Ciaran walks in carrying a tray.

'Good morning,' he says, placing the tray on the bedside table and leaning over to kiss me. The luminous dial of my alarm clock says ten, so we've had just four hours' sleep. 'I thought I'd pop out and buy some fresh croissants and see if I could get a couple of lattés anywhere. I know it's your favourite.' He hands me a silk dressing gown that's hanging on the back of my bedroom door. 'And you'd better put that on or I'll never get away. Too many distractions.' He smiles, surveying my breasts.

Get away?

'You're going?' I say, trying to keep my tone casual as I break up one of the croissants. My mouth feels dry. What does this development mean? Was last night just a one-off?

'Yep, sorry. I'm meant to be going away for the weekend to stay with some friends I haven't seen since Wall Street days. They've got a place in Sussex, and I did say that I'd be down there by midday, which I obviously won't be.' He looks at me carefully. 'I'm godfather to their son and I really can't let them down. I'm disastrous enough about remembering my duties! You do understand, don't you?'

I nod slowly and smile. Keep it calm, Trixie. Don't let him know that you're all confused.

'Look,' he continues, 'I really didn't expect last night to happen.' What does that mean? 'But it did and I'm so glad,

148

because I've wanted it to happen since the first time I spilled coffee on you!' Good answer! I feel my smile radiating up, reaching my eyes. He's not running out on me. This really is a valid excuse.

'It's all right,' I eventually say. 'I've also got things to do today.' Oh shit, Trixie! Wrong answer! He looks crestfallen. Go for a change of strategy. 'Although obviously if you hadn't already got plans, I could have fitted you in.' I lift the duvet cover suggestively, revealing a naked thigh.

'Don't!' he exclaims. 'You're driving me crazy. I really can't be late.'

'Really? I could always put this clock back and then you'd be on time.' I move forward, pressing the buttons on the alarm, watching the luminous dial jump back to nine, and revealing just a little more naked flesh.

'You mean I wouldn't be late in Trixie time?' I sense he's warming to the theme.

'Or we could say you were still on Wall Street time.' The dial moves back through eight and seven. 'It takes a long time to adapt.'

'But that's five hours behind us.' He moves forward to the bed, and I reach out for his hand as the clock finally reads five. 'But seeing as I'm here, I should really take advantage of the time difference!' And he does!

Afterwards we lie there, wrapped in each other's arms, just talking. I learn about his siblings, we talk about past relationships, the items we'd take to a desert island, our favourite foods. But three hours later guilt sinks in and Ciaran really *does* have to leave. He promises to ring tomorrow, but I nonchalantly wave away such ideas, encouraging him to concentrate on his friends and their son. Trying to indicate that I won't be a clingy girlfriend. Ciaran's girlfriend. I like the sound of that, but I know all too well that one night of making love doesn't constitute a relationship.

I watch as he gathers up his clothes and dresses, enjoying the sense of intimacy, and finally I pass him his wristwatch, which had lain on the bedside table as a reminder of real time. Then he leans over, gently kisses me, wishes me a successful trip to New York and promises to ring.

'I wish I hadn't made plans. I'll call, honest.' He kisses me again. 'And not just once!' Then he turns and leaves, slamming the front door behind him. I lie there not moving for what seems like hours, remembering every moment we shared, thinking over our conversations, and finally I drift off back to sleep.

I dream of Ciaran, not in his Sir Galahad attire like the last time, but sitting in a psychiatrist's chair. He's analysing relationships and that age-old question: When is the right time to call?

Actually the psychiatrist bears a remarkable resemblance to Sigmund Freud. (Well, it is a dream, and you might as well get the best candidates for the roles; after all, they don't cost anything.) He is sitting upright in a black leather chair, and Ciaran is prostrate on a white bed. Luckily that doesn't really require much imagination!

'So,' asks Sigmund, 'when do you call a woman after your first date?'

'It all depends on whether I'm keen or not. If I am keen, probably a week! Don't want to seem desperate.'

'What if she rings you?'

'Wouldn't like that. She'd seem too serious and I'd definitely worry about the ticking of a biological clock.'

'What if you've slept with her?'

'Got to be careful then. Don't want them to think that you've been making love or it opens a huge can of commitment worms.'

'And Trixie?'

'What a girl! Beautiful, talented and fun to be with.'

Well! It is *my* dream.

'You'll call her immediately?'

'Don't know what to do. I'll see her at work.'

'But she's in New York this week.'

'I'll see her when she gets back.'

'But you promised to ring her there? She'll be hurt and I don't think you should treat her like that. She deserves more!'

150

Hurrah for Sigmund!

'I don't know. Trixie knows how to play the game, and anyway she's more interested in saving her career at the moment. We'll see how things go when she gets back to London.'

What!!!!

I wake with a start. My alarm clock says one, but I'm not sure what time zone it's now operating in. I reckon it must be six. The room is dark, and from a chink in the curtain I can see that outside the night has begun to close in. I pull my dressing gown around me and reach for the phone to call Julie.

'Julie,' I say. 'I've just had a nightmare. Can you come over? This is a two-bottle discussion!'

'Don't tell me! It's Ciaran, and you've just had your Sigmund Freud dream!' How well that girl knows me! 'I'll be there in about an hour.'

The voice of reason arrives in a new woollen jacket and leather trousers, which delays the start of our conversation, as I have to examine the quality and listen to the full extent of the shopping expedition she enjoyed today.

'I guessed something had happened when you didn't ring to confirm lunch at Joe's,' she says. 'Fill me in on the gory details.' So I do! Suddenly Julie bursts out, 'Que sera, sera.'

'Sorry. How did we get on to Doris Day songs?'

'We didn't. I'm just saying that if it is going to happen with Ciaran, then it will. There's nothing you can do to change that. You, probably more than anyone, should know that. Look,' she adopts a more soothing tone, 'Ciaran is not Sam. Don't make Sam the bellwether that you judge everybody by. If you jeopardise future relationships just because you're worrying that the man will behave like that rat, then you're going to be letting him keep ruining your life. He isn't worth it. Ciaran will ring because he wants to ring, and not because Sigmund Freud told him to.' Hmm. Sounds pretty stupid when she puts it like that.

'All right. I'll relax,' I promise. 'It's just that this is the first time since Sam that I've felt something for somebody. I don't want it to go wrong.'

'It'll only go wrong if you play it heavy. Honestly.' How on earth did I manage to have such a sensible friend? 'Anyway, enough of all this unnecessary worrying. Open another bottle and tell me. Was he any good?'

Oh God! Oh God, yes! Yes! Yes!

Monday, October 23
(D Day minus 22 – if I can make it here, I can make it anywhere)

New York! Any temptation to cancel the trip went quickly out of my mind when I remembered two salient facts. Firstly, absence makes the heart grow fonder. And, secondly, whilst the streets in London may be paved with gold, in New York they are paved with shops.

The limousine arrives on the dot of eleven (I told Jim that it was coming at nine and it wouldn't be worth venturing into the office first), and transfers my luggage, laptop and me to Terminal Three at Heathrow Airport, where I swiftly check in and do a quick tour of the duty-free shops before arriving at the lounge for Virgin Upper Class passengers.

I sign in with the receptionist and go to the bar, perch on one of the cream stools and order a glass of champagne whilst casually doing a quick recce of the lounge. Checking if any other City bankers are here. I nod at a couple that I recognise as working for a German bank as they walk through towards the office area. Anybody who looks like a potential client? Oh, how gross! A small man sitting on the red armchair against the far wall is surreptitiously picking his nose with his little finger. I don't care if he's the Sultan of Brunei – I'm not doing business with him. And if I find that he's seated next to me on the plane, then I will refuse to shake hands or share any equipment with him. Even if we have a crash landing and discover that there's only one oxygen mask.

I sip my champagne and nibble delicately on the sushi laid out on the chrome bar top. I can spot only one potential client. He's got long straggly hair and thick glasses and is wearing faded jeans, trainers and a rather filthy T-shirt. That's filthy rude, rather than filthy dirty. He's tapping away on his laptop, which he has hooked up into one of the phone sockets in the floor. Obviously an Internet geek. I shall have to introduce myself.

I rummage in my handbag to find my glasses. They've only got clear glass in them, but everybody tells me that they make me look so much more intelligent. And nerdy! Well, as nerdy as someone blessed with my looks could ever be!

I've barely reapplied my lipstick when a massive man comes up and struggles to sit on the stool beside me. He's the sort of man that you spot in those seaside postcards weighing himself. The ones where the scales shout back: Will the coach party get off now? His face is pouring with sweat following the exertion, and he pants out an order for a large gin and tonic at the waitress.

'Cheers.' He raises his glass to me. His fingers, huge like bananas, are adorned with large gold signet rings, and I catch a glimpse of a gold identity bracelet under his shirt cuff. This man must have set off every alarm in the airport when he came through Passport Control.

I nod in response to his greeting, signalling the waitress to bring another glass of champagne.

'Where you headed to today, then?' he asks me. Shit. He's so close that I can't even pretend I didn't know he was talking to me. And I definitely can't pretend not to notice him. I mean, the floor beneath me is practically listing towards him under the weight.

'New York. Manhattan. On business.'

'Me too. What line of business are you in?'

'Investment banking. I work in the City.' Now go away! I don't want to talk to you.

'I'm in the food line myself.' No. Couldn't tell. You hardly look like you touch the stuff. 'Off to New York to meet a few big food companies to see if I can get any contracts. Looking promising, though.' He calls the waitress back and orders a plate of steaming egg noodles with mushrooms and water chestnuts. 'Missed breakfast,' he explains. 'Feel like I'm wasting away.' Hmm. How true! 'Jimmy Munroe,' he says, extending his hand.

'Trixie.' I put my hand forward to be swamped in his.

'Trixie what?'

'Long story, but my colleagues call me Trixie Trader. It's a sort of a nickname, but my real name is Trixie Thompson-Smythe.'

'So is that what you do? Trade?'

'Not really. It was just a good example of alliteration.' I watch his eyes glaze over. 'I help companies raise money. Through bond issues.'

'What? Like premium bonds?' Stick with the food industry, Jimmy.

'No. These are eurobonds. I advise companies on how to raise money through eurobonds, a bit like the government raises money through premium bonds. But premium bonds don't mature and only pay out cash prizes. Eurobonds make a fixed annual interest payment to investors and mature in a specified period, but there is much more complicated stuff going on behind the scenes.' Blind him with science.

'How much can they raise?' Jimmy throws his head back and tosses a handful of cashew nuts into his mouth. 'The companies?'

'That depends. If the company is well enough known then it could raise a billion pounds. Maybe more.' His eyebrows lift at this, and I can see he is now looking at me with respect. Don't like to tell him that I've never, personally, organised a billion-dollar deal. 'But generally it's a few hundred million.' Why am I explaining all this to Mr Eat-All-The-Profits? 'I wouldn't really want to do much smaller than that because it gets quite complicated. Investors generally like to get involved in big bond issues. They perceive them as more liquid.'

'I see. And do you have a card, er, miss?' He looks quizzically at me. Don't say that he is going to hit on me.

I rummage in my bag, find my card holder and hand over a business card to him. He looks carefully at it before putting it into his jacket pocket.

'So, if I wanted to raise any money, I would come to you?'

'Do you?'

'No. Not for me to say anyway. My friend owns the company. By rights he should be doing this trip but he's scared of flying.

155

So I have taken his place. I'm sort of his right-hand man.' He waves his dumpy right hand at me. 'He thinks he's getting value for money given the size of my hands, eh?' I laugh politely.

'God, that reminds me,' I say hastily. 'I'm booked in for a manicure in the beauty salon. In,' I look at my watch, 'oh my. Two minutes' time. Will you excuse me?' He nods, looking slightly dejected, but then his food arrives and the light shines from his eyes. 'I hope to see you on the plane,' I lie.

'Wouldn't it be funny if we were sitting together?' he says, trying to roll his fork in his noodles. 'I'm seat 1A. What number are you?'

'Sorry, really got to rush. They hate it if you're late for an appointment here. See you later.' I dash off towards the beauty salon, hoping that they can fit me in for a quick manicure. Must check my boarding pass. Only hope I can change my seat if need be.

Monday, October 23
(Still D Day minus 22 – working on New York time now)

I landed at JFK Airport without encountering Billy Bunter again. I did spot him as I climbed the steps to my seat on the plane, but he was merrily emptying three packets of savoury biscuits into his enormous palm and hardly noticed me. It's not that I actively dislike fat people as such, it's just that they bring back too many sad memories for me. I find myself attacking them as a protective mechanism. I think Kate understands, but a seven-hour journey with a total stranger would be a nightmare. I don't know who would hate it the most!

I arrive at The New York Palace, on the corner of Madison Avenue and 50th, barely an hour after landing. I quickly make my way through the main entrance, but then turn right through the doorway to the reception for the more exclusive The Towers, 'a hotel within a hotel,' as the blurb puts it.

Julie recommended this hotel to me. She stayed here on her last business trip, and said that I would love it. For a start, it's élite and carries the highest rating for any American hotel. And secondly, it is just minutes from the shops! I've followed her advice and opted for a room on an odd-numbered floor. It seems even top-rated hotels can be quirky. Rooms on even-numbered floors in The Towers are decorated in a classic European style, whilst those on odd ones are art deco.

I have just settled into my 'exquisitely appointed' suite when the doorbell sounds and there, standing in my portal, is a vision. A blond Adonis, dressed in hotel uniform, is telling me that he will do anything that I want during my stay to ensure my comfort. Anything? Will it be included in the bill? I don't know how Brenda in the accounts department will react to 'personal services'.

But Sebastian swiftly brings me back to the real world. He describes himself as my personal butler. My very own Jeeves.

157

Sadly, they never do anything that might be construed as over-friendly. Pity. Oh for goodness' sake. Get a grip, Trixie. Remember Ciaran. The man that you spent Friday night with. That reminds me. Has he called?

'Are there any messages for me?' I ask Sebastian, who opens a leatherette folder and takes out several pieces of paper. He hands them over to me with a little bow. I scan them. Jim, Julie, Lily with some long, detailed saga about her supermarket loyalty card (bet the operator loved that) and Candice. She's the first client I am scheduled to meet, a recommendation of Ciaran.

'Oh.' I look up at Sebastian. 'It seems that I won't be needing my booking at Le Cirque as apparently my client wants to go somewhere else to eat. Are diners fashionable again?' He smiles but shakes his head before informing me that I am missing out on a fantastic meal. And all because the lady loves hash browns.

'Do they serve alcohol in diners?'

'It really depends, but generally no.'

What! I instruct my butler to fill a small flask with vodka. Neat. I can always order orange juice there. Sebastian nods, and then gives me a quick guided tour of my room. This is the mini-bar. These are three dual-line telephones. The mini-bar. Fax machines. Mini-bar. Printer and scanner. Mini-bar. Safe for your laptop. Mini-bar. Is he trying to tell me something? Or does my mind only focus on the relevant bits?

Sebastian moves to leave the room, but first hands over a batch of my very own personalised business cards, with the hotel address, phone and fax numbers, so that my New York clients can contact me at any time. Wow. How cool is that? He promises to return with a hip flask of vodka within the hour. Just time to unpack, hang my clothes up in the bathroom while I have a quick shower in the hope that the steam will make any creases fall out, and get ready to meet Candice. In Chelsea. Hmm. I may be thousands of miles away but nothing really changes.

I ask the cab driver to re-check the street and door number

when we pull up outside Candice's chosen venue. It looks disgusting. All Formica and paper napkins. I can see waitresses walking around, stainless-steel coffee pot in one hand, dressed in pink nylon overalls and bobby socks. Sadly the driver is convinced that this is the right place, so I get out and enter. In her message, Candice said that she would be wearing a red jacket and holding a copy of *The Road Less Travelled*. When I rang her back to confirm the change of venue, I told her that I would be wearing Armani.

Heads turn as I enter the diner. Although not a new phenomenon for me, I'm somewhat disconcerted by the quality of the stares. Beady, piercing eyes gaze out from a forest of bushy beards and brushed-cotton check shirts. I am just waiting for Grizzly Adams to walk in. But towards the back of the diner, there is a change in style of clientele. Black replaces red checks. Grease, or perhaps gel, replaces frizz. And skeletal replaces well fed.

It looks like I have walked into a ward filled with consumptive patients. But instead of them lying down in iron beds made up with starched white sheets, they are sitting up around chipped Formica tables, sipping black coffee and sniffing.

Sniffing. All I can hear is sniffing. I just hope that I don't catch anything. It might be wise to have a hot toddy tonight at bed time, with a double dose of Echinacea to ward off any germs. I spot the red jacket at a corner table. Candice? She waves her book at me. The poor girl appears to have a terrible cold. Her eyes are streaming, and it looks as though she's spilled a packet of Lemsip on the floor. No wonder she didn't want to go to Le Cirque. Poor darling probably can't taste anything at the moment. But I do think that she could have chosen a slightly more salubrious venue.

I try to remember what Ciaran told me about Candice. She's an accountant, recently returned from a two-year posting to Colombia. Perhaps that explains her clothes, which are definitely not from the latest collections. Candice stands as I approach, and offers her hand to me. It's thin and bony, and her nails are chewed down, almost to the cuticles. Imagine.

Hands like this in New York – the cheap manicure centre of the world.

'Trixie?' she asks, as we shake hands. Her dog-eared copy of the self-enlightenment bible has been placed face down on the table. Best place for it.

'Pleased to meet you, Candice. I've heard so much about you.' Sucking up to potential clients. It'll be the death of me.

'Coffee?' She beckons a passing waitress over.

'What'll it be?' drawls the waitress, who pauses chewing on her gum to look up at me.

'Orange juice,' I reply. 'Is it freshly squeezed?'

'Well, I opened the carton only an hour ago. Can't get fresher than that.' She laughs and makes her way back to the serving counter.

'Do you want anything to eat?' Candice asks. What, here? She must be mad. 'I can recommend the omelettes. But don't go for the burgers. Patsy,' she points over at the waitress, 'tells me that they haven't fully defrosted yet. Think I'll have another black coffee.' She waves her empty mug at Patsy. 'So. You've come over from London?' I nod. 'God, that was brave.'

'Why? Are you scared of flying? Ciaran said you recently returned from a posting in Colombia. I imagine that was fun, but scary. You hear such awful stories about Colombians.'

'Ciaran. How's the lovely Irish one? Is he still wedded to his career?' She tells me about how the women threw themselves at him when he worked on Wall Street. 'He wasn't really interested. I thought he was gay at first, but as I got to know him, I realised that he just wasn't swayed by pretty faces. He was more of a character man. Unfortunately, as I never tired of telling him, characters are usually pug ugly. What do you think?'

'I've never really thought about it.'

'Is he seeing anyone now? That'll break a few hearts here if he is.'

'I don't really know him very well,' I fib. 'He heard about my trip to New York and suggested a few people I should meet. He wasn't sure, though, who you work for now.'

'God, Ciaran really is out of the loop. When I returned from Colombia last year I got a job as finance director of a company based in New Jersey but things didn't really work out. I'm looking around at the moment.'

Shit! My first meeting, and the client is completely useless. I pour nearly all the contents of my flask into the beaker of orange juice. I think I'm going to need it.

'You never told Ciaran that you're unemployed?'

'I haven't spoken to him for a while. Actually, I was surprised he had my number to give you. He must have got it off a mutual friend. When you called I didn't think it was relevant.'

'Not relevant,' I retort, heaving my briefcase on to the table. 'When I have gone to the trouble of bringing you my deal?' I rummage for the carefully prepared report that I'd drawn explaining why Trixie Trader was extremely qualified to handle any deal that was offered to her.

'Careful!' She tries to push my briefcase down on to the floor. 'Can't we do this somewhere a little more private. Jerry over there is watching.' She indicates a pallid youth, clad all in black, sitting two tables away. 'And I'm sure that he's an undercover cop. I might be wrong, though. He might genuinely want to meet Charlie.'

'So what? I'm hardly doing anything illegal.' I search the briefcase for my report. 'Who's Charlie? Would I want to meet him?'

'You Brits. You're so damned cool.' Candice is tugging the briefcase out of my hands. 'I can't cope with this. I'm off to the bathroom. See you in there.' She stands up, lifts her book and walks off toward the back of the diner. Americans. So dramatic. I look around the diner. Jerry is definitely watching us. Or maybe it's just me. He's probably never been this close to real Armani. After five minutes or so, and several 'whaddya wants' from Patsy, I move towards the rest rooms to check on Candice.

'Candice!' I yell. I knock on the only closed door of the stalls. Suddenly it opens and a skinny arm reaches out and yanks me into the cubicle. 'What are you doing?' I exclaim as I rub my arm. I'm sure that it will bruise. Luckily it's autumn and long sleeves, or I would be seriously peed off with Miss Weirdo. Ciaran's got a lot of explaining to do!

'Didn't want anyone to see. Now did you bring the stuff?'

'Of course I did.' I reach into my briefcase and at last find the document that I've been searching for. 'Here you are.' I thrust it into Candice's hands. 'My credentials. What I can do for you, although after everything you said earlier, I doubt you need my services.'

'What is this?' shrieks Candice. 'Bloody mail order?'

'Sorry?' This woman may be a friend of Ciaran's but I think she's a nutter. I look at her and say very slowly. 'What are you talking about?'

'Where's the goods? You said you were coming here to deal.' She opens the buttons on her jacket to reveal a money belt tied around her naked torso. It looks like it's crammed full with dollar bills. 'Ciaran didn't say anything about pricing, but I assumed we're talking several grand, right?'

'I have no idea what you are talking about,' I tell the mad woman, whilst studying her belly-button ring. She must have really pushed hard whilst doing her abdominal crunches. She's as flat as a pancake. I didn't know ribs were back in fashion.

'You said you were coming to New York to deal. So deal.' She's unzipping her money belt and pulling out a handful of dollar bills.

Suddenly the penny drops, hitting Colombia, Charlie, red eyes and dealers on its way to full comprehension jackpot. My God. She's a junkie. And I'm in a bathroom stall with her and an overstuffed money belt, and a possible undercover cop outside. Help! I must be jet-lagged! How could I have been so naïve?

I reach my hand out behind me and fiddle with the latch as I take a small pace back from Candice and her pierced belly button.

'I think there has been a terrible misunderstanding. Ciaran doesn't know about your,' I hesitate on the correct terminology, 'new friendship, does he?' She shakes her head. 'I'm afraid he thought that you were still in the market for doing bond

162

deals.' She shakes her head again. 'That's what I'm here to do. Bond deals. Not, er, Charlie deals.'

She looks at me, tears welling in her eyes. God, the girl is thin. For a fleeting moment I wonder about cocaine as a quick-fix way to lose weight, but then I look at Candice and know that I could never do it. Alcohol will remain my drug of choice.

'Are you all right?' I gently ask her. She nods. 'I'm truly sorry about the mix-up.' I unlock the door and walk out. Candice has sunk on to the closed toilet seat and is now sobbing into her cupped hands. I want to help her but there's nothing I can do. She makes me promise, through her sobs, not to tell Ciaran about the confusion. I agree, walk briskly through the diner and hail a cab to take me back to civilisation. And a well stocked mini-bar.

Tuesday, October 24
(D Day minus 21 – and they call the Americans financial wizards!)

Ciaran did ring last night, while I was downtown at a diner with drug-crazy Candice. It wasn't until I returned to my room and lifted the phone to order a club sandwich from room service that I realised he had called. Thank you, Sigmund Freud. You actually got through to him. He sounded friendly. Breezy even.

'Hi there, Trixie. It seems you're not around, but I just wanted to touch base as promised. I'm well. Had a busy day today; there were some inflation figures that spooked the market. You might have heard? God! I sound so boring and uptight. I just wanted to say that I enjoyed Friday night. Okay?' Then a second message, delivered seconds after the other one. 'It's Ciaran, by the way. Sorry. Should have said that at the beginning of the last call. Bit presumptuous to have just assumed, etcetera. Ciao.'

As if I didn't know who it was. Did he think I could have forgotten? I listened to the message four times. Carefully. Analysing intonation. Was that a deep breath before he started? Did he sound disappointed that I wasn't around to take the call? 'Touch base as promised.' What did that mean? Was this just a duty call? Did he really want to ring? Enjoyed Friday night! What about Saturday?

It dawned on me that this was the real reason that I don't go in for serious relationships. Not Sam, although he played a huge part, but this. This mating game, with its confusing rules and strange etiquette. The need to wait and analyse your opponent's moves. Careful not to make a false start. It's pure agony.

And despite years of practice I still haven't conquered it. But it seems that Ciaran, along with the rest of the male species, has. I get inflation numbers and thanks for a pleasant evening. No nice little message about missing me.

I wrote the words of his message down on a piece of my very own personalised stationery, courtesy of The Towers, and stared at them. It called for a girlie chat, so I rang Julie and we spent an hour (well, I'm sure that my employers wouldn't want me to be lonely, or confused) analysing Ciaran's mumblings. Her sipping Black Russians whilst I indulged in a club sandwich and a cocktail of bottles from the mini-bar. Plus a Toblerone. Well, it was an emergency. And our conclusion? Our findings were indecisive. The prosecution (me) found that there was no real evidence of affection. The defence (Julie) found that the call itself plus the mention of Friday was evidence of affection, along with his hesitant, nervous tone. An open verdict.

I was proud of myself this morning. I only glanced over Ciaran's message once, whilst I sipped my freshly squeezed orange juice and ate a croissant. The rest of the time I went over my notes for today's meetings. I have four. One cancelled late last week, and I didn't have a chance to arrange a substitute. Still, the panic is over. Dr Noriko's deal is in the bag. But I want to make a good impression because I hope that they will switch some future business my way. And because I am rebuilding my professional pride. Yeah!

This trip is really about installing a pipeline that will guarantee me a steady flow of deals in the future. Something to ensure that I never get into such a severe mess again, to a point where the rug is about to be pulled from beneath me. I think I have been successful in establishing one back in London. My old clients appear pleased to hear from me again, and I've met new ones. They don't want to do any deals this year, but that's understandable. After all, it's nearly over. But I'm hopeful for the next. The old Trixie, as Jim liked to call her, is definitely back.

The first meeting does not go well. As I am ushered into the company's boardroom, I notice a silver trinket box on a sideboard containing a mass of business cards. The six men sitting around the oval table are hosting a beauty parade. I am just one in a long queue of bankers who will enter this opulent room today. We will each give our sales spiel, our pitch for their business, and they will go off and decide on just one lucky winner. I had come here with the hope that they might expand the list of bankers that they do business with to include me. But it looks like an all-or-nothing situation. And from the disapproving glances at my ever-so-slightly-too-short skirt, I sense that I have lost before I have even begun. These dinosaurs, with their grey hair, monogrammed shirts and Ivy League qualifications, would prefer to do business with a man. An older man. Someone who can visit them in their Long Island homes at weekends. And bring the wife. Me? Hmm. I can just *see* their wives welcoming me with open arms.

After twenty minutes of presenting what I thought was a pretty fine pitch, the most senior of the company's directors interrupts me.

'Thank you, Miss Thompson-Smythe. Most interesting,' he drawls in a Southern accent, whilst puffing on a pipe. A rebel! Breaking New York City's rules about smoking in public places. Next he'll be telling me that sometimes he doesn't wear a tie. 'Have you got a copy of your presentation for our files?'

'Well, yes, I suppose.' I hesitate. I have worked darned hard on these ideas and I am not going to have a bunch of geriatrics rip them off. Pass them on to the winning pitcher; give him something to work with. Yes, I know it sounds arrogant. But hey, I'm certain that what I have just shown them is a pretty unique proposal for a deal. 'I'm sorry,' I tell them. 'Parts of the presentation could be construed as the property of my employers and I won't be able to leave them with you. But you're welcome to the report on my bank and its strengths and a résumé of my career to date.' I smile and shrug my shoulders, as if to indicate that it is all really out of my hands. Rules are rules.

'Short résumé, is it?' Ooh. Nasty.

'By definition a résumé always is,' I respond sharply. What have I got to lose? These men don't want me here. I flick through my presentation, withdraw the pages that I deem proprietary, place them in my briefcase, and hand over the abbreviated version. He takes it without a word, but the requisite stretch of his arm reveals a massive diamond cufflink.

Put that diamond in a platinum setting, place it on the third finger on my left hand, and I would be in heaven. Well, as long as it wasn't him doing the placing.

I fasten my jacket, lift my briefcase and shake hands with the other gentlemen. Then I carefully take a business card out of my holder and place it with a flourish in the silver box with all the others. I move forward to the Southern gentleman and vigorously shake his extended hand. Then I wish them all good day, and turn to leave. I have my hand on the brass door handle when Mr Pipe Breath shouts out:

'By the way, pass on my regards to your chairman. We were at Harvard together.' Shit! Well played, Trixie, but I think you lobbed too wide. His game. Bloody chairman. Is there anybody that he doesn't know?

The next meeting is hardly more successful. I can tell immediately that the gentlemen I've come to present to have no real desire to borrow money on the bond markets. They keep asking me about stock-market flotations, and whether they should list the company on the London or New York exchange. 'Read my card,' I want to yell at them. 'Does it say anything about equity markets? No. It says I am a bond market specialist. Did you not read the letter of introduction?'

And then I have a brainwave. I realise that this trio of turgid tossers have never left these shores. They holiday in Florida. Europe is a country over the ocean. London is the place where the Queen and Tony Blair live. In Buckingham Palace. Together. And Fergie is confined to the Tower of London for treason. Or toe-sucking. And wasn't she married to that guy who invented liver salts? It's time to broaden their horizons.

'Of course,' I interrupt the dullest member of the threesome, who is spouting forth on the inflated valuations of Internet companies that have distorted the marketplace for companies like their bottling factory. 'That phenomenon is not yet apparent in the bond markets. Indeed, I consider it an ideal time for you to borrow money through this route for that very reason. It's much cheaper.' There is murmuring around the table, but I feel a spark of interest has been ignited. Time to deliver my winning strategy. 'I don't need to tell you gentle-men that European investors are not very familiar with your company and its business. It would obviously be necessary for one, perhaps two of you to accompany me on a whistle-stop tour of the Continent to assuage their concerns. And the London-based investment community would also welcome such interaction.' Hook, line and sinker. I can almost feel them mentally clearing their diaries in anticipation of an all-expenses-paid trip. I can imagine the internecine fighting to decide the lucky traveller, and the battle I will have with Jim to gain approval for such a trip. I'll have to bump their fees up. Discreetly, of course.

I leave with assurances – 'You have our word on that, ma'am' – that they will contact me regarding a large bond issue during the second quarter of next year. 'Sadly, ma'am, our financing needs are not immediate. And besides, the weather will be milder then.' Great. If I had wanted my career to be decided by the weather, I'd have become a hot-air balloonist.

My lunchtime appointment is with another contact of Ciaran's. Once bitten and all that, so I ring first just to make sure that she is not a drug addict, without making it obvious that I'm asking such a thing. Carol seems surprised when I enquire if she'll be bringing Charlie along to the restaurant. In fact, she doesn't know any Charlies. Apart from her grand-father but she wouldn't dream of dragging him out of the home for lunch.

We meet in the marbled entrance to her office on Wall Street. A grim, grey street that I find hard to believe is one of the world's major financial centres. Where is the hustle and bustle of high finance? The only movement I can see is the steady stream of young rookies spat out of the lifts to embark on the most important job in their current calendar: getting the coffee for the boss. I watch them walk through the reception area on a mission to Starbucks, mouthing the words: 'Three skinny lattés, two large filters and a double espresso.'

Carol's pleasant-looking, in an innocuous sort of way; the sort of woman that I usually love walking alongside. We make our introductions. She seems friendly enough, but blanches when I suggest grabbing a sandwich and a bottle at a local wine bar. Her office operates a non-drinking policy for staff. It would be quite wrong for her even to visit any premises that sell alcohol, just in case a colleague saw her and reported back. It's a sackable offence.

'Besides,' she adds, 'It's like a desert here. I don't think there are any wine bars within five minutes' walk. Shall we just go for a coffee?' Whoopee. Lucky us. Can I have syrup with mine? Really push the boat out.

Strangely enough we don't bond – no pun intended – although I learn a bit more about Ciaran and those days when he worked on Wall Street.

'He was driven,' says Carol. 'First in, last out. Never a day off sick in the time that I knew him. He set himself such high standards, and expected everybody else to match them. He had no time for any slackers, but what am I telling you this for? You work with him, and know all this.' I sort of nod in startled agreement. 'By the way,' she adds, making the past hour all worthwhile, 'I heard he had got together with someone in London. Jerry in my office, who's in contact with him, says he seems quite keen on her, but you know how men are. She probably hasn't got a clue. I think her name's Tracy something. Do you know her?'

I express my regrets that I don't know any Tracy, apologise for having wasted Carol's time when she has no immediate financial requirements (she confided that she was meeting me as a favour to Ciaran) and drop a ten-dollar note on the plastic table top to pay for our two mocha coffees. Then I leave the shop, walk down the road for a few minutes, and suddenly punch the air, yelping out the words 'quite keen'. I should have realised from the phone message!

My last meeting is then blown out on me. The client has flu but his secretary informs me that he would be willing to reschedule. Could I come back Wednesday week around noon? Er, no. I extend my sympathies to her boss on his illness, thank her for the offer but decline, thanking God once again for Dr Noriko. Who would have thought it? Me and a lecherous Japanese businessman, with a penchant for multi-coloured women, actually helping each other out! And not in the most obvious way. I'd kiss him if he wasn't so obnoxious. Ah well! Better save them all for Ciaran. Anyway, no point in wasting time. The shops are open and my credit card still has a few thousand pounds left on it. I walk briskly off in the direction of Saks Fifth Avenue.

Wednesday, October 25
(D Day minus 20 – pride comes before The Fall)

It hasn't been fruitless, this trip to New York. I have only to look in the wardrobe of my art deco suite to see that. And my Trish McEvoy make-up folder has been replenished with badger-hair brushes and new eye shadows. But on the business front, it has been a bit of a disaster. I think the clients like what I'm showing them – the eyes of my guest at dinner last night almost fell out at my décolletage – but they are unwilling, or unable, to commit themselves to anything for the foreseeable future.

I should just accept this trip as an investment for the future. And what a future it now looks. Why should I worry about any second deals? I was only asked to bring in one – and I have. Dr Noriko has saved my career whilst Ciaran has saved my personal life. He rang last night, but again I was out. This time the message sounded friendlier. He moaned a bit about his team, said that he'd been tearing his hair out trying to motivate them on some big transaction or other, but then it contained the words 'I miss you', so I seized the moment (well, a bottle of wine and two brandies does have that effect on me) and left a message on his voicemail in the office. 'Ditto,' I said. Short and sweet. Enigmatic, I thought, although I probably ruined the mood when I rang back a minute later and added: 'It's Trixie, by the way.' Still, at least I didn't leave the time that my Virgin Atlantic flight was scheduled to arrive the next morning, just in case he felt like meeting me at Heathrow Airport with a bouquet of flowers and a beaming smile.

It would have been silly anyway. The flight touches down at some ungodly hour, and the airline's courtesy limousine will be waiting at the airport to speed me back to the bank and my desk. No rest for the wicked, as they say.

After the third meeting of the morning, where I received yet another 'don't call us, we'll call you' message, I decided to pop back to my hotel for a quick work-out in the fitness center, as the hotel insists on calling it. I wanted to energise myself in anticipation of the long journey back, and the report that I must write this afternoon. An appraisal of my trip. I've been thinking hard about what to put, and I expect Jim would like something more than 'waste of time'. I mean, he has to justify this trip to the accounts department.

Strangely enough, when I arrive back at my suite and see the mini-bar and the room-service button on the telephone, all thoughts of exercise suddenly go from my head. I fetch my laptop from the handily sized safe, change into some sweat pants and T-shirt, open a mini bottle of champagne and switch on.

Sixteen e-mails. Wow. I never knew I was so popular. I scroll through them. The first is from the bank's IT department about some boring virus that could infect our computers. A couple are from Julie and Bloodhound. Ten are from Lily, who recently discovered the e-mail facility in the computer I have at home, but completely forgets about time zones.

From: LilyS @ hotmail.com
Date: October 25, 2000 9.05 a.m.
To: TrixieT @ hotmail.com
Hello, Trixie. Are you there?

From: LilyS @ hotmail.com
Date: October 25, 2000 9.07 a.m.
To: TrixieT @ hotmail.com
Can you hear me?

From: LilyS @ hotmail.com
Date: October 25, 2000 9.08 a.m.
To: TrixieT @ hotmail.com
Are you receiving me? Over and out.

From: LilyS @ hotmail.com
Date: October 25, 2000 9.11 a.m.
To: TrixieT @ hotmail.com
I'll be back in ten minutes. I'm just off to vacuum your bedroom.

From: LilyS @ hotmail.com
Date: October 25, 2000 9.26 a.m.
To: TrixieT @ hotmail.com
What happened in there? It looked like a bomb hit it. All clean now, though. Put on some clean sheets as well. Thought it was best.

From: LilyS @ hotmail.com
Date: October 25, 2000 9.28 a.m.
To: TrixieT @ hotmail.com
Did you not want clean sheets? Talk to me.

From: LilyS @ hotmail.com
Date: October 25, 2000 9.50 a.m.
To: TrixieT @ hotmail.com
I don't know what I've done wrong. Stop giving me the silent treatment.

From: LilyS @ hotmail.com
Date: October 25, 2000 11 a.m.
To: TrixieT @ hotmail.com
Are you lying there unconscious? Is that why you haven't responded? Oh my God. I better call the hotel.

Ah! So that explains the phone call from reception just after six this morning. I thought it was a bit strange that they woke me up just to ask if I was having a nice day. But then this is America. They're obsessed with service.

Jim's message is just as strange.

From: JimK @ bankmail.com
Date: October 25, 2000 12.15 p.m.
To: TrixieT @ hotmail.com
Call immediately. Difficulties with credit approval for Noriko deal.

173

What difficulties? This man's company is one of the most prestigious in Japan. How can there be problems with its credit? It must be a wind-up.

I ring Jim, and after some muttering from his personal assistant Mary about the time I choose to call, get put through.

'Ha, ha. Very funny, Jim,' I tease. 'Next you'll be telling me that the company is in financial difficulties and has a big black hole in its accounts.'

'Almost,' he answers softly.

'You're kidding, right?' Suddenly I see another black hole looming. In my bank account. I can feel the panic rising in my stomach – either that or the champagne bubbles are gassy – as I repeat the question. 'Right?'

'Sorry, Trixie.' Jim is attempting his 'if I speak nice and slowly then it may defuse the bombshell' voice. 'The credit department have done a very thorough check of Dr Noriko's company, and they've discovered that it owes a fortune. Their conclusion is that it may well not be able to pay back its existing debts.' He pauses for a moment, letting the message slowly sink in. 'Under those circumstances, I am afraid, there is no way the bank can justify managing a bond issue on the company's behalf.'

'This isn't a wind-up?' I ask, just checking once more. Suddenly champagne seems a really silly idea. And my nonchalant attitude to clients on this trip even more so. Where is my fallback position? I have nothing in reserve. I feel like a magician tugging on the string of handkerchiefs hidden up his sleeve, only to discover that it isn't there. He's left standing on stage, telling jokes, repeating old tricks until the curtain falls. There will be no curtain calls for me. It will fall. Whoosh. Down. Over. No applause. Leave the theatre by the stage door. Pick up your wages on the way out.

'Are you there? Trixie?' Jim's voice cuts into my thoughts. 'When are you back?'

'Tomorrow,' I answer. 'Leaving tonight on the red-eye. Should be in the office by ten, at the very latest.'

'Okay, we'll speak tomorrow. I've got to go now. My wife has got opera tickets and the curtain goes up in fifteen minutes.' Oh rub it in, why don't you? 'Come to my office as soon as you get in. Bye.'

I sit there, phone in hand, dazed, for several minutes. Then slowly I replace the handset. I am not sure how long I sit, but pins and needles soon arrive in my foot to jolt me into walking around the suite. I look out of my window down on Madison Avenue, watching people stroll along, shopping bags strung idly across their shoulders. How much longer will I be able to do that? Just shop when I feel like it, or when a subliminal message emanates out from the pages of Italian *Vogue* saying, 'Buy these outfits. Now. You'll look fantastic in them.' I stare down at St Patrick's Cathedral. How many people know that, viewed from above, the gothic masterpiece is shaped like a cross? Not many, I guess, because firstly, nobody is taller than it, and secondly, few people can afford these room rates.

I suddenly know what to do. I throw my feet into a pair of J. P. Tods, grab my room key and purse, and run out of the room, into the lift, down through the foyer, out on to the street, cross the road and race up the few steps into St Patrick's. I pause for a moment to catch my breath, move purposefully through the crowds of tourists to an official-looking woman standing behind a trestle table littered with leaflets on various saints. I almost knock over a Japanese tourist examining the literature on St Bernadette and St Theresa before I point at a rack of candles, which carries the sign *For your intentions*.

'How much?' I gasp.

'Only one dollar,' replies the woman, who is wearing a badge saying *Warden*, as she takes a note from the tourist who apparently has decided on both leaflets. 'The box for the money is right beside them.'

'No. I mean for the lot,' I say. 'I have a big intention to ask for.'

'Madam, you can't buy the lot. It's one candle per person.'

'Where? Where does it say that?' I demand. 'If there are restrictions placed on purchases then I believe they should be displayed prominently.' That's right. Sound legal. The Americans hate lawyers. Mutter something about suing the church for restrictive practices.

'Well it doesn't actually say that. But everybody knows that it's one candle per person.'

'Did you know that?' I demand of the Japanese tourist.

'I sorry,' she replies, before turning to the warden. 'I no want to get involved. Did St Bernadette see Our Rady at Rourdes?'

'Lady,' I correct.

'I told you. I no want to get involved,' she repeats, before turning away and marching off to join a line of Japanese tourists following an umbrella around the cathedral.

'So?' I look the warden straight in the eye. Try the old withering look. 'How much?'

'There are probably a hundred candles scattered around the church on various stands,' she eventually says.

'So one hundred dollars?'

'I suppose that would be correct. Yes.'

'You don't give a discount for bulk orders?' Ah. She has a good withering look herself. 'And when do you think it works better?'

'Sorry?'

'Prayers for intentions. Would the candles be more effective if they were lit on a Sunday? When is the force with you?'

'Madam. This is not *Star Wars*. This is the House of God. It is a Catholic church – we do not operate on a peak-rate basis. Prayers work at any time, or in any venue. Now do you still want the candles?'

'Yes please. And if I slip you an extra tenner, would you light them for me?' She gives me such a look that, if this were not a church, I would swear that I was face to face with the devil incarnate. 'Maybe not, then. I'll just get a taper.'

And that's how those Japanese tourists ended up praying with me for my intentions. Me and my job. I was totally unsympathetic to their cries that there were no candles left for them. The Japanese got me into this mess and they can damned well help me get out of it!

176

Thursday, October 26
(D Day minus 19 – hit me again, God; I don't think I felt it the last time)

My luggage feels heavier. Much heavier, as I drag it into the bank foyer, nod at the security guards as I hold up my entry pass and make my way to the lifts. It can't just be my shopping. No! It's me. I feel leaden and tired. Not jet-lagged tired but the tiredness that comes from depression. The tiredness I felt when my world with Sam fell apart. The tiredness you think you'll never recover from.

And, of course, he had to be the first person that I see. Standing by the bank's reception desk, chatting up one of those glamorous females who spend the day welcoming guests, signing them in and offering directions to their meetings. This one's obviously new. Young, blonde and pretty. I bet she doesn't worry about her calves. She's giggling away at some comment from him, throwing her head back as she flicks her hair out of her eyes. She resembles a horse. Swap the flagpole for a hayfork, I want to shout, and fly some manure from it.

Jim beckons me into his office as soon as he spots me leaving the lift. I dump my luggage and laptop by my desk, murmur greetings to my colleagues and make my way to my fate.

'Close the door,' Jim instructs as I enter the glass-walled room. 'Sit down.'

I obey both orders. Is this it? The moment when he tells me to pack my black bin bags and leave. Do not pass Go. Do not collect £200. Just leave. Quickly. No fuss. The redundancy package will be fair.

'I'm sorry that I had to break the news of the credit department's decision while you were abroad.' He looks at me. 'I know how much this deal meant to you.' Understatement of the century. 'Do you want me to inform Dr Noriko of

177

the bank's official decision?' I nod. 'So where does this leave you? Have you any other potential leads?'

I pause before replying. I choose my words carefully, trying to get across the message that I have plenty more irons in the fire. It is just that the fire will not be lit until the New Year.

'Many clients have fulfilled their borrowing requirements for this year,' I begin, keeping my hands locked in my lap. 'But a significant number have indicated that they like my proposals and are keen to do business with me next year when their borrowing calendar permits.'

'So what you're telling me, Trixie, is that you have no other real leads at the moment.' I nod. Jim sighs. 'Didn't you listen to what I said, what, three or four weeks ago? The decisions are being made next week. I will have no option but to put your name forward.'

'But Jim, I've been *trying*. It just hasn't been as easy as I thought it would be. But the old Trixie has come back, honestly. Ask me anything about the markets over the past three weeks. I can answer any questions.'

'That's not the point.' He shakes his head. 'You were set a task and you haven't achieved it. Admit it. You rested on your laurels as soon as Dr Noriko signalled he would work with you.'

'That's not true.' I'm irritated by his assumption. I only rested a few times, generally after alcohol. 'I have explored other leads. Nobody seems to want to borrow any money. But I thought you said I had six weeks. I'll get something. I promise. I've got two more weeks.'

'No, I said that final decisions would be made at the beginning of November – that's next week – with the announcement mid-month. I'm sorry, Trixie. I've kept your name off the semi-official list that was drawn up weeks ago, but I can't make any more exceptions for you, much as I may want to.' A constant beep of e-mails arriving disturbs a few moments of silence, before he adds: 'If you don't have a deal in the bag by Thursday then I'm afraid I'll have no option but to submit your name for redundancy. I'm sorry, but it's only fair to your colleagues.'

He lifts a report off his cluttered desk, signalling that the meeting is over. I stand, bend my head as I straighten my skirt for a few moments, gaining time while I compose myself. Then I fling my shoulders back and march out of his office to my desk.

I can barely concentrate on my screens, though. I'm mentally rerunning the meetings that I have attended over the past three and a half weeks, trying to recall if any client indicated that perhaps, if the price was right, they might be willing to borrow this year. Correction. Borrow within seven days. But it's no good.

Bloodhound must know what's going on. I haven't told him and I'm sure Jim hasn't, but he seems to understand. Every so often I look up to find a Styrofoam cup of steaming coffee at my side. So engrossed in my dream world am I that I never notice him putting them there. No questions are asked about my meeting with Jim, although I'm sure that Bloodhound has received a few internal messages from colleagues desperate to know what went on behind closed doors.

Suddenly I awake from my reverie and notice a flashing message on my Bloomberg screen. It must have been there for ages. It's from Ciaran, asking whether I fancy popping out for coffee at eleven. The time is now noon. Blast. He'll think I'm playing it cool. Potentially, the only good thing about my life at the moment, and I'm going to blow it through no fault of my own.

I immediately send a response. Friendly but not overly keen. Explain about the faulty screen I have, which fails to display messages immediately, and ask whether he fancies meeting at the Coffee Republic across the road. In ten minutes? He responds in one word. *Five*. Great!

So five minutes later, I touch up my make-up, leave the bank and slip across the road to Coffee Republic. A queue of bankers stand at the counter ordering their coffees. I recognise one or two and nod at them. Ciaran is already seated, facing the wall, two large lattés in paper cups resting on the chrome surface in front of him. I tap him on the shoulder, smile and take the seat beside him, discarding my cashmere coat on another one.

'Oh, thank God,' he exclaims.

'What?' I look at him in horror. He's looking good, in a black coat and grey suit. Armani man, or what.

'You left a message on my machine saying "ditto".'

'Yes,' I answer, blushing at the memory.

'I got worried 'cause in my message I mentioned something about pulling my hair out.' He lifts up a curl and places it back behind my ear. 'But yours all looks in place. Still,' he continues in a softer tone, 'even if you were bald I'd still fancy the pants off you.'

What's a girl to do? I blush! A vibrant crimson colour it feels like. It mightn't be the sort of compliment my mother would like, but it sure works for me. If only we could bunk off now. And yes! I did say BUNK!

'Nope. No problems with my hair.' I bunch up a tress in my hand and pull firmly on it. 'See, strong through to the roots.' He reaches over. To the others in the coffee bar it looks like he's pulling on it too, but I can feel the fingers softly stroking my cheek.

'I missed you,' he mouths.

'Ditto.' We laugh.

'How did it go? Were any of my leads useful?' I shake my head, and recount the story of Candice. I know she asked me not to but there's an intimacy now between Ciaran and me, and it won't be helped by secrets. I sip my coffee.

'Have you heard the news? About Dr Noriko's deal?'

He nods slowly.

'Were you surprised?'

He hesitates, sweeps a loose hair out of his eye. 'Not exactly, Trixie. But . . .' His voice is different now. The humour in his tone has gone. He sounds almost nervous.

'But what?' What's going on? Why is he studying his cup so carefully? Look at me! 'What's going on?'

'This is going to sound much worse than it is.' My stomach churns. Why is he acting like this? 'I was the one who told the credit department about the extent of Dr Noriko's borrowings.'

'What?' My voice sounds distant to me. Sharp. I don't understand what Ciaran is saying. He ruined my deal for me? I'm vaguely aware that a couple perched nearby on chrome stools are looking over. 'Why?'

'You asked me to sound out investors about Dr Noriko's company, right?' I fail to acknowledge the question. I just stare coldly at him, daring him to return my gaze. 'I tested them out about your bond idea. They loved it.' He examines my face for any pleasure at the compliment. 'Unfortunately they couldn't buy any. They had already bought as much of Dr Noriko's bonds as they could justify. Look, we knew that his company was a heavy borrower.' He searches again for grudging acknowledgement. 'So I sounded out some of the more sophisticated guys, put the idea to them, but nothing. I couldn't understand it. Here was a great idea and they were walking away from it, so I asked a few clients confidentially what was wrong. It seems the company has also borrowed bucketloads through small private bond issues, things we'd never known about. It owes billions.' He pauses. 'There's no way Dr Noriko's company can pay back what it owes. I had to tell the credit department. Make sure they were examining the full picture, not just the frame.'

I let it sink in. I lift my coffee cup and drain the froth that has settled at the bottom, using my plastic spoon to ladle out the last persistent wisps. I'm buying time. And Ciaran knows it. He shifts awkwardly on his seat.

'When did you do your Sherlock Holmes act?' I eventually ask, before shoving the spoon into my mouth for one last lick.

He's buying time now. But I'm *not* selling.

'When?'

'I started probably . . .' Pause. Deep intake of breath. Pretence at mental recollection. God, this bastard can act. 'Last.' Small shaking of the head to settle the answer. 'Tuesday.'

There. It's out. No turning back. I remove the spoon from my mouth and use it to point at him.

'And when did you solve the case?'

Another pause. Hole is dug. Say it quickly. 'Thursday.' He sounds anxious.

'One day before our date?'

'Yes.'

'One day before you shared my bed?' The neighbouring couple can barely disguise their interest now. They're not sure of the reasons but they know that one hell of a fight is about to take place. And Mike Tyson is not even here.

'Yes.' He sits there, stirring his spoon around an empty cup. Like a naughty schoolboy who has been caught out by his teacher.

'The day after you sent me a huge bouquet of flowers. What was that? A sweetener?'

'No! I was pleased for you. I didn't know this would happen.'

'But you knew you couldn't sell the deal?'

'I thought I might have difficulties.' He is looking at the wooden floor now.

'You knew you couldn't sell the deal,' I repeat.

'Yes,' he admits, glumly.

'But you still thought you would wine and dine me?'

'That was different. That was personal. I haven't been able to get you out of my mind since I got here.' The words that just twenty-four hours ago I would have longed to hear.

'And sleep with me?'

'I didn't plan for that to happen. And once I'd set this thing in train with Noriko, I couldn't halt it.'

'So I ended up with the consolation prize. Looks as though it's the only thing I'm going to get.' I stand up, ignoring his denials, rummage in my wallet and remove three pound coins. I place them on the surface in front of him as payment for my coffee. Then I lift my coat from the adjoining seat, and put it on.

'You're despicable,' I tell Ciaran. 'You're just like Sam, but you don't even know it.'

Then I walk slowly out of the coffee shop, across the road, into the bank and back to my desk. Bloodhound looks over at me as I arrive, and opens his mouth as if to say something, but then thinks better of it. I spend the rest of the day in silence, pressing buttons and staring at moving charts on my screen, but not really taking anything in. Bloodhound passes me three Post-It notes, indicating that Lily and Julie have both rung. I look at him quizzically. Three notes but two calls? And he jokes that it was his very own three-for-two offer. I smile but then crumple the messages in my hand and drop them in the bin. I don't want an audience to watch my world falling apart. Not again. But I must know the answer to one question.

'Did you know?' I turn to face Bloodhound. He looks uneasy, and I can sense that he's been waiting for this question. Watching the clock since I arrived back from the showdown.

'I found out this morning . . . after the meeting. Ciaran told me about his discovery.' His tone changes as he finishes the sentence, and a burst of anger appears to erupt from within him on the final word.

'What did you say to him?'

'I called him all the names that I should have called Sam.' He smiles at me. 'And some new ones that I learned from you. And Julie.'

Friday, October 27
(D Day minus 18 – so it's D Day minus 10 now that Bloody Jim has changed the rules)

Brian, the headhunter, leans back in his chair, checking the notes in his lap. He agreed to this emergency breakfast meeting late last night. I rang him from home after debating the likelihood of me pulling off a major deal in seven days. For once, the nays had it. Well, every nay should have its day.

But the meeting has turned out to be a disaster. I would have thought that a large headhunting firm like this would be glad to have me on their books, and that breakfast would be something more than a chipped mug of instant coffee. And not even in the dining rooms. No. Brian directs me to a small, windowless office without art or paint to brighten its walls. He rang the receptionist from the phone on a small corner table to alert her as to his whereabouts just in case Mr Whisper-his-name-so-low-he-must-be-important arrives early. Could she show him through to the Monet room, please?

'Which room is this?' I ask pleasantly, as I sit myself on a rather tatty office chair. Perhaps it's a new artist. A modern one, like Tracey Emin.

'This?' Brian takes a quick glance at his surroundings. 'Oh, it's the old store room. So. How's Christopher doing these days? Haven't seen him for a while, but then I shouldn't be telling you that, should I? No. Ha, ha.' He giggles like a constipated hyena. 'And Manfred? Such a nice chap, for a German. Very English, if you know what I mean. Very . . . what's the word I'm searching for?' His mind flicks through his vocabulary Rolodex.

'Uptight?' I suggest. 'Anal?'

'I don't think that's very nice, Trixie.' Brian frowns at me. 'Particularly after everything he said to me about you recently.'

'Really?' I'm intrigued. Nice chap, Manfred. Always thought so. 'What did he say?'

'I don't know if I should tell you.' Brian leans back even further in his chair and looks at his reflection in the mirror opposite. 'Well, all right. But don't tell him.' I shake my head, accepting the rules. 'He said that you deserved everything that was coming to you. That the effort you have put in over the past few years totally justifies the announcement soon to be made.' He smiles at me. 'There now. Wasn't that nice of him? Are you being promoted? Have you come to update your curriculum vitae?'

I look at him flabbergasted. Manfred knows. Everybody knows. They expect me to lose my job. And they think I deserve to. I struggle to regain my composure, before making a mental note never to invite Manfred to dinner again. Never to speak to him again.

'Not exactly.' I hesitate over the words. 'I came to discuss my future career path. To analyse a possible move to another bank. To check what is out there. I mean, I don't think anybody should stay in the same place too long. They become institutionalised.' Look at Manfred.

'Oh dear. I must say, this is unexpected. If I'd known that this was the reason for your visit then I don't think that I would have agreed to it,' bleats the insipid Brian. 'There's just nothing out there for you.'

'Nothing? Surely there are a few vacancies that I would be ideal for?' Other banks should be pleased that Trixie Trader is even considering working for them. 'After all, I once received an award for a deal that I constructed. I have a reputation out there.'

'Yes, well.' Brian looks awkward, checking his wristwatch. 'Unfortunately your reputation is – how can I put it delicately? – not quite the standard to encourage job offers to flow in. People say that you have become,' another pause, 'lazy. That you don't work hard and just bitch, I think the word is, about people.' Only people like you, Brian. Walking caricatures. 'And as for the award, well, unfortunately, whilst it was a great deal

185

at the time, a tremendous coup to open up a new financial market, not many other companies really want to borrow in Albanian lek. Your skill set is not exactly transferable.'

'Look, Brian. You're my headhunter. I need your services. So service me.' Perhaps I could have worded the last part better. 'Get me some interviews. Let me show people what I can do given the chance.'

'I can't,' he protests weakly.

'Yes you can. Come on.' I smile encouragingly.

'I'm sorry, Trixie. I really can't.'

'Why?' I explode. 'Why not?'

'Because we've now been retained by your bank to recruit staff. It would be totally unethical of us to then poach its staff as well. I recently placed a nice Irish chap with your bank. What was his name again?' His sieve-like memory conducts another search. 'Yes. Ciaran. Ciaran Ryan. Do you know him?'

'So, now you can't work on behalf of any of its staff?'

'That's right. I'm sorry.'

I don't believe this. 'Could you recommend anybody that I should take my impressive curriculum vitae to?'

'Sorry, but I think they will all tell you the same thing. Unless you are prepared to lower your standards, and the salary that you're willing to accept, then I'm afraid you'll find it extremely hard to get another job in the City.' Brian has missed his vocation. He should have been an actor. He almost looks sad to be passing on such news. 'And now, if you'll excuse me. I have another client along in five minutes, and I need to prepare myself.' He extends a plump hand towards me. I stand, accept his hand and then leave to begin my final week in the City.

I'm the last person to arrive at the desk this morning. But why should I care? It's not as if I have to impress anybody. Bloodhound is engrossed on the telephone but nods at me, mouthing the word 'hello', as I take my seat. The markets seem calm today. No sudden movements that just might allow a uniquely structured deal to emerge. Bloodhound ends his call and turns to me.

'Lily has rung three times for you.' He hands over several

yellow Post-Its. 'She says it's urgent and that you didn't answer the phone last night.' He looks accusingly at me.

'Don't tell me. Tesco has a special offer on. Three packets of dishcloths for the price of two. Ring her back. Tell her that I've already spent my money on a bulk order of marmalade and can't afford the dishcloths. Go on.'

Bloodhound looks at me carefully before telling me that I sound cruel, mocking Lily's quirky habit. 'It's not hurting anybody, is it?' She's just trying to be nice and helpful. And by the way, Julie rang. She's also worried about you.'

'Oh right, yep. I'll call her back now. Perhaps I can tempt her out for some lunch.' I move to press her direct-dial button on the screen before me.

'Wait,' says Bloodhound. 'She's not there this morning.'

'Oh?'

'No, she's on some sort of course today. That was her on the phone when you arrived. She was ringing during the coffee break.'

'Why didn't you put her through?'

'Because . . .' He hesitates. His face scrunches up, as if he is calculating some tricky equation, and starts to turn red with the pressure of it. 'Because she didn't ring for you.'

'Well, whom did she ring for?' Stupid boy. Why else ring here? Who else is there?'

'She rang for me.'

'To see how I was?'

'Nope.' He pauses. 'To see how I was.' Another pause. 'After last night.'

'What?' I barely notice the screams from the foreign exchange desk. Something about the yen going into a kamikaze dive.

'After our third date.'

'What? You're joking?' I look carefully at him. Third date? But the third date's the stopover date!

'No.' Such a small word. It's amazing how damaging it can be. It finds its target immediately. My best friend Julie going out with my colleague. My world is falling apart and all they can think about is hearts and roses. 'We didn't know how to tell you,' he adds. No wonder she defended him when we lunched at Joe's Café. And I bet he went with her to the Met Bar that night I couldn't. Why do pennies take so long to drop? Perhaps they're not made as well as they used to be.

'Well, I think this way was a winner. Great timing. Perfect pitch. Thanks.' I turn back to my screen, noticing that the yen is sinking faster than a bottle of Krug at lunchtime. Ironic. All that angst about Dr Noriko's deal and it now looks as if I wouldn't have been able to pull it off anyway. The mathematics just doesn't work when the yen is at these levels. Poetic justice, is that the phrase? Bloodhound looks at me for some time before adding, in a softer voice, that Ciaran had been looking for me. He wants to talk. Let him call a Chatline then. I've got seven days of work to complete.

I am still staring at the screens two hours later when an internal phone rings and one of the receptionists from the foyer informs me that a Mrs Lily Smith is waiting in reception to see me. What the hell is she doing here?

I tell the receptionist that I will be down in five minutes – buying time – but all she can say is not to worry. Lily has been giving her some tips on getting greasy fingerprints off the reception's counter.

Four minutes later I'm walking through the security barriers to the reception area. Lily is standing there, spouting forth to the receptionist about the flower arrangements that sit on both ends of the desk.

'I don't like these exotic ones,' she's saying, pointing at the splendid birds of paradise, standing erect in the glass vases in all their gold and purple splendour. 'No. Give me a plain old carnation or chrysanthemum, that's what I say. Wonderful flowers. So long-lasting. I got some pink carnations from the garage only last week and they're still as perky as ever.' She breaks off as she sees me approach, but then decides she simply must tell the receptionist the best part. 'And only one ninety-nine for ten.' She points at the birds of paradise and tuts, shaking her head as if considering the needless waste.

Then she sweeps an imaginary crumb off her black bouclé coat. Her best coat. Made by Marks & Spencer when it knew how to make clothes. Not like today. Her hands grip a pair of black kid gloves, an old Christmas present from me, and her handbag. Like a barrier between us. She's nervous. Lily has never turned up at the bank unexpectedly.

'Trixie.' She smiles shyly at me.

'Hello,' I say, in a matter-of-fact tone. 'What are you doing here?' Something is wrong. Not with Lily but with here. The bank. I can't put my finger on it. Something is different. Then it dawns on me. Muzak is playing in the background. Muzak! In an investment bank? We're not a bloody hotel. I turn to the receptionist. 'What's with the music?'

She moves her head upwards, in an angle with her ear outwards, straining to hear what I am talking about. A tinny sound echoes through the reception hall, bouncing off the marble walls and floors. It sounds like . . . like 'Greensleeves'. Then I spot it. The ice-cream van. Parked outside the entrance. Music blaring to alert potential customers. I move towards the doorway to get a better look. A queue of City bankers stands patiently, waiting to buy an ice cream. And Kate. Right at the front of the queue.

Lily watches me as I move back towards her.

'Sorry,' I say. 'I don't think I've ever seen an ice-cream van in the City. It must have got lost. Mistaken this for a school, which is an easy mistake considering some of the juveniles who work here.' I decide to cut to the chase. 'What are you doing here?'

Lily shuffles uncomfortably from one foot to the other. Her coat swings slightly open, revealing that for once, she is not wearing a tabard. And now, come to think of it, there's something different about her. I look closely at her.

'You're wearing make-up.' It sounds accusatory, not like I'm merely revealing my discovery. She blushes, and mutters about it being old stuff that I had been throwing out but that it seemed such a waste. Years of life in the pots yet. I wave my hand to indicate that I don't care about her using

189

my make-up, and then I notice it. On her left hand. Sparkling on her third finger. A small ruby and diamond ring. Accentuated by the nail polish that covers her nails. Nail polish? When did Lily ever wear nail polish? She always used to say that if God had wanted us to wear nail polish then he'd have coloured our nails scarlet, which I thought was a bit silly, because not everybody suits scarlet. And what about French manicures? My mind wanders, ignoring the burning issue at hand. I pull it back to order and focus. Lily is wearing a ring. An engagement ring.

'You're wearing an engagement ring! Why?'

She laughs nervously, and then digs into her handbag and pulls out a walkie-talkie.

'Romeo. Romeo. Come in, Romeo,' she says into the mouthpiece.

'Receiving you, Juliet. Loud and clear,' comes the reply. A faint echo of 'Greensleeves' in the background.

'Have apprehended Trixie.' What! This woman has watched too much television. 'Please come through, Romeo. Juliet is waiting.'

'Ten. Ten,' comes the reply. What the hell does that mean?

I look up. Kate is entering the rotating doors, a large Mr Whippy in one hand. She's followed, like the Pied Piper, by several colleagues, desperate to get back to their seats after brief lunches. Keen to check their positions and make sure that they have not lost any money while they sipped their Chardonnay. I spot Ciaran in the crowd. He looks tired, but that could just be wishful thinking on my part.

Suddenly Kate sees us. She waves and comes bounding across the reception area.

'Hiya, Trixie.' She smiles at me. If she knows anything about what has happened to me over the past few days, her eyes are not betraying it. They seem genuinely friendly. 'And Lily,' she exclaims, as though they're old friends. 'How lovely to see you. You were right,' she lowers her voice, 'a bit of bleach did the trick. Isn't it wonderful? Ice-cream vans in the City.'

Lily is replying, but I don't catch what she is saying. I'm

watching Ciaran. Lily breaks off, follows my line of sight, and waves enthusiastically at him. Traitor.

'Hello, dear. How nice to see you again,' she enthuses, as he hesitantly walks over. He shakes her hand and nods at me, keeping his eyes down. I remain impassive. Kate seems to sense something is wrong, but before she can move off, I hear a yell.

'I'm here, Lily. Where is she?' I turn to spot a tall man, dressed in white overalls and a white hat, like an upside-down paper sailing boat, approaching, clasping a walkie-talkie in one hand. He comes right up to us and stops. The words *Larry's Luscious Licks* are embroidered on his breast pocket. In navy blue. Kate licks a bit faster on his arrival, in case he's brought any samples. Ciaran just stands there, not knowing what to do. The new receptionist that Sam was chatting up yesterday has returned from her lunch break and is watching our party with interest. A spy in the camp.

'Ooh,' says Larry. 'I didn't expect an audience.' He smiles at Lily, and then gently takes her hand in his.

'Trixie,' says Lily, facing me, 'meet Larry. My future husband.' He gives her a little peck on her cheek as she announces this. 'Larry,' she continues, 'meet Trixie. Your future stepdaughter.'

A gasp escapes from Kate's mouth, before she breaks into a round of applause, calling me a dark horse for not saying anything before. I'll never be able to get rid of her now. She'll always be round for samples. Ciaran says nothing for a moment, but then offers his congratulations and walks off towards the lifts. He's probably relieved that things didn't work out between us. Imagine. Dating the stepdaughter of an ice-cream-van man.

And me. I can say nothing. I watch my mother squeal with delight as her fiancé squeezes her hand. And I feel nothing but shame. But for the first time in my adult life, I don't think it is at her. Or them. But at me. Eventually, after Larry smothers me in a bear hug, I offer a poor imitation of hearty congratulations, then mutter something about how I shouldn't leave my desk for too long, and after agreeing to meet them in the Old Parr's Head in Islington for a celebratory drink later, I turn and walk back towards the lifts.

Saturday, October 28
(D Day minus 9 – it was just a little white lie)

I don't remember much about yesterday afternoon, and for
once it wasn't because of a long lunch. My mind was in
turmoil. I was certain that every time I looked at clusters of
people gathered around the trading floor they were discussing
me. Trixie Thompson-Smythe – the fake. Only I'm not really
Thompson-Smythe. It's Smith. Like Lily. I am not the product
of a wealthy middle-class background as I'd led them to
believe. No. I'm the product of the unhappy union between
Lily and Alfred, a feckless fly-by-night who disappeared one
night when I was three. I don't really remember him, but
apparently I look a bit like him. Particularly around the
calves!

Lily supported me by taking in laundry and offering her
services as a domestic. I used to go with her, examine all the
beautiful antiques, stroke the fabulous furs, finger the wonderful designer clothes that her employers usually owned, and
dream of the day that I too would own belongings like these. I
saw the City as the key to the door of respectability and
affluence. But the doormen were selective. Not everybody got
the key, and the chances of receiving it could depend on
background. So I invented one. Big deal. I'm sure I'm not the
first. And I know I'll not be the last.

But the big problem was Lily. How to deal with her? How to
explain her presence in my life? Julie knew, of course, that she
was my mother, not my housekeeper. But though she did not
approve of the situation, she did not let others in on the secret.
Sam never knew. He was born and bred posh. His mother
would have had a fit if she thought he was consorting with the
lower ranks. Strangely enough, he was also a fake. He pretended to his colleagues that he was a geezer, dropping his
aitches and peppering his sentences with cockney rhyming

slang, in an effort to be 'one of the lads'. It would almost have been worth it to stay with him to see his reaction when I finally dropped my familial bombshell. I was the genuine article. A commoner!

I never really explained the situation to Lily. She knew I was ambitious to move on from my background. I told her that all wealthy people called their parents by their first names. A sort of quirk of the upper classes. She got slightly confused one day when she saw Prince Charles refer to the Queen as his mother and not Elizabeth. I explained that it was an affectation of the monarchy. Nobody could call the Queen Elizabeth, not even her husband. She went away muttering about posh people and their strange ways. And, of course, I tried to avoid situations where the truth might be revealed. There were one or two awkward moments at my dinner party – that was risky, and the longest period I have ever exposed Lily to work colleagues – but I think I got away with it, just.

It wasn't her fault that she ruined it all yesterday. She was excited. In love. Wanting to share the news with her only daughter, who had not exactly been easy to get hold of over the previous days. Larry, it turns out, was a childhood sweetheart. Somebody she had known long before Alfred. Her first love. But they had drifted apart, married other people and lost touch. Until two months ago, when she hailed an ice-cream van after the taste for vanilla had overcome her. There was Larry, smiling down, offering her extra raspberry sauce and pushing three Flakes into the soft creamy ice when she had only asked for two. Kismet. A meeting of minds.

It did not take long for the two of them to realise that they still had feelings for each other. And every Sunday afternoon they would take the van out to Primrose Hill, blare out 'Greensleeves' and watch as a trail of small children came running over for their weekend treat. And if they had a few slabs of raspberry ripple left over at the end of the afternoon, then what better use to put it to than to shove it in the freezer of her only daughter, who had always been partial to a cone as a child. And besides, Lily told me as we sipped our glasses of wine and nibbled on the peanuts in the Old Parr's Head, she was worried that I did not eat enough dairy products.

Larry is a genuinely nice man, and he seems besotted with my mother. I didn't have an instant rapport with him. I could sense that he was intimidated by me, by the fact that I had made something of my life and progressed. We got on but it was slightly stilted. There's only so many ways you can discuss the ice-cream industry, and I didn't think that high-powered finance would be his thing. Still, I only hoped that he could provide for my mother now that I might be forced to stop supporting her. Buy her new tabards every Christmas, and enough lavender water for her to splash behind her ears, which she moaned were always burning.

Julie and Bloodhound also came. Lily insisted. 'Tell Julie to come for a Cinzano,' she told me, 'and that nice colleague of yours. What's his name? Dalmatian?' Kate had a prior engagement. She was very apologetic, passed on her congratulations to Lily (with a big bear hug) and was tactful enough not to mention the fact that Lily was my mother. Ciaran, however, had turned down the invitation. Politely. Feigning pressure of work. But I could see his mind working overtime. 'Trixie is a fraud. Bloody lucky escape.' Larry said he quite understood. A friend of his, Jimmy, was also meant to be coming, but was up to his eyeballs in documents and said he couldn't leave the office.

In the end it was a nice evening, I think, as I settle down on the sofa, munching a bowl of fresh fruit salad and watching children's Saturday morning television, dressed in my old tartan pyjamas. I have barely seen the latest chart release when Julie rings.

'Hi.' Her voice sounds clipped.

'Hi.' So does mine.

'How are you today?'

'Fine. You?'

'Fine.' And they say it's good to talk. Then suddenly she starts like a floodgate, bursting to let the relentless tide through. 'Look, I'm sorry I didn't tell you about Christopher. I wasn't sure how you would react, and he was nervous that you might be upset, thinking that the two of us would be talking behind your back when we are together, and then you got all upset about Ciaran, and we didn't like to say anything then in case you thought we were rubbing it in, and then you found out yesterday when you had enough shocks to deal with.' Golly. When Julie wants to get something off that chest of hers, there's no stopping her.

'And were you?'

'Were we what? I think there are some parts of this relationship that should remain personal. It's only fair to Christopher,' she retorts indignantly.

'I wasn't talking about sex, stupid. Were you talking about me behind my back? But now you have brought it up, blow "fair to Christopher". If he wants to bonk my best friend then I'm at least entitled to some details, such as good, bad, indifferent and is he good in the doggy position?'

'I don't like the way you talk about him. If you must know, I think you've always had a soft spot for him, and this is the way you hide your true feelings. That's why I was worried about telling you about Chris and me. I thought you might be jealous.' I have to put the phone down, because I am so shocked at Julie's idiotic suggestion that I have dribbled fruit juice down the front of my pyjamas. It's trickling between my breasts and I search for a towel to dry it up.

'Julie,' I say in a tired voice, 'I can assure you that I do not, let me repeat that, NOT, that's N for nobody, O for orange, and T for Trixie, fancy Bloodhound. Or whatever the hell you want to call him.'

'I hate it when you're like this,' she shrieks. 'You're in denial.'

'No I'm not. He's not my type. Got it. End of story. Although, and I will only say this once and I will deny that I did if ever anybody asks, I will admit that he has grown on me in recent weeks. He has helped me,' I nearly choke on the word, but there, it's out now; better out than in, as Lily would say, 'a lot. I have almost forgiven him for the Sam débâcle.' I can hear a sigh of relief through the earpiece. 'Even though he lied to me.'

'But you lied to him too,' came the immediate retort. 'So it's evens.' Her voice adopts a softer tone. 'I told you to tell people, that they wouldn't care about your background, but you cornered yourself into your upper-class fantasy and now look what's happened.'

'Gee, thanks, Julie, for your support. Have you ever thought of joining the Samaritans?' Bloody Julie. She's always right. Like maths teachers or agony aunts. I then ask cautiously, 'What does Bloodhound say?'

'Christopher,' answers Julie, pointedly, 'is confused. He wonders where you actually went to all those weekends that you claimed you had gone home to the country.'

'What did you say?'

'That usually you were with me, and we went on lots of short trips. But he's also concerned about the raffle tickets you constantly flogged him, claiming that the proceeds would go to your mother's Women's Institute.'

'Look, the money did go to my mother's Women's Institute. She's a member, just not in Gloucestershire, and besides, she's always collecting money for charities. You know that.' I hear my doorbell ring. 'Look, Julie, I've got to go. If you're happy and all that jazz, great. Tell Bloodhound that I'll explain to him on Monday.' Along with everybody else, I think to myself. 'Speak later. Bye.'

I place the phone back in its station and walk to the front door, pulling my The Towers fluffy white dressing gown around my well-worn pyjamas. It must be a recorded delivery. I throw open the door to discover Ciaran. Dressed in jeans, black polo neck and calf-leather jacket, with just the right amount of designer stubble, he looks gorgeous. But out of place. He shouldn't be here. What do I do? Shut the door in his face? Spout forth a stream of obscenities, which is always a vote-winner with the neighbours? Or invite him in?

'Can I come in?' There. The decision is taken out of my hands. I cannot do anything about it. I pull the door back further, take a step to the side and watch him enter the hallway. I then close the door, without saying anything, and stand there. In my BLOODY pyjamas. Thank God I didn't go for the face-pack effect too.

He shifts uneasily from side to side – his new Patrick Cox loafers must be pinching – until he realises that we are not moving from the hallway. Only twenty-four inches from the front door, with my right hand just itching to grab the handle.

'You look well,' he says, the beginnings of a twinkle appearing. But it quickly dissipates when my face retains its impassive expression. 'Considering.'

'Considering what?' I say icily. 'That I'm from a poor background? That my mother worked morning, noon and night to scrape together enough money to support me? That my father was feckless and ran away with a Pearly Queen when I was three?'

'No. I didn't mean any of those things. I meant considering those nasty old pyjamas that you're wearing.'

Just one week ago I would have exploded with laughter (at least I think I would have – after all, it is an insult) and told him all about my slob weekends, when I spend the whole two days in these pyjamas, eating junk food and watching old movies and soothing American detective series like *Murder She Wrote*. But I can't. He's hurt me and now he's come to gloat. And I'm not going to help him.

'Really?' I say. 'How kind of you.' He looks uncomfortable again.

'Look, Trixie,' he starts. 'I just wanted to see if you were all right. It was quite a bombshell yesterday. Congratulations to Lily, by the way. She looked very happy. But . . .' he pauses. 'It wasn't a surprise to me.'

I look at him uncomprehendingly.

'I knew. Well, at least I didn't know but I sort of suspected.' What a liar! Any moment now I expect to see his nose start to zoom out. God! That reminds me of another part of his body! I shut the memories of our night and morning together tight away. When do men learn how to become bastards?

'How?' I say sarcastically. 'Did I eat with the wrong fork when we were out?'

'No. Don't be silly. And even if you did, I wouldn't have cared. Wouldn't have noticed either. I only had eyes for you.' Oh, pass the sick bucket. I forgot how grovelling turns my stomach. 'I sort of knew for certain when the bouquet of sunflowers that I sent weren't in your flat. You explained that you'd given them to Julie because Lily was allergic, and then I vaguely remembered that you'd said something another time about how your mother was allergic to sunflowers. It seemed too much of a coincidence, and I sort of put two and two together.'

'So you bought them specially, as a trap?'

'No,' he says, smiling at the recollection. 'I asked for the most stunning bouquet that they could produce for the most stunning woman that I knew. And then there were the family portraits. Your ancestors.' Ah. How red can a blush get? I'm now going for the world record. 'I recognised them from a catalogue I had for Lots Road Auction House.' Get Norris McWhirter here quick! 'You did buy them there?' I look at the floor. Embarrassment. Humiliation. Whatever word you want to call it by. It just feels shit. Ciaran moves forward, gently catches his thumb under my chin and moves it back to its rightful position. He smiles awkwardly at me and then continues in a softer voice than before. 'But the real reason that I knew you weren't so high and mighty is because we got on so well. I had never felt like that before. A connection. An empathy. An attraction. A brilliant attraction. And I knew then that I could never have felt that with somebody who didn't share my sort of humble background. Knew that I might never feel it again.'

A small tear drips, like a traitor, from the edge of my right eye. Ciaran keeps his thumb under my chin but gently moves his forefinger on to my cheek to wipe it away.

'So, why did you use me?' My voice sounds small, choked.

'I didn't mean to. I was scared to tell you what I'd done. I thought you would cancel the date, and I didn't want that. Hell, it took all my self-restraint to walk away on the Saturday before. I couldn't bear to miss out again.' He pauses, as if

199

embarrassed by his admission. 'But I felt that I had some duty to my employers. Work always used to come first with me. You were suddenly sharing that position and I didn't know what to do. I didn't want to feel that I had compromised the bank's trust in me. They pay me hundreds of thousands of pounds and I at least owe them loyalty.'

'And me?'

'I'm so sorry. I guess I never really thought the bank would keep its threat to you. I thought it was idle – a sort of wake-up call.'

'Yep, well I've woken up now.' I take a step back, removing my face from his gentle touch. 'I appreciate you coming around. Really.' I nod as I say this to emphasise that there are no hard feelings. 'But I think you should go now.' I move my arm out, to loosen the door handle and pull it open. Ciaran looks at me carefully, checking that this is not a joke, a test to see his reaction, but I stand there resolute, ignoring the trickle of tears that follows the escape route mapped out by that first little deserter.

'Is there any hope for us?' he asks quietly.

'I don't honestly know,' I tell him. 'You did do the right thing, though, by the bank.' Then, after stopping for a moment in the doorway, just in case I collapse into his arms like they do in the movies, Ciaran walks out into the autumn brightness. I shut the door, lean against it, feeling its coldness on my cheek, and watch all the other deserters drip on to the wooden floorboards.

Monday, October 30
(D Day minus 6 – Shoulders back, pert little breasts out and left, right, left, right)

I hear Sam's voice as I emerge from the lift. Coming through the trading floor loudspeakers. 'Okay, everybody,' he rasps. 'On my count. One, two, three.' And then suddenly everybody is facing me and singing: 'Just one Cornetto, give it to me, delicious ice cream from Italy. La, la, la, la, la.' Well, not everybody. Kate and her colleagues are sitting at their desk with their fingers in their ears. Like children in primary school. I knew I could rely on her to give Sam the finger. And Ciaran and his team are just carrying on working, pointedly ignoring the dawn chorus. It's a kind gesture but it's not going to catapult him into my good books.

I take a deep breath and then march determinedly to my desk. Bloodhound too is sitting with his hands over his floppy ears.

'Remind me,' he says as I take off my coat and settle into my seat, 'to tell Sam not to give up the day job. He'd never make a conductor. They're all off-key.'

'Please don't mention giving up day jobs,' I reply. I haven't quite decided how to treat Bloodhound today. I'm still angry with him for dating my best friend without telling me first. Or asking my permission. And Julie for keeping secrets. Like, is he any good?

'Sorry.' He looks shamefaced. 'Are you okay?'

I nod.

'Fine. Why wouldn't I be?' Focus. Focus. Focus. Stare at the screens and pray that an idea jumps out at you. Watch the markets carefully. Examine the way that the graphics are changing. Can you sneak a deal through the gaps?

'Why didn't you tell me?' Is he persistent, or what?

'Back to you.'

'Sorry?' A furrow has appeared in his forehead as he scrunches up his shiny nose in a quizzical expression.

'Why didn't you tell me? About Julie. My best friend. The person I bitch about you to. Can't do that now. Can I?' I press a few buttons on my keyboards to send new graphs on to my screens.

'Sorry,' he mutters. 'I always bitched to her about you but I suppose that I can't really do that now. It would seem disloyal.'

'Disloyal. Pah! You don't know the meaning of disloyal. Get your own friends, Bloodhound. Leave mine alone.' And then it hits me. Nathan. Internet nerd. Bloodhound's other friend. Could he be my saviour? 'Have you got the number for Nathan?'

'Nathan?'

'Your friend. The one you brought to my house for dinner. Remember? Or did you use the services of Rent-a-Friend?' Jim's voice bellows in the background, summoning people into the morning meeting. Blowed if I'm going. That will be the best thing about losing my job – I won't have to listen to colleagues blathering on about what the day is likely to hold, and then blathering the next day about why their predictions of the previous day have backfired but how they could turn it into an advantage today. And then the next day coming in and blathering on about why their advantage has turned into a disadvantage and that their initial prediction might actually have been correct – just premature. Nah. Won't miss that baloney.

Bloodhound is slowly gathering his papers for the meeting.

'Why do you want Nathan's number? You're not going to date him just because I am dating Julie, are you? That would be silly.'

'Would it make you feel awkward?' I push. 'Knowing that one of your colleagues is dating one of your closest friends, and might actually discuss you? Now you know what it feels like.' He looks uncomfortable. 'But sorry. I'm not going to date him. I'm going to ask him out for dinner. To discuss business.'

'Look, I've got to go to this meeting but I really don't think you should go out for dinner with Nathan. He's strange.'

'I assumed that, if he was a friend of yours.'

'No. I mean really strange.'

'Look,' I say, putting my hands on my hips. 'Don't you want me to get a deal? To keep my job? Or do you want to keep Nathan to yourself? Get him to do any deal with you.'

'No,' retorts Bloodhound. Manfred, who has just stood up on the other side of the desk to go to the morning meeting, looks over the bank of trading screens to see what the argument is about. Bloodhound lowers his voice and brings his face closer to mine. 'That's not true. He's weird. I've discovered some things about him . . . Oh God.' He looks at me. 'It's like talking to a brick wall. Here's the bloody number.' He hands me a card from his Rolodex and walks off to the meeting.

I dial the number. Nathan answers it after one ring.

'Nathan?'

'S'right. Who's this?'

'Trixie. You came to a dinner party at my house?' I adopt my hesitant tone. Don't want him to think I'm pushy, or that I'm desperate to see him again in a romantic light. God. It was bad enough seeing him in candlelight. I wasn't sure if the wax on the tablecloth came from his hair or the spent candles.

'Ah yes. Remember now. How's Trix? Boom boom.' Never heard that one before.

'I haven't done them for a while,' I answer, 'not since my regular clients moved abroad. Focus more on City work now to make a living.'

I can almost hear the confusion down the phone line. He doesn't know if I'm joking or not. And he could be worth millions? Sometimes life is strange. Suddenly the penny drops.

'Ah, right. Joke. Good one. Got me fooled there. So to what do I owe this honour?'

'I was wondering,' I falter. Deep breath. Ignore Bloodhound's warnings. 'If you'd like to come out to dinner with me. I have some, er, ideas for your company. To help you raise finance.' Well, I haven't at the moment, but I can get some if needed.

'Great. What about tonight? There's a new Internet café that I want to try out.' That wasn't quite the venue I had in mind.

'Okay.' Be pleasant. Remember this is a potential client. And he is always right. Even if he does have terrible taste in clothes, hairstyles, restaurants and deodorants. 'What time would you like to meet? And where's the café? Should I book?'

'Man, you're funny. I remember that about you now. It's on the Holloway Road.' He gives me the number, mentions something about it having some great service providers and agrees to meet at seven. Then hangs up because 'I just got in some great DVDs and I really have to try them out. Catch ya later.'

I ignore Bloodhound, who tuts and shakes his head sorrowfully after I confirm that Nathan and I are meeting for dinner tonight. Actually the day passes quite quickly. I get a bit tired of the chorus that greets me every time I leave my seat to visit one of the other trading desks or the loo. But so does everybody else, and by five it is only Sam who sings. And everybody discovers he is tone-deaf. I even ignore the Wall's Ice Cream pennant that flies from his pole, until the end of the day, when I walk over to him and mutter the magic word 'harassment' in his ear.

Soon it's time to meet Nathan. The Internet café is situated near the Archway end of Holloway Road, between a mini-cab firm and a shop which promises to 'clear out houses quickly' and pay cash. God knows who lived in the houses it has cleared but the furniture went out with the Ark. At least I would have said that it came from the Ark but I don't think they had orange plastic in those days.

Nathan is already there when I enter, engrossed. Playing on a computer. I tap him on the shoulder, and he twists around, jumps up and shakes my hand vigorously. He's got his awful bottle-like glasses on, and his hair is as greasy as the day we first met. But I think to myself – this is a millionaire, he has an Internet company, and he might now want to borrow some more money. Repeat it to myself like a mantra.

'Good to see you, Trix.' He pulls out a plastic chair – bet it came from next door – and beckons me to sit down. Ah. How romantic. We're going to share the computer. I look around for the waitresses, but I can't seem to see any.

'Where are the service providers?' I ask Nathan, who looks at me, puzzled.

'What?'

'The service providers?' Again nothing. He looks at me like I am talking another language. 'Waitresses?' I translate.

'Oh, those.' He nods his head, waving his finger in the air as he at last understands the question. 'Good joke. Like it. Clever play on words. Nah, there aren't any. It's self-service.' He points at a counter at the back of the café, where a man stands, back to me, frying sausages on a grease-covered cooker. Circa 1970s. Bet that came from next door too.

'And the menu?' I ask, guessing the answer as the words leap from my mouth. Nathan points at a white board hanging over the counter.

'I'm having the all-day breakfast,' he tells me, 'with white bread, tea and spotted dick for afters. What do you fancy?'

'I think I'll just have a vodka tonic.' He shakes his head. 'What?' I ask. 'Don't tell me. It hasn't got a licence.' He nods. 'I'll settle for a coffee then. Shall I go and tell the man in the striped apron?' Another nod.

I walk to the back of the café, past hordes of nerdy youngsters completely absorbed in the computers in front of them. The chef rests his hands on the counter – he's holding a grubby damp cloth in one of them – and asks me what I would like.

'Decaffeinated espresso, please,' I reply.

'What's that when it's at home?' he asks gruffly.

'Coffee?'

'Oh, right. Nescafé all right. Or I've got Gold Blend.'

'Either would be fine, thanks. Black.' He puts a spoonful of granules into a mug, with the address and phone number of the Internet café printed on the outside, and tannin staining on the inside, and fills it from the tap of a big water boiler. He hands it to me, along with a sugar shaker (which I decline, obviously) and then passes me a plate with Cholesterol City swimming on it.

'And could you take this breakfast to your mate. Eggs scrambled not fried. I'll bring the tea and bread over in a mo.'

Nathan tucks eagerly into his meal, muttering something about not eating all day because he's been busy working out the costings for a new project.

'In fact,' he says, 'it's great that you called. I want to branch out into a new area and need to raise more funds. The last lot has run out, we're expanding so fast.' My ears prick up. Ha, ha, Jim. The joke is going to be on you. 'I want to set up a chain of Internet cafés like this.' He waves his hand around.

'Oh.' I can't keep the disappointment out of my voice. 'I thought you wanted to raise a serious amount, not just a couple of hundred.'

'Very funny. Not exactly like this. It will be more upmarket, and I've already got contracts with some great service providers. Probably need about ten or twenty million to start.' Hmm. It's smaller than I'd originally hoped for – isn't that always the way? – but Jim didn't set any limits on size.

I go straight into investment banker mode. Telling Nathan what I could do for him. Explaining that the time might be right to do a bond in the sterling markets. I've been watching the markets all day, and I think I see an opportunity to squeeze one through. I've been chatting for about ten minutes when Nathan throws his hands up.

'Whoa, whoa, whoa,' he says. 'I haven't said that I'll give you the business.' I look at him stunned. Why agree to dinner, and I use the word loosely, then? 'I have some special requirements.' No. I am not going through the saga of hiring prostitutes again. No way! I start to protest, but he cuts me off. 'No, it's not that,' he says. 'It's something that you can do. Come with me.'

He takes my arm and leads me through to the back of the café to a door with a brass etching of a girl sitting on a potty on it. Nerd boys snigger as they watch us. Nathan pushes open the door and pulls me in. A waft of air freshener hits me.

'You have something I want,' he says. Panic begins to overtake me. Don't tell me that he thinks I'm a dealer. I couldn't bear to go through that scenario again. Then realisation dawns as he starts to undo the buttons on his jeans. No! I don't need the job this badly. Do I? 'Go on,' he says. 'It'll only take a minute.' What? No wonder he's single.

'I – I don't know.' I speak hesitantly, my mind vacillating between saving my job and saving my dignity. He starts to loosen his belt.

'I bet you think I'm weird.'

'Yes.' Remember, the client is always right.

'What?'

'Sorry.' And sometimes he or she is not. 'Look, I don't know.' Should I kneel down and think of Prada? In my wardrobe. For ever.

'But you have some lovely ones. The nicest I've ever seen.'

'Eh? Lovely what?'

'Underwear.'

'What?' I shriek. 'You. You. You were the one who rifled through my underwear drawer the night of the dinner party.' He looks embarrassed.

'I'm sorry. But I could tell you were a Rigby and Peller girl, and I just couldn't resist them. You can have them back now, as long as you'll swap the ones you have on today for them.' He drops his jeans to reveal MY knickers. I can't believe they fit him! I'm *definitely* starting a diet tomorrow. 'I haven't taken them off since I got them.'

'You're disgusting,' I yell, throwing open the door so that the Nerd Boys can see what happens when you grow up into a Nerd Man. 'Find some other banker to give you knickers.' And I storm out of the café.

207

Tuesday, October 31

(D Day minus – oh I've lost track: just know that I'll be out on my ear on Friday unless a miracle comes to pass)

'Don't say anything,' I caution Bloodhound, as I take my seat. Glancing at my screen, I notice that the markets seem a bit calmer today. Tokyo and the Hong Kong stock markets seem to have closed firmer than expected, and the world's currencies have finally completed their roller-coaster ride. The perfect time to do a deal, I think ironically.

'What, like . . .' he starts teasing, but I butt in before he can say the words 'I told you so.'

'Don't.' I hold my hand up in warning. 'I'm not joking.'

'I'm sorry. Ciaran and I only discovered his weird hobby on the way home from yours. He showed us his trophy in the cab. Believe me, he wasn't like that at university.' I look at him sceptically. 'Anyway,' he continues, 'you've had a few calls already.' He hands over some scraps of paper. 'Don't think anything is important. Lily wants to know if you'll be her flower girl.' I glare at him. 'Look, don't shoot the messenger.' He holds his hands up as if to defend himself. 'Just telling you what she said. Apparently she bought a bolt of material in the Liberty sale, and thinks it would make up a treat.' I decide to cut him off before he gives me the whole message. 'Oh, and Julie rang.'

'For me? Or you?' I ask, watching the colour flood his face.

'You.'

'Was she at yours last night?' Her answer machine had cut in when I rang from the cab after my disastrous meeting with Nathan. I'd wanted her to come out to the Met Bar, to drown my sorrows in celebrity heaven. He nods, looking awkward. I shrug.

'And there was a message from some bloke called Jimmy Munroe.'

'Who?' I ask, trying to recall where I've heard that name before.

'He said he met you in the Virgin departures lounge and that you told him that you were a banker.' Oh, him. Fatso. The man who doesn't need to bring a rubber ring to the swimming pool because he's already grown his own. Five of them. 'He wants to borrow some money.'

'Don't tell me. He's buying a car.' Bloodhound shakes his head. 'A house?' Another shake. 'What?'

'Apparently,' says Bloodhound slowly, savouring the moment, 'he wants funds because the firm he works for is embarking on a major expansion project. They've just signed some sort of distribution deal in the States. I don't know any more, but he was keen to talk to you. You must have made an impression on him.' Not as big as the impression he left on the bar stool.

He passes over the number. It has an Islington prefix. I dial it immediately. What line of business did he say that he was in? Food, was it? Or am I just getting confused because he ate so much of it. I have never known a plane to run out of savoury snacks.

'Who left this latté on my desk?' I ask, while waiting for the phone to be answered.

'Ciaran,' replies Bloodhound, without looking up. I place the Styrofoam cup in the bin beside my desk.

'Triple L Foods,' answers the receptionist, just as I turn back.

'Jimmy Munroe, please.'

'Whom shall I say is calling?' Her voice has that irritating singsong tone that receptionists seem to think people like. A bit like the landlords who hang the signs *You don't have to be mad to work here but it helps* behind their bars, receptionists have no idea as to what really impresses their callers.

'Trixie Thompson-Smythe.' Bloodhound shoots me a glance. 'Look,' I hiss at him, putting my hand over the mouthpiece, 'that's what it says on my business cards and I'm *not* going to get into a huge explanation with a total stranger about why I've changed my name, am I?' He shrugs and turns back to his screens. 'Greensleeves' plays down the phone line. Bloody 'Greensleeves'. Everywhere I go. Bet Lily will have it for the wedding march.

I hear muffled voices as the phone is answered, and then a breathless Jimmy Munroe.

'Trixie, is that you? Thanks for returning my call.'

'Pleasure,' I say, crossing my fingers. 'How can I help?' Keep it businesslike, Trixie. Matter-of-fact.

'Well I wondered if I could buy you some dinner.' Might have known food would be involved. 'My boss would like to meet you.' I'm so pleased that I had the foresight to include my photograph on my business card. Not that the bank approves, but as I told Jim, a picture is worth a thousand words. Of course, he was rather rude and said my clients would appreciate less than a thousand words, just a call once in a while to say hi. But that was then. Now they can't get me off the phone, and it still makes no difference.

'Right,' I say. 'Can I ask what this is about?'

'We need to raise about fifty million pounds,' he says. 'I know that is less than you're used to, but it's just the start of a rolling programme of borrowings. If things go according to plan then we might eventually need to borrow an equal amount every month. Maybe more. We have great plans.' My heart is beating so hard now that I am sure he can hear it down the phone line. This man, this obese man, with his penchant for big jewellery, might just be my lifesaver. I could kiss him.

'When were you thinking of?' I keep my tone casual and businesslike. I hear a flicking of pages, and some more muffled discussions, before Fat Boy comes back to the phone.

'Tomorrow?' What about tonight? I want to scream. Tomorrow only gives me two days to sort everything out. I compose myself and agree, but swap it to a lunch – gives me an extra afternoon. 'Right,' he says. 'We'll meet you in Frederick's in Camden Passage, just off Upper Street. Do you know it?'

'Yes. Love it.'

'About one?'

'What about twelve?' Go on. An extra hour for me, and an extra three courses for you to get through.

'All right. We'll see you then. Bye for now.' He hangs up.

'Bloodhound!' I scream. He looks over in panic, scared that he's done something to upset me. 'I may actually beat the odds. I may actually beat the odds,' I repeat, in a stunned voice. He beams at me, and I settle back to analyse the markets and just how Billy Bunter can raise his money. It's going to be a long day.

Wednesday, November 1
(D Day minus 3 – sorry, I didn't recognise you with your clothes on)

I arrive just before noon at Frederick's in order to do a quick recce of the place. Check for escape routes in case I am asked for my knickers, or other undergarments. Actually I'm wearing Marks & Spencer ones today as a deterrent. Big white ones that skim my tummy button.

The maître d' smiles when I walk through the door. For one awful moment I think that I have actually tucked my skirt into the ghastly passion-killing knickers, but then I remember that the last time Julie and I came here, we did get rather out-of-hand on the Cloudy Bay sauvignon blanc. I glance at the cream walls, just to check that the chocolate mousse did not stain.

'Hello,' I say, blushing. Surely he doesn't remember. He is just smiling because I'm a paying guest.

'Good afternoon, madam,' he replies.

'Table for three in the name of Munroe. At noon.'

He checks the book on the stand in front of him, dragging his finger down the list of bookings until he suddenly stabs a name with his finger.

'There,' he exclaims, lifting up a menu. 'Got it. You're in the private room. Would you like to follow me?' He gestures to the doorway with his right hand. I remember the days when I was nervous about business lunches. On my first one, I shook hands with everybody – including the maître d'. He was really chuffed, kept bringing me extra bread rolls.

The large round table is set for three, and the remaining unwanted chairs are set to one side of the room, the primary colours of their fabric covers making a stark contrast against the white walls. I take a seat facing the door.

'Something to drink?' he enquires, as he shakes the linen napkin into my lap.

'Kir royale, please.' I open the menu and pretend to study it, checking for the lowest-calorie options.

'Certainly, madam. And some water?'

I nod.

'Sparkling, please. A large bottle.'

He makes a small bow and leaves to fetch the drinks. It's ten past but there is no sign of Roly Poly and his boss. Suddenly I hear a commotion outside the room, in the bar area. It sounds like a mutual backslapping event. The maître d' is saying stuff like 'customers just love it' and 'raspberry ripple has never been so popular' and finally 'our desserts sales have increased threefold'. Then something is said that I can't quite make out, as the door opens.

In wobbles Jimmy, followed by . . . followed by . . . I blink, but no. It's true. Larry. My mother's intended is standing in front of me, dressed not in white jacket with a splattering of raspberry sauce, but Armani. I look him up and down in amazement, taking in the Church's shoes, Thomas Pink shirt and Hermès tie, as Jimmy rocks from foot to foot saying, 'Surprise.'

Eventually I find my voice – whatever that means. I hadn't lost it, it just wouldn't come out when I wanted it. I stand slowly, placing the menu on the table in front of me.

'Is this a wind-up?'

'No, it most certainly is not!' says Larry. 'Sit down, please.' He looks at the maître d' – 'A bottle of your finest champagne' – and then at me. 'Your bank hasn't instigated one of those stupid no-drinking-at-lunchtime rules, has it?' I shake my head. That's not strictly true. It tried to a few years ago, but everybody pretended that the memo hadn't arrived, and then we got the chairman's secretary drunk at lunchtime and she never had the audacity to type it up again.

'I suppose you wonder what's going on,' he continues. I nod. 'Well, Jimmy here,' the fat one beams at me, 'was telling me about this banker he met in the Virgin lounge whilst he was waiting for his flight to New York. Extolling your virtues, he was, telling me what a pleasant woman you were and that we should enlist your services. It was only when I saw your business card that the penny dropped.' He pauses, while the maître d' pops the cork and fills our glasses.

'Can I just interrupt for one second,' enquires the maître d', 'to tell you the specials? Right.' He launches forth with news of poached haddock and soft poached eggs, saffron risotto and I don't know what else. I can't take things in. But then he adds: 'And I'm sorry to inform you all that chocolate mousse is off.' With a glance at me, he leaves the room.

'Right, shall we all quickly decide and then I'll explain everything,' says Larry. So we do. And he does.

'Right. I'm the chairman of Larry's Luscious Licks, or Triple L Foods as we call it now. Rebranding,' he adds conspiratorially, 'the bane of my life. Larry's Luscious Licks served me perfectly well for twenty years but then some young upstart management consultant came in and told me that it would have to change. Apparently we wouldn't be taken seriously if it didn't. They did some consumer testing, and would you believe it, some people thought we were a company that produced sex aids.'

'And are you?' I ask, sipping my champagne.

'Of course not. We're a producer of fine ice creams and other frozen desserts. You must have tried our chocolate profiteroles?' I shake my head. 'Funny, Lily told me that you had. Strange.'

'Are you a pervert?' I continue with my cross-examination.

'I beg your pardon?'

'A drug addict?'

'What is this?'

'Do you ever wear ladies' knickers?'

'Now hold on.' Larry puts his glass down, and even Jimmy is stunned enough to stop munching his way through the bread basket. 'I know you're only trying to protect your mother's interests but I think you may be going too far.'

'No. I'm trying to protect my interests. Could you carry on?'

We pause as the starters are carried in. Not surprisingly, Jimmy has ordered the largest on the menu. He looks at my green salad in horror. 'Not dieting, are you, dear? There's nothing of you. I've never looked at a calorie counter in my life.' He rubs his bellies in admiration. Larry holds his hand up for Jimmy to stop talking and carries on, as per my request.

'Right. We rebranded about five years ago,' he looks at Jimmy for agreement, 'about the time that we won a huge contract from a major fast-food outlet, supplying them with real Cornish ice cream made in London. And it all sort of spiralled from there. We now have the frozen dessert contracts for, ooh, hundreds of restaurants. That's right, isn't it, Jimmy?' Jimmy nods, his cheeks stuffed up with risotto, like a hamster preparing for hibernation. 'Plus we maintained our ice-cream van franchise, which has been booming like Billy-oh.'

'I'm sorry,' I say, pushing my empty plate to the side. 'I really don't know what you're on about. I meet you for the first time, what, five days ago?' He nods. 'When you're dressed up like an escapee from *Happy Days*, driving a silly little van with a painted sign warning drivers that children may run out into the road, and a dreadful version of "Greensleeves" blaring out, but today, you sit down to lunch looking like a City slicker, discussing major contracts and talking about food distribution and rebranding. Could somebody please tell me what's going on?'

'When you put it like that, I suppose it does sound confusing,' admits Larry. I might have known it. My mother has landed a delusional nutter. 'Right. I'm the chairman and chief executive of Triple L Foods, one of the largest privately owned food companies in the country.'

What?

'So, are you a millionaire?' And there I was when we first met assuming that finance wouldn't interest him.

'Yes. On paper anyway.'

I don't believe this. My mother, who has never cared about money in her life, is about to marry a MILLIONAIRE. And I, who have watched the film *How To Marry a Millionaire* fifty times, am single. Where's the justice in that?

'So why didn't my mother tell me that on Friday?'

'She doesn't actually know,' he responds sheepishly.

'You're kidding. Right?' Larry, who I can admit now that I liked, nay loved like a father, from the very moment I laid eyes on him, shakes his head.

'Every so often,' he explains, 'I go back to my roots. Try to remember the days when it was just the ice-cream van and me. See the smiling faces of children spending their pocket money with me.' Oh, please. Pass the sick bucket. Surely you mean see the smiling faces of your accountants as they tot up the pocket money. 'So I borrowed one of the old vans, put on the uniform and visited my old haunts around Bethnal Green. I had only just stopped down Columbia Road when who should arrive to buy a cone with a Flake but Lily. We couldn't believe it. She was so excited that I'd achieved my dream – I always told her that I wanted to be an ice-cream man – that I hadn't the heart to tell her the rest. Next thing I knew we were stepping out and, well, I learned all her concerns about the evils of money. And how,' he looks at me carefully, 'it's changed you. And I just couldn't tell her. Could I, Jimmy?' He looks over at Jimmy, who has just fitted a complete bread roll into his mouth. 'And she thinks my house is an old council one that I bought. It's just down the road, actually. Duncan Terrace.'

What? My favourite road in the whole of Islington, where the weeping willows sweep along the rockeries and protect the fenced gardens that divide both sides of the street.

'So she still doesn't know?' I ask, as the waiter puts our main courses before us.

'No. And you mustn't tell her. Not at the moment. I'll tell her when I'm good and ready. For now, she just thinks that I have an ice-cream round. As you saw last week, she seems happy enough with that.'

'But . . .'

'No, Trixie.' He holds his hand up. 'As I said, I'll tell Lily when I'm good and ready. And you'll keep quiet, especially if you want my help to save your job.'

'What?'

'I know all about it. The deal you have to bring in, and the timescale. Your friend Christopher told me about it in the Old Parr's Head. No.' He holds up a hand again to silence me, since I've begun to protest. 'I forced him to tell me. You looked so miserable in the bank when we told you our good news that I knew something was on your mind. I made Christopher spill the beans. Anyway,' he points at the plate in front of me, 'don't let your food go cold.'

I pick at my Dover sole. Imagine. I'm to be the stepdaughter of a multi-millionaire. There really is a God!

'Anyway, it's only right that you benefit from the company. After all, you were the main reason for our latest business deal,' he confides, shovelling his peas on to his upturned fork and opening his mouth wide, like a child about to experience the food aeroplane. See. You can take the man out of Bethnal Green, but you can't take Bethnal Green out of the man.

'What do you mean?' I'm completely baffled. Jimmy is rifling in his briefcase for some papers, which he places on the table in front of him.

'That dinner party you held a few weeks ago. Lily said you were taken aback by the ice cream she served up, although she did tell me that your friends seemed to love it. Apart from that awkward one. The venereal one?' I nod, and mutter the name Liz. 'Anyway, she said you were moaning that it wasn't American, and she was quite insulted. Couldn't see what the Americans could produce that was better than mine, so we did a blind tasting. And mine came out tops. So we sent Jimmy out there with samples and, well, he landed a big deal, eh, Jimmy?' His colleague nods enthusiastically, and the chairs at the perimeter of the room bang against the wall. 'They just loved our ninety-nines and the lemon meringue pies were a real winner. So we now have to raise funds to set up a joint venture over there, with one of the major ice-cream makers, to produce our Cornish line.'

I put down my fork. I can't eat any more. My stomach is racing in excitement. Perhaps I could just give up working. Forget about Jim's stupid deadline, and just live on the trust fund that my beloved future stepfather is bound to set up for me.

Jimmy interrupts my daydream.

'I've taken the liberty of producing a presentation, detailing our financial information and projected sales in America and listing the other countries where we are thinking of setting up factories.' He passes me the papers. 'As you can see, we are likely to need funding in Japanese yen, Greek drachma, Albanian lek . . .' He looks at me. 'Yes, really. Albanian lek. They've gone crazy for our Tootie Fruitie. And one or two others, but our main need now is for American dollars. About fifty million of them.'

I start to flick through the pages. The projections are amazing. This company is really going places.

Jimmy continues, 'And we took the liberty of applying for a credit rating from the two major agencies.' He passes over two separate reports. 'As you can see, they have been more than fair with us.' I check the rating. It's good. Very good, in fact. This has just made my task so easy. Investors like to buy bonds from companies that have been graded by credit agencies. It's a bit like department stores offering store cards to customers after checking with credit companies first, just to see if they've ever been bankrupt or have outstanding county court judgments for non-payment of bills. Nobody likes to lend money to a debtor, and bond investors are no different.

I wave at the waiter through the open door.

'A bottle of your best vintage champagne, please. And,' I fumble in my wallet and pull out my corporate credit card, 'could you put the total bill on this?' He nods and scurries off. 'Right, gentlemen.' I smile at Larry. 'I must be off. The bond markets wait for no man, or woman, and I assume you want these funds in a hurry. And I definitely want to do this deal in a hurry, but not,' I add hastily, 'if it's not at the right price. So I'm off. Enjoy the champagne, and I look forward to raising another glass when this is all over.'

I stand, shake hands with Jimmy and place a small peck on the cheek of Larry, who blushes, and then grabs his handkerchief to wipe off any tell-tale lipstick marks. 'Can't have Lily thinking she's got competition,' he laughs. 'Keep us informed, and if you want us to come in and meet anybody, just name the time. Actually, I think I know your chairman; we produced the desserts for his daughter's wedding. Nice do, that. A marquee. Might suggest that to Lily.'

'Tell her,' I say, 'that I'll wear anything she wants for her Big Day. Even a meringue.'

Wednesday, November 1
(D Day minus 3 – Lily has such wonderful taste in men)

I'm sitting in a black cab, willing it to go faster, to whisk me back to the bank and let me start work on the deal-to-beat-all-deals. So engrossed am I reading the presentation that Jimmy gave me that I barely hear the cab driver telling me who he had in the back of the cab last week.

I rush into Jim's office, without knocking, and rock impatiently on the balls of my feet as he signs off his phone call. Mary rushes in after me, standing in the doorway muttering about how she couldn't stop me. Get lost, Mary.

'Well, what is it, Trixie?' Jim asks irritably, as he hastily pushes some papers into his desk drawer. 'And no. If you're asking if you can leave the bank two days early, the answer is no.'

'Don't be silly.' I wave the presentation under his nose. 'I've got a deal. For Triple L Foods. You know, the large private company. They want to borrow about fifty million dollars, but that's only for starters. Their ice cream is selling like hot cakes. Sorry,' I apologise as Jim cringes. 'But it is. All over the world. Look at page two.'

He opens the presentation, and examines the colourful graphs and pie charts.

'Look at the projections for sales in Japan,' I point out, 'and Ireland. This company is going places. They want to establish a rolling programme that will enable them to borrow in the bond markets at regular intervals, and they want me to co-ordinate it.'

Jim looks up at me, and shakes his head sorrowfully.

'What?' I exclaim. 'What is it? I've got a deal. Take my name off that list. The one you just shoved into the drawer.' He blushes at the last sentence, but continues to shake his head.

'Have you got credit approval for this deal?' He flicks through some more pages of the presentation.

220

'No, but the company has got a credit rating, from two major agencies. That should count for something.'

'And have you organised the swaps that will underpin the bonds?'

'No, but that shouldn't take long. Just as soon as I get the go-ahead from the credit department,' I persist, feeling less confident of my position now. His tone does not sound quite as pleased as I had expected.

'Have you asked the sales force if they can sell bonds on behalf of Triple L Foods?'

'Well, no, but . . .' I pause. Where are the open arms? The tearful welcome back into the fold? The 'I always believed in you, even when you didn't in yourself' speech? I suppose now would be the wrong time to ask for a pay rise. 'But look at the credit rating. It's a good one. This is exactly the type of company that our investors lap up. Hey, we can even throw in a couple of cartons of ice cream with every purchase.' Jim remains aloof. 'Okay, so maybe not,' I continue. 'But isn't this great?'

'Why,' asks Jim in a tired voice, 'didn't you get this deal earlier?' I didn't know that my mother was marrying the chairman and chief executive of the company earlier, stupid. I'm working as fast as I can, given the circumstances. 'There is no way that this deal will be signed, sealed and delivered by Friday, is there?'

I can't believe it! He's actually going to keep to his threat. I have a deal, finally, but it's too late. Maybe just twenty-four hours too late. I feel as though I've been kicked in the teeth as I slowly shake my head. The bank will retain Triple L Foods as a client, but I'll not be here to see it. Somebody else will do this deal. I lean forward, close the presentation, place it under my arm and walk out of Jim's office in silence, ignoring Mary's stony stare.

I walk past my desk until I am standing beside Bloodhound. He looks up, startled. Then I place the presentation on the keyboard in front of him.

'Have a deal on me. I probably owe you it.' Then I return to

221

my seat and stare without seeing at the screens in front of me. Larry rings to check that I got back to the office okay and to find out when he has to come in and sign any legal documents or official agreements. I tell him that I'm back and will call with further details as soon as possible. 'Why didn't you call me on Monday?' I want to scream at him. 'At least then I would have had a chance.' But I already know the answer. It's in the presentation pack. The contract with the American company was not signed until Monday evening. A copy was faxed to Triple L Foods at nine in the evening, London time, with a written note to say that the originals were being couriered over. Anyway, be honest, Trixie, even if Jimmy Munroe had rung on Monday you wouldn't have seen him that night. No! You were too busy chasing rainbows with a pant-wearing pervert.

Bloodhound looks through the papers that I have given him, then turns to me.

'I don't understand. It's a deal. You've got several deals. Achieved the objective. Why are you handing it over to me?'

'Because I didn't get it early enough. I threw my towel into the wrong corner and was eventually knocked out by the bell. There's no way that I can get that deal done by Friday, and Jim is in no mood to grant me an extension. Go on. Take it. Use the bonus to buy a new wardrobe. Please.' I place special emphasis on the last word.

'But Trixie.' Bloodhound is persistent; I'll say that for him. That's probably how he won Julie over. He wooed her into submission. 'Isn't it worth a shot?'

'Look.' I am now tired with this conversation. Take the deal, Bloodhound, but please *shut up* about it! 'There's no way the credit department will grant approval by Friday. I haven't primed the sales force, worked out a structure or got the lawyers to draw up the necessary documentation. We're talking at least three days' work. There's just no way!'

'But,' he insists. This must drive Julie crazy. He's like a dog with a bone, always gnawing, gnawing, gnawing, until he's drained the final bit of marrowfat. 'What sort of structure were you planning? You must have had an idea.'

'Sure,' I answer. 'I had an idea. Thought of it in the cab coming back from lunch. I'd go for a plain sterling deal, sell to domestic investors who know this company and love its products, and swap the proceeds into dollars. The most simple deal there is. Nothing fancy, and in these markets,' I press a few buttons and watch new graphs spring to life on my screen, 'I guess the company could borrow at a rate of . . .' I suggest some figures, point out some graphics on the screen to Bloodhound and then continue, 'And now, if you wouldn't mind. I've got some people to ring to say goodbye to.'

I turn away from him, struck by the injustice of the situation, and slowly the tears drip down my cheeks. Tears of frustration. Of anger, with myself and my silly, stuck-up attitudes. I'm *really* going to miss this job.

Friday, November 3
(It has arrived, but even condemned men get a last request)

I was like an automaton yesterday, calling headhunters, ringing old friends who might know of a vacancy, a job for somebody who once became blasé about her career but who now would give anything to have it back. Everybody was polite, but news of my potential downfall had stretched outside the environs of the bank into the City streets, which thrive on gossip. An acquaintance, I couldn't put it much firmer than that, told me that her bank couldn't employ me because it had a no-drinking-at-lunchtime rule and she had heard that I was an eight-bottles-a-day kind of girl. If only. Another had heard that I was enjoying a torrid affair with Jim, and that the chairman had caught us in flagrante delicto. I didn't know what I was more annoyed about – the slur on my character or on my taste. I mean, Jim!

I'm a great fan of all things Chinese – especially those little Mao jackets that were in fashion several years ago – but I hate the whispers. The way they feed into fact, into general acceptance, giving colleagues and distant associates the belief that they know the root cause of my fall from grace. Of course, it was her morals that caused it, they whisper in the wine bars, and did you hear that she was a product of a broken home? QED

Lily comes over this morning to see me off. We spend ages searching through my wardrobe for the right outfit – the one that says I may be down but not out. But she doesn't come to the door to wave me goodbye. She can't.

Julie sends flowers, with a card telling me not to let the buggers get me down, and offering Krug tonight. She must have paid a fortune to get the bouquet delivered before I leave for work at six thirty. And I'm determined to leave for work early – to stand defiantly in front of Jim in the morning meeting.

I didn't hear from Larry or Jimmy, but they must know what is happening. Bloodhound will have informed them that he's now their banker, and knowing Lily, she'll have been prattling on for the past thirty-six hours about the injustice. I told her that I had got a deal (but not who it was for) but that I was still going to miss the deadline. Poor Larry. I think I'll buy him earplugs for his wedding present.

I arrive at six fifty, smile politely at the security guards, who look rather awkward. They must know. Probably got the black bags ready under the counter in front of them, just waiting for the signal to run around the building slipping them on the desks of the condemned. I just hope they are bunny bags, with convenient little tie handles, and recyclable. Just because people are losing their jobs there is no need for the bank to neglect its principles.

Bloodhound gives me a tight little smile as I sit down and pull out my drawers, searching out the belongings that I must take home. I find a photograph of Sam and me in happier days, and instinctively look over to his desk. He's not there but it is decked out in bunting, with tinsel flying from the flagpole. Don't tell me. He bedded a team of cheerleaders!

In the event, my final act of defiance against Jim isn't necessary. He's not in the morning meeting – apparently he is in conference with some new clients – but Ciaran hosts it, so perhaps my early appearance is worth it. He can't look me in the eye, particularly when he inadvertently asks what I think the markets will do next week, and I reply, survive without me.

Bloodhound and I sip our final cup of coffee together, and just as I drain the last ounce, Jim's personal assistant Mary arrives and asks me to follow her. I stand, and tell Bloodhound to make sure the security guards don't just toss my belongings into the black sack. They may be acting like removal men today but they don't have to emulate them completely. He promises that I'll find my belongings in the same state as I left them.

I follow Mary into the lifts and up to the fourth floor, where the personnel offices are located. Several years ago the bank had panic buttons installed in these offices, in case a member of staff learning of his or her redundancy became violent. They will not need that safety device this morning. I am calm. Resigned, no pun intended, to my dismissal.

Mary turns right out of the lifts, and I shout to her that she is going in the wrong direction, but she ignores me. No change there, then. Instead she walks down the corridor, with its walls covered in prints of the City of London through the ages, towards the meeting rooms. She stops at the Fitzwilliam Room, named after a former chairman of the bank, whose major claim to fame was that he installed ladies' toilets on the floor where the boardroom is. No longer could fuddy-duddy codgers argue against the promotion of women to the board on the grounds of inadequate facilities. Still, I think it was ten years before they were ever flushed.

Mary knocks, and Jim calls out, 'Enter,' so I do. Ah, if only I'd been this obedient in the past none of this would ever have happened. He is sitting behind the massive oak table, pouring coffee from one of those silver thermal pots into a china cup for . . . Larry?

'Larry?' I exclaim. He looks up at me and smiles. Jimmy Munroe is also in the room, helping himself to a Danish pastry.

'Trixie.' Larry comes forward and shakes my hand, pulling out the chair beside me and beckoning me to sit down.

'Larry,' I repeat, sounding like a parrot. 'What are you doing here?'

'Oh, come now, Trixie,' interrupts Jim. 'You know as well as I do that Larry and Jimmy have come this morning to sign the documents, just before we press the button on their bond issue.'

What? I mentally retrace my steps this morning before I arrived in this room. No. I'm sure I haven't drunk anything. So why is Jim talking gobbledegook? Perhaps if I keep quiet it will all start to make sense.

'Good work, Trixie,' continues Jim. No. Still not making sense. 'I must admit that I never thought you had it in you, but Larry told me what an amazing proposal you came up with on Wednesday afternoon and how you both realised that speed was of the essence to achieve a borrowing rate of . . .' And then he says something that is vaguely familiar. 'That idea of yours to . . .' Extremely familiar. 'It was inspired.' Hmm. That bit is slightly less familiar.

Jim has just outlined the bond structure that I mused over with Bloodhound, just after I was told that I would definitely lose my job, when I told Bloodhound what I would do in his shoes.

'So,' Jim hands his Mont Blanc pen to Larry, pushes some papers towards him and points to a dotted line, 'would you like to sign there? And there? And Jimmy, could you come and sign here?' Jimmy wobbles over to do his duty. 'Well,' says Jim, 'I think we can now press the button. Trixie,' he turns to me, 'I saw that you have all the telexes and faxes ready to alert other banks. I'd say we should send them out at about, ooh,' he checks his Rolex, 'nine thirty?'

I nod, because I know that if I say anything it will sound like 'What the hell is going on?'

Jim turns back to the bank's newest clients. 'Will you both join me in the boardroom at noon for a celebratory glass of champagne? And you, Trixie,' he turns to me, eyes laughing, 'I suppose you'd like a bottle.' Well, it might make this morning make sense. 'Go on now, Trixie.' He shoos me out of the room. 'Get this bond out there. Larry and Jimmy will be here all morning.'

It is only when I am in the lift back to the trading floor that it hits me. I didn't say a word in the Fitzwilliam Room. I might just have got away with it. I rush out of the lift back to my desk, where Bloodhound is sitting, chatting away on the phone. He hangs up quickly as I arrive. Must have been talking to Julie. Does she know what's going on? 'Cause I'm damned if I do.

'Can you tell me what the hell is happening?' I ask him. 'I've just been in the Fitzwilliam Room with Jim, my future stepfather and Mr Eat-As-Much-As-You-Like, listening to them telling me that a bond for Triple L Foods will be launched today. And that I'm responsible. Now I know that I often have

227

memory lapses, but hell, I'm sure I would remember something like this.'

Bloodhound takes a deep breath, opens the drawer beside him and withdraws a small notepad.

'Look at that,' he says. It looks like scribbled notes of the conversation that we had on Wednesday afternoon, when I told him what I would do given the chance. 'I wrote it all down and it looked so easy. As you said yourself, it was just a simple little deal. So why should a simple little deal take so long?'

'Still with you, just,' I say. 'But apparently I've primed the sales team, credit team, organised a currency swap and pre-arranged the notices for other banks. And all without moving a muscle.'

'You had done the hard part. You got the client and worked out a structure for the deal. Some of your friends here,' he pauses, and lowers his voice, 'decided to do the rest of the work.' As I stare at him in shock, he adds: 'Well, it just didn't seem fair that you would lose your job. You did what Jim wanted, but then he was a bastard and changed all the rules.'

'So what happened?'

'Well,' he looks awkward here, 'I spoke to Ciaran and explained the situation. I figured he owed you one after his last efforts to help your career, and he agreed to prime the sales force and tentatively sound out investors. Guess what?' If you think I am guessing anything else, you have another think coming. I'm already working in a parallel universe. 'They loved the idea and the company. You might actually be able to increase the size of this deal, but don't count any chickens,' he hastily adds, as he sees my eyes light up. 'And then it was just a matter of calling in favours.'

'What do you mean?'

'Well, the credit department were overworked and told Ciaran that they couldn't do anything until Monday, but he went ballistic, discovered they were working flat out on six deals for Manfred and then laid some pressure on the German one to allow your deal to leapfrog his queue.'

'How did he do that?'

'He got the canteen to agree to take sauerkraut off the menu, and then said that his sales team wouldn't be able to sell any of Manfred's deals for a while. He told him that investors were bored with German companies.'

'And are they?'

'I don't know, but Ciaran sure sounded convincing. Manfred allowed his deals to be rescheduled and the credit department found time to analyse Triple L Foods. It's a really good credit, miles better than the ratings agencies have judged. Ciaran even pulled some reports off the Internet that Larry forgot to give you, which made great reading.'

'Seems like Ciaran was quite involved with all this.'

'Oh, yeah, couldn't have done it without him and Julie. She came around this morning at two, when we were finalising last-minute details, with pizzas. We actually roped her in to type and send out all the faxes to the other banks. Took her ages; she doesn't really know her r's from her . . .'

'Elbow?'

'Actually I was going to say t's. We called Larry at midnight, told him what we were doing, and the lawyers arrived about two this morning. So,' he looks at me and smiles, 'when you give the signal, the début bond issue for Triple L Foods will be released on to an expectant audience.'

I can't believe it! Ciaran, Bloodhound and Julie working to save my career. I can see Ciaran in the distance, shouting at his team, encouraging them. He looks good, perhaps even a little slimmer, in his dark trousers and cream shirt. He turns around, catches my eye and grins.

'But what about the redundancies? Jim has to cut the head-count. If I'm not going, then . . . who is?'

Bloodhound slowly lifts his hand and points in the direction of Sam's desk. The bunting. It is not to commemorate a night of passion. His colleagues have hung it over his desk to commemorate his departure.

'Sam?' I look at Bloodhound. 'Has he really gone? But why?'

'He was becoming a liability,' explains Bloodhound. 'The bank was already getting really worried about the threat of sexual harassment cases, and then when the rumours went around about gonorrhoea, the powers-that-be got really panicked.'

'But he made a fortune for this bank. Is there no loyalty to anybody?'

'Actually, he didn't.'

'What do you mean?'

'He has made some bad calls on the foreign exchange markets recently. Apparently one of his many lovers was into astrology and convinced him that he should establish a proprietary account, and use the bank's money to trade according to when the Sun was in the ascendant and all that stuff. You know that joke about Uranus? Well, he fell for it. Actually Ciaran discovered the truth. He was at a drinks party recently, chatting up some girl, and she turned out to be a former lover of Sam's.'

Chatting up some girl! Bloodhound's words dig into me like a dagger, but he carries on oblivious to the damage he has done and I learn that Sam was escorted from the bank early this morning. Before even I arrived. He was so shocked and angry by the move that he took the keys for his company Porsche, which was parked in the bank's underground garage, and, in front of the security guards, dropped them down a drain outside. Chutzpah!

'Anyway,' says Bloodhound, 'we can talk about all this later on. I'll fill you in with more details tonight, over a drink with Julie? But we'd better get cracking if we want to get this deal out on time. Come on. All hands to the pump!'

He gives my hand an encouraging squeeze as I lean forward to plant a small peck on his cheek.

'Julie's a very lucky girl,' I tell him. And then I turn away from Bloodhound and walk towards Ciaran's desk. He sees me coming and moves towards me, so that we meet in a space, away from the prying ears of his team.

'I guess I owe you thanks.' He looks down at me, but there is no twinkle in his eyes. Instead he looks tired. Haggard.

'There's no need,' he replies graciously. 'I guess we can call it quits now.'

Quits. Why does that sound so awful? So final. The end. An affair over before it really began.

'I guess. But thanks anyway.'

I turn and start to walk back to my desk, reciting the word 'quits' to myself, psyching myself up for my deal, putting my personal life behind me. Suddenly I hear my name called out. I turn. Ciaran is still standing where I left him, and he's saying something that I can't quite hear. I take a step back towards him.

'Sorry? What did you say?'

'I asked if you'd give me another chance, Trixie, please. I'm so sorry for what I did.'

And then I remember the times that I had hurt friends, especially with my cutting barbs. I think of my superior attitude towards my mother. My insecurities and pretensions. And I know that I am not the right person to judge Ciaran.

'Maybe. But only if there's no more lies.'

'I promise.'

'Good! Because I have to tell you something.'

'What?'

'I hate café latté!'